Between a Wok and a Dead Place

Spice Shop Mysteries

ASSAULT AND PEPPER
GUILTY AS CINNAMON
KILLING THYME
CHAI ANOTHER DAY
THE SOLACE OF BAY LEAVES
PEPPERMINT BARKED

Between a Wok and a Dead Place

A SPICE SHOP MYSTERY

BY LESLIE BUDEWITZ

SEVENTH
STREET
BOOKS®

Published 2023 by Seventh Street Books®

Between a Wok and a Dead Place. Copyright © 2023 by Leslie Budewitz. All rights reserved. No part of this publication may be reproduced, stored in a retrieval system, or transmitted in any form or by any means, digital, electronic, mechanical, photocopying, recording, or otherwise, or conveyed via the Internet or a website without prior written permission of the publisher, except in the case of brief quotations embodied in critical articles and reviews.

This is a work of fiction. Characters, organizations, products, locales, and events portrayed in this novel either are products of the author's imagination or are used fictitiously. Any similarities to real persons, living or dead, is coincidental and not intended by the author.

Cover images © Shutterstock
Cover design by Jennifer Do
Cover design © Start Science Fiction

Inquiries should be addressed to
Start Science Fiction
221 River Street, 9th Floor
Hoboken, NJ 07030

Phone: 212-431-5455
www.seventhstreetbooks.com

10 9 8 7 6 5 4 3 2 1

ISBN: 978-1-64506-061-1 (paperback)
ISBN: 978-1-64506-075-8 (ebook)

Printed in the United States of America

*For those who work to preserve the past
and give us all a better future.*

The Year of the Rabbit Parade Line Up

Wishes for good luck and fortune from the cast!

AT SEATTLE SPICE

Pepper Reece—Mistress of Spice
Sandra Piniella—assistant manager and mix master
Cayenne Cooper—creative cook and problem-solver
Reed Locke—salesclerk with a secret passion
Kristen Gardiner—Pepper's BFF
Arf—an Airedale, the King of Terriers

THE FLICK CHICKS

Pepper
Kristen
Laurel Halloran—widowed restaurateur and houseboat dweller
Seetha Sharma—massage therapist with a mystery man
Aimee McGillvray—owner of Rainy Day Vintage

MARKET MERCHANTS, RESIDENTS, AND FRIENDS

Nate Seward—the fisherman
Chuck and Lena Reece—Pepper's snowbird parents
Roxanne Davidson—assistant curator of small, weird things
Aki Ohno—the eyes and ears of Chinatown
Oliver Wu—a would-be hotelier with eyes for Seetha
Bobby and Abigail Wu—sitting on history

THE LAW

Detective Michael Tracy—Major Crimes, cookie thief
Detective Cheryl Spencer—they've heard the jokes, and they aren't laughing
Officer Tag Buhner—Pepper's former husband, on the bike patrol
Officer Paula Ohno—walking the beat

One

Contrary to its soft, vulnerable appearance and quiet personality, the Rabbit is confident and strong, always moving toward its goal, regardless of criticism and obstacles. Though careful and attentive to detail, the Rabbit often spices things up in surprising ways.

—The Year of the Rabbit, in Chinese astrology

"TRY ONE OF THESE, PEPPER," MY MOTHER LENA SAID, POINTING at the fat, transparent steamed dumplings, her souvenir teacup tipping at a dangerous angle. "Shrimp, with ginger and scallions. Divine."

The short, dark-haired woman running the booth plucked a perfectly pleated morsel from a bamboo steamer and set it on my plate. Behind her, an elderly woman slid another steamer onto the table. Lifted the lid and released a warm, heavenly fragrance.

If you've ever been to a cocktail party where you've had to juggle your wine glass, a too-small napkin, and a plate of appetizers, all while avoiding elbows, trying to hear and be heard above the music, and nodding when introductions are made because you can't possibly free a hand, you've got an idea what the food walk during the Lunar New Year celebration in Seattle's Chinatown–International District is like. What Seattleites call "the CID," spelling out each letter. But for that dumpling, I'd brave it all. I stuck my bamboo chopsticks in my pocket to reduce the risk of putting out an eye—my own or a stranger's—and took the dumpling with my fingers.

"Har gow," the woman said. "Best in the city." A vinyl banner in the back of the booth, accented by a string of small red lanterns, repeated the claim, attributed to the *Seattle Times* food critic. Though I didn't agree with all the critic's reviews, her raves about my spice shop in Pike Place Market convinced me of her good taste. One bite and I knew she'd nailed it.

"Total yum," I said. She rewarded my praise with another morsel. I held up my phone. "Selfie with dumplings. Lean in." My friend Seetha, in her puffy white coat, bumped shoulders with my mother while I, several inches taller with short spiky hair that exaggerates the effect, stood in back and snaked my arm between them to snap a couple of shots. Three dark heads, three happy faces.

"I always thought dim sum meant dumplings," Seetha said. "But they've got all kinds of things."

"Dim sum is a broad term." Our host wore a white chef's jacket, the name of her restaurant embroidered in red, in English and Chinese, over the left breast, and gestured to the array of dishes on the cloth-covered table with a graceful hand. "Dumplings, yes, but also rolls, small buns, cakes, and other dishes. And the tea. Always tea."

I took a sip of mine. Green, scented with jasmine, perfect for the overcast January day. A good beginning for the Year of the Rabbit, though the new year didn't officially start until tomorrow. Saturday afternoon was the better choice for a food walk and art fair, followed by an evening parade. My spice shop sells a similar blend, not quite as smooth, and I wondered where they got theirs. We supply herbs and spices to hundreds of the city's restaurants and food producers, from a crepe cart to a fourth-generation butcher known for his sausage and salami to an internationally renowned chef's empire, but I'd only managed a small inroad in the CID. Hadn't tried very hard. Many of the restaurateurs in this part of the city, just south of Pioneer Square and the business district, have long relationships with other suppliers. They guard their sources like the bronze lions and dragons guard the gates of the Forbidden City.

"Traditionally served at brunch, but these days," our doyenne of dumplings continued, the rest of her explanation lost in a cacophony of sound. Barely ten feet from us, in front of the ceremonial gate that was as tall as some of the nearby buildings, a man dressed in red and black banged on a barrel-shaped drum. On either side of him, musicians clanged cymbals small and large. A trio of four-legged lion dancers prowled the urban jungle, two in yellow and one in red. Everyone in the crowd packing the street stopped to watch. The man carrying the giant head of the red lion swung it from side to side, then up and down, to the steady beat of the drum, while the man in back controlled the cape-like body. For a moment, I forgot the lions weren't real. Not that they were particularly realistic. Not at all. Stylized, puppet-like, their red, yellow, and black eyes the size of saucers, the yellow-bearded tongues painted to match. Long furry fringe hung from the cape and wound around the men's pant legs, swaying with their movements.

Mesmerizing.

The beat grew more pronounced. The man in the back end of the red lion scooped the front man up on his shoulders, holding tight as the mounted dancer swooped low, pretending to charge a small child who shrieked in delight. The dancer leapt back to the ground and the men resumed their intricate footwork.

Then a team of dancers swarmed around them, more modestly dressed in red and yellow pants and T-shirts. Each held a small lion head with a long tail that swept down his back. As the two-man teams had done, they swayed and swung, stomping their feet like the kings of the jungle whose spirits they were meant to invoke, lifting the heads high above their own and waving them in the air before pulling them back down over their faces.

"Oliver!" Seetha cried, and though I couldn't imagine how he could hear her over the bang of the drum and the din of the crowd, the dancer nearest us stepped closer. Lifted the head of his costume and bowed to her, his long yellow and red tail sweeping the pavement. I caught the quickest glimpse of jet-black hair and dark eyes before he clapped the lion mask back in place and the troupe moved on.

"That's him? That's your mystery man?" I said. "That's why you were so keen on coming." The flush on Seetha's brown cheeks answered for her.

"The lions dance to bring good luck and fortune," the dim

sum woman said, an impish smile on her face. Behind her, the old woman muttered something in Chinese, then bent and turned away.

The street dancers were a preview to tonight's parade, though we didn't plan to stay that long. The festivities in the CID are the biggest and best attended in the city, fitting for the heart of Seattle's Asian community, but celebrations would be held all over town during the next two weeks. Even in Ballard, the historically Scandinavian neighborhood near Fisherman's Terminal. And it wasn't all furry frivolity. Art exhibits, cooking classes, and lectures on the history of Pan-Asian Seattle filled the calendar. Fundraisers abounded, from sequined galas to 5Ks. My former employee Matt and his girlfriend were taking part in tomorrow's Rabbit Run, raising money for a community health center, and they'd hit up my shop for a healthy pledge.

Me, I was in it for the food and the friends, and the bright colors and sounds and energy that kept me from missing my guy, Nate Seward. Ha. As if anything could. But at least keeping busy kept me from obsessing over the danger he faced every day, fishing the icy waters of the North Pacific off Alaska.

My mother handed Seetha and me small paper plates of treats nestled in red paper cups.

"Oh, I love sesame balls," I said. "And egg tarts."

"I've got dessert for your dad, if we can find him," she said, scanning the crowd. "There he is." She nodded toward my father, Chuck Reece, on the far side of the street. As she says, a tall spouse is useful in a crowd, especially a man who likes to wander off by himself. I get both my height and my curiosity from him.

I bit into a sesame ball, warm and crunchy on the outside, sweet and smooth inside. Finished it off. Wrapped the rest in my napkin and tucked them in my tote bag for later. Teacups in hand, we wound our way through the throng to watch a well-organized group of children, mostly Asian but not all, in red pants and shirts demonstrate martial arts moves.

My father, over six feet with a full head of dark hair despite being past seventy, stood beside a woman who did not reach his shoulder. Her gray and black hair was streaked with the same regal purple as her puffy parka, and both matched her pronged metal cane.

"Aki," my mother cried.

"Lena!" The two women embraced. "And this must be Pepper. I haven't seen you since—well, whenever it was, you were shorter than I. Now even my granddaughter towers over me."

I'd hit five feet in the fourth grade and reached my current five-seven at fourteen. No wonder I didn't recognize Aki Ohno, though I'd heard the name many times.

My mother introduced Seetha, then explained. "We met Aki and Ernie ages ago, when we were setting up the free meals kitchen at the cathedral. They'd created a similar program down here and were so helpful. That led to several joint projects." She put a hand on the older woman's arm. "We were so sorry to hear about Ernie, and to miss his funeral. He was a wonderful man."

Now I remembered. My parents moved to Costa Rica a few years ago and my brother handles their finances. They'd asked him to make a contribution in Ernie Ohno's memory last winter, to an emergency housing fund for elders, and he'd mentioned it to me.

"You've moved on," Aki said. "Enjoying life."

"We're moving back now," my mother said. "Part-time. Snow-birds. House-hunting, so if you hear of anything . . ."

Aki gestured toward the stage. "Good to see the younger generation continuing the traditions."

We turned our attention back to the demonstration. Two girls, fourteen or fifteen, dressed in white, red scarves at their throats, wielded swords with the confidence of a chef slicing a tomato. They lunged, pointed, parried, and poked. Terrific, and a little terrifying. Though neither blade touched the other girl, it was not hard to imagine either of them lopping the head off an enemy in a moonlit alley, or taking down a trio of attackers, like Tom Cruise's character in *The Last Samurai*. Aki's cane made small movements in her hand, as if it harbored a secret desire to be a fearsome sword but had been cast a different fate, helping a little old lady make her way through the streets.

I glanced at my watch, a pink Kate Spade splurge from a few years back. "We've got to run. Seetha and I are meeting Reed and his family in Maynard Alley to watch his sister's dance troupe. You two coming?" I asked my parents.

"We'll stay here," my mother said, and looped her arm through Aki's. "Reconnect with our old friend."

After a round of "nice to meet yous" and "good to see yous," Seetha and I took off. I opened my mouth to quiz her about Oliver when a familiar figure whizzed by on a bicycle.

Seetha saw him, too. "Was that Tag?"

My ex-husband, a Seattle police officer on the bike patrol. "Yep. Picking up an extra shift, I imagine. The bikes make it easier to work the crowds when it's this congested."

Everywhere, the festivities continued. We passed a booth with the largest wok I'd ever seen, clouds of ginger-scented steam filling the air. At the next corner, a Filipino dance troupe performed—bare-footed, bare-chested men playing shells and marimbas. We passed food trucks and booths selling jewelry and art. Everywhere, the rabbit ruled. Rabbits flew on brightly colored flags. They perched on tables and filled window displays. And stuffed rabbits endured the sweaty clutches of small children.

I knew where we needed to be, but the crowds and the street closures blocked our path. Reed Locke is a college student who's worked in the Spice Shop since high school, long before I bought it. His dad's acupuncture clinic is one of the few medical offices left in the Market, and Reed grew up prowling the Market's nooks and crannies. He works afternoons at our warehouse and production facility and weekends in the shop, which means I don't see him as much as I'd like. Business was slow this time of year, so I'd readily agreed when he asked for the afternoon off to cheer his sister on. The Locke family is one of the oldest and largest Chinese families in the city, and his grandfather had long been a mainstay in the Locke family association, though family, in that sense, meant a cultural connection rather than blood ties, defined by a shared name and region of origin in China.

"Let's go that way and work our way around." I pointed.

But though I'm a Seattle native and make occasional deliveries in the neighborhood, the CID is a bit of a maze. Within minutes, we were standing at the entrance of a narrow alley, the four- and five-story buildings on either side plunging it deep into shade though the sun wouldn't set for another hour. The CID and adjacent Pioneer Square were shaped by the Great Fire of 1889 and the regrades, a mind-boggling early-twentieth-century engineering campaign that sheared off tops of hills and filled in low spots. In some blocks, streets were lowered, creating a new ground floor, while in others, streets were elevated. The resulting labyrinth led to the city's ever-popular Underground Tour, a mash-up of fact and fiction. There were plenty of hills left, enough to make you wonder why the white settlers who came here in the 1850s ever imagined it a livable place. Some alleys had functioned like streets well into the 1960s. Thanks to a recent reclamation project in the two neighborhoods, Nord, Maynard, and Canton Alleys bustled once again.

But this alley had none of their charms. Dark, the brick cobble grease-stained, garbage and recycling bins obstructing any traffic that might have dared enter.

"Let's go back," Seetha said, and started to turn. I was about to join her when a flash of light caught my eye. Low, almost at ground level—on, off, on, off. And a muffled sound, like a door clanging shut. I waited, but no more lights and no more sounds. A rat shot out from beneath a garbage bin. I stifled a shriek and quickly followed Seetha to the sidewalk, where the red lantern streetlights were coming on.

"Which way?" she asked.

The crowded sidewalks and well-lit store fronts were a welcome relief. More red lanterns had been hung on wires crossing the street, bright and festive.

"Now I know where we are. That tea shop is one of my customers." I pointed. We hadn't gone far when a door at the top of a short flight of steps burst open and a woman emerged.

A woman I knew.

"Roxanne?" I'd never seen her look anything but perfectly polished, whether she wore a stylish pantsuit, a summer sun dress, or as now, jeans and a turtleneck. Running shoes. No coat. She was breathless, her eyes unfocused, her thick brown hair falling out of its twist.

"Pepper! I'm so glad to see you. I don't know what to do."

"About what?"

"The body. I think I found a dead body."

Two

The fortune cookie, now an after-dinner ritual in Chinese restaurants across the United States, originated as a Japanese treat brought by bakers who immigrated to the West Coast around the turn of the 20th century.

IN HER PANIC, ROXANNE HAD LEFT HER CELL PHONE BEHIND, so I called 911. Seetha stayed outside to direct the first responders while Roxanne dragged me inside.

"What are you doing here?" I asked. "What is this place?" Retail shops, offices, and restaurants occupied the street level, but nothing about the exterior gave a clue to what went on up the steps.

"The Gold Rush Hotel," she said, as the wood-framed glass door closed behind us.

My eyes struggled to adjust to the dim light. I made out a few chairs in the compact lobby, heavy brocade curtains with velvet tiebacks at the windows. Glass-front curios filled with old jars, wooden boxes, and figurines lined two walls. Above the stairway to the upper floors hung musical instruments, ready for a guest to take down and play, a dark red carpet runner on the steps. I could just make out the wood paneling of the front desk, partially screened like an old-time bank, separated from the lobby by a maroon velvet rope.

I'd been transported to another era, or the set of a Bogart and Bacall movie.

Roxanne led me to a door, partly open. "The hotel occupies the central section of the block. The rooms are upstairs. It's been closed for decades, but the owner is considering some changes and asked me to catalog the furniture and artifacts. I was finishing up for the day and thought I'd grab some dinner and catch part of the parade, when I noticed the basement door was open. It's never open."

"You went down there? You could have been in danger."

"I wasn't thinking about that. I had to make sure—you'll understand when you see. It's a treasure trove."

"Like the Panama?" I asked, fumbling on the wall for the light switch. The Panama Hotel, once workingmen's lodging and now a national historic site, where Japanese Americans sent to the camps left suitcases and trunks. Some reclaimed their items, but others never did, and the basement storeroom had been catalogued, studied, and preserved, a window on a shameful past. Then I remembered a more recent discovery, where renovation uncovered long-lost murals from an African American jazz club that thrived during Prohibition. "Or the Louisa?"

"No. Nothing like that."

I found the switch. A brass button on a brass plate. Held my breath—I love old buildings, but antique electricity is a tad scary— and pushed it. An overhead bulb on the other side of the door flickered, then stayed on.

"They seriously need to update their electrical system," I said. "Or at least install decent light bulbs."

Roxanne had draped her navy coat over a wooden armchair near the door, her black leather briefcase beside it. Clutching my phone in one hand and fumbling for the handrail with the other, I followed her down the narrow stairs. At the bottom, she led me through a small area lit by a single bulb. A few stray bricks lay on the floor, alongside a stack of old lumber.

"What is this place? Is it safe to be down here?"

The air was damp, filled with the odor of mold and mildew. A heavy wooden door, its brass hardware darkened with age and disuse, stood open a few inches.

Roxanne wrapped her arms around herself, her eyes wide.

"I can't go in there. He—the blood. Everything. It's too horrible."

I pulled my gloves out of my coat pocket, drew them on, and took a deep breath. Pushed the door all the way open. Flicked my flashlight app and slowly scanned the room. No windows—an interior room. Images began to emerge from the darkness: rough wood shelves, stacked with small wooden boxes. Cabinets reminiscent of the red-lacquered apothecary in my shop. A large work table. An old-fashioned scale, a heavy weight in one pan holding it permanently off-balance.

Not a storeroom. Not like the Panama. The bottles and tins behind the glass doors spoke of another history, another era. A Chinese herbal medicine shop or clinic?

I took a step forward. Then another. My foot crunched on broken glass and I aimed my light at the floor. A broken bottle. Two bottles. Three, four. A mortar, used to grind medicinal herbs. I raised the light. Tins and porcelain jars had been opened, their lids tossed carelessly aside. Wooden drawers, labeled with Chinese characters, had been jerked out of their cabinets, some emptied and dropped on the floor, the herbs inside scattered.

As though a search had been interrupted.

I panned the light slowly across the wreckage. Gasped as it found the body, even though I'd known it was here somewhere. A man, wearing yellow pants. A red brick. An arm, a shoulder, a red and yellow shirt. A pool of blood spread from the man's skull, an open wound visible through his short dark hair. I could not see his face, and for a moment, I was grateful, not wanting to see the broken bones or lifeless eyes. The taste and smell of death nearly overwhelmed me as I made out the long red and yellow tail of a lion dancer.

Something glinted. Though the man's neck was twisted, his head facing away, I saw a silver chain, and hanging from it, a tiny silver pendant in the shape of a fortune cookie.

"Good luck and fortune," the dim sum seller had said of the lion dancers. Maybe so, but the charm hadn't worked for this one. Had Oliver, the dancer who'd flirted with Seetha, been wearing a pendant like this? I couldn't recall.

Heavy footsteps thudded on the floor above us. I heard Roxanne scurry to the staircase. "Down here. In the basement," she called.

I stood and surveyed the room. Broken glass aside, not much damage. An open door led to a small room, empty but for what looked like a doctor's exam table, unpadded and even more uncomfortable than most.

Despite my coat, a chill swept through me. Was the man on the floor the interrupted, or the interrupter? What had the searcher been hoping to find?

We'd seen no signs of anyone upstairs, and Roxanne had been sure she was alone, the doors locked. Who knew about this place? Who had keys?

Who was the lion dancer, and who had killed him?

And where was the killer now?

My questions would have to wait. First to arrive were two patrol officers, an average-sized white man and a small Asian woman. I watched as they took in the scene, their gazes pausing briefly on the damage. The man crouched and touched a blue latex-gloved hand to the dancer's neck.

"I think we can call off the EMTs," he said, but it was too late. First one medic, then another, came into view, lugging the boxes of gear I had seen far too often, and much too recently. I flashed on the memory of watching them work on young Beth Yardley in my friend Vinny's wine shop two days after Thanksgiving. Nearly two months ago, but the memory still haunted me. As the EMTs sized up the situation, the woman officer gestured, and I followed her out of the old pharmacy.

Roxanne was waiting at the foot of the stairs. "Is he—?"

"Yes, ma'am," the officer replied. "He is unfortunately deceased."

Roxanne let out a sound, halfway between a choke and a gasp, and clutched her throat. She swallowed hard, pressing her lips together, then exhaled and raised her chin. "They won't touch anything they don't have to, will they? That place is like a museum."

"No, ma'am," the officer said, then ushered us up to the hotel lobby where she took out a notebook and introduced herself.

"We'll need you to stay for a bit," she told Roxanne after we'd answered her questions about who we were and why we were here. "Until we can confirm your story. You're sure neither of you recognizes the victim?"

We did not.

"The owner lives upstairs," Roxanne said. "I think he's at the festival. I'll call him."

She rummaged in her briefcase for her phone.

I peered outside. Where was Seetha? "Did you see where my friend went? The woman who was waiting to direct you. About five-three, straight dark hair. South Asian—Indian. Wearing a puffy white jacket. She knew one of the lion dancers. Though I can't imagine it's him. There are dancers all over today."

"Sorry, ma'am. No one was waiting. The door was unlocked."

"I have to find her. She doesn't know this area and it's super busy today." And there might be a killer in the crowd. Roxanne had finished her call and returned. "But I don't want to leave you alone."

"Don't worry about me," she said. "Come back when you find her."

I looked to the officer for confirmation, noticing the name tag on her uniform. She'd introduced herself earlier, but the name hadn't pierced my rattled brain.

"Ohno. Are you related to Aki?" The purple streak in the officer's hair was the same color as the older woman's. "You're her granddaughter, aren't you? My parents are Chuck and Lena Reece, friends of hers from the old days. She's a pistol."

"That she is," Officer P. for Paula Ohno said. "Always with a cause. My role model."

The patrol sergeant entered as I left. I knew him vaguely, from when I'd been married to Tag.

Outside, other officers had cleared and blocked off the area. Night had fallen. The temperature had dropped and it felt like rain. The mood had turned, too. No sign of Seetha. If I called or texted, could she hear the phone in all this chaos? People wandered by, in pairs and clusters, many sipping from the souvenir teacups that came with our tickets to the food walk, unaware that a man had been killed behind these doors. A brick to the head—it had to be murder, didn't it?

Tea. Roxanne could use a good cup. Maybe I could snare some as I scouted for Seetha. What if the dead lion dancer was Oliver?

Maybe it wasn't. It had been no exaggeration to say lion dancers were everywhere—a pair were entertaining a cluster of children across the street right this minute.

I scanned the crowd, expecting to spot my friend watching for me. But no.

I ducked under the yellow tape and headed for the tea shop. Family-owned, like most restaurants in this area, with a long history that had almost ended when the pandemic started. When the income stopped but the rent was still due. The owners' fortyish son, Keith Chang, had come home and taken over, reopening with a new name and a new look. And a menu he called "modern traditional." Basically, anything he wanted, with an Asian flair. In our conversations, he'd made clear his intent to introduce a wide range of flavors. "The only spices my parents used were star anise and Szechuan pepper," he'd told me, "and a bit of ginger. But we are turning over a new leaf."

Not a new tea leaf, though. For that, he was keeping their long-time supplier, and no, he couldn't be prodded into sharing the name.

I made my way through the throng to the Fortunate Sun Café. The first time I'd been here, Keith had been deep-cleaning the kitchen and the smell of old grease had about knocked me over. Nate and I had come to the reopening, complete with a blessing dance.

Soft light spilled out the windows. A high-top counter lined the front window where customers sat on tall Zen stools, sipping their drinks and chatting as the world went by. Keith had pulled down the cheap vinyl wallboard and scrubbed the old brick behind it, now hung with artwork, all eye-catching and all for sale. A mezzanine level offered additional seating. Light and airy, modern and semi-industrial, with more than a nod to the past.

I stepped inside. There she was, sitting at one of the gleaming new wooden tables, her back to me, speaking earnestly to a man in yellow.

"Seetha? What are you doing here? Why did you leave? I was worried sick."

"Pepper! What happened? Are you okay? Where's Roxanne?" Seetha stood as if for a hug but stopped herself. "I came in here to get out of the cold—I was just about to text you. I couldn't believe I ran into Oliver."

"Oliver?" Ripples of shock, relief, and anger ran through me. "So it's not you?"

"Pepper, what? Sit. This is Oliver Wu." Seetha slid over and patted the vacant stool. It was still warm, and I was still half speechless, a rare affliction, as anyone who knows me can tell you.

"Roxanne?" Oliver said, glancing between us. Poor man, lost in the volley of our conversation.

"She did find a body," I said to Seetha, "in the basement of the building where she's working. The police and EMTs are there now, but I—I don't think there's any hope."

"You mean—he's dead?" she asked.

I nodded.

"Pepper! Happy New Year!" Keith Chang stopped at our table, his short black hair almost as spiky as mine. "I'll bring another cup. What else can I get you? We've got ginger scones, red bean cookies, and green tea ice cream, all spiced to perfection, thanks to you. We're serving our classic green tea and our winter hibiscus blend."

Tea. The reason I'd come to the Fortunate Sun. "Could I get two large go-cups of green tea? Right away? It's kind of an emergency."

"Sure." He beelined for the service counter.

I turned back to Seetha and Oliver and, for the first time, noticed the giant black tote bag on the stool next to him, overflowing with bits of red and yellow fluff. "I thought the man in the basement might be you. He was dressed in yellow and wearing a lion dancer head like yours."

"The basement? Where?" he demanded.

"Next door. The Gold Rush Hotel."

He blanched. Pushed back his stool. Rapidly thumbed his phone, scrolling for—what?

"Here you go, Pepper." Keith returned with two large white paper cups, lids in place. I started digging for my wallet when he stopped me. "No worries. Tea emergencies are on the house."

But before I could thank him, Oliver found what he wanted on his phone. Raised his head, eyes wide, neck rigid.

"Roxanne texted me. I hired her. I own the Gold Rush."

Three

Chaos never picks a good time.

—Anonymous, that wise old philosopher

BY THE TIME WE GOT BACK TO THE GOLD RUSH, THERE WAS no question that it had become a crime scene. More lights, more patrol officers, more yellow tape.

Seetha and I followed Oliver inside. A uniformed officer asked Oliver for his ID, then spoke into his radio. The small lobby was overrun, and Roxanne had taken refuge in a chair in the corner, next to the windows with their view of the comings and goings in the street below.

"Tea," I said. "The oldest medicine known to man. Or woman."

She took the cup and sniffed the steam. "Thank you, Pepper. I don't know what I'd do without you."

My usual wisecrack—"lie in the gutter and weep"—was completely inappropriate under the circumstances, and I resisted the urge to spit it out. Roxanne and I didn't know each other well enough for my sense of humor. She was my boyfriend Nate Seward's ex-wife's younger sister, if you follow all that. We'd met last summer when a stone-studded silver trousse set, a sheath holding a knife and chopsticks, dating from eighteenth-century China became evidence in a murder in a vintage shop in the building where Seetha lives. Roxanne is an assistant curator at the

Seattle Asian Art Museum, and Nate had sent me to her for help. Since then, we'd become friendly, if not quite friends.

And she mattered to Nate. A lot. That meant she mattered to me.

"Where's Nate?" she said. "He didn't come with you to the festival?"

"Alaska. Fishing." I took the chair next to her and popped the lid off my tea. "Seetha and I came down for the food walk. We were going to meet Reed, who works for me, to watch—oh, parsley poop."

I thumbed Reed a quick text. *Sorry. Got held up.* Wrong words; I x'd it out. *Something came up. I'll explain tomorrow. Good luck to your sister!* Although her performance was probably long over. Outside, the light was fading. The afternoon had plumb slipped away. A white medical examiner's van pulled up.

"I don't understand why you went downstairs," I told Roxanne, pent-up emotion spilling out. "You're lucky you didn't get hurt. You don't have any idea who that poor man is?"

"No. Like I told the officer, I consult with private owners sometimes. Oliver hired me to catalog the artifacts in the building. But the real find is that pharmacy. I told him he needs to bring in an expert to evaluate it and help the family decide how to preserve it, but his parents—"

"Well, if it isn't our good friend, Ms. Pepper Reece. Why did it not occur to me, when we got a call about a body in the basement of a rundown hotel in the International District, that I would run into you?"

"Detective Tracy," I said. "I can explain." The detectives had just come up the basement stairs. I'd encountered Tracy, a short Black man, and his partner, a tall blond woman, several times in recent years. They were good cops, even if they didn't always have much patience for me.

"I'm sure you can. Meanwhile, tell me who your friends are and what you're all doing here. Ms. Sharma, we know," he said, glancing at Seetha, standing between Oliver and Officer Ohno.

I introduced Detectives Tracy and Spencer—yes, they've heard the jokes, and no, they're not amused—to Oliver and Roxanne, who explained her project. The forensics team arrived, and Spencer took them downstairs.

"You own this building?" Tracy said to Oliver, and I heard his skepticism. Oliver was around thirty-five, his hair in a trendy cut. His bright yellow outfit, on the other hand—well, I suppose the king of the jungle look is always in style. Though I hadn't spent a lot of time in the CID, I did know that most of the property down here is owned by families, some by family associations who manage the group assets. The street-level businesses, like the tea house and the barber shop and grocery store I'd passed, were rentals, though the hotel itself didn't appear to have been active for decades. It was remarkably clean, though, and I detected a hint of incense.

Wait. Hadn't Roxanne said the owner lived upstairs? Did Oliver live here?

"Yes," Oliver said. "No. Actually, well, it's in the family."

"Your parents? Grandparents? Where are they?" Tracy surveyed the room with his usual sharp eye, as if expecting the elder Wus to materialize out of the woodwork or the faded rugs.

"I'll call my parents," Oliver said. "But I'd like to know more first."

"Wouldn't we all?" Tracy said.

"Detective," Roxanne interjected, "can we talk about the artifacts in the basement? I'm very concerned—"

"We'll get to that, Ms. Davidson," Tracy said. "Meanwhile, I have a dead body to identify." He held out his phone. There are times when the screen is more humane than the real thing, and asking someone to identify a dead man is one of those times.

Oliver stared at the screen. "No. No."

"So he wasn't part of your dance troupe?" I asked. "The lion dancers who were at the food walk earlier? Where you saw Seetha and me."

"No," he repeated. "It's the Lunar New Year. There are lion dancers all over the place."

As I'd seen myself. But if my doppelgänger were killed in my building . . .

"So you don't have any idea what he was doing in your hotel, in that basement that Ms. Davidson is so concerned about?" Tracy asked. "Who has keys, besides the two of you? Your parents and who else?"

"It's Dr. Davidson," Oliver said. "To the hotel, no one. As you can see, we haven't rented rooms in decades. I moved in a few weeks ago. That's when I decided we needed a professional assessment. We—the family. We're considering the options."

Officer Ohno spoke up. "What can you tell us about the pharmacy? I've been around the CID most of my life and I've never heard a word about it."

"Hmph," Tracy grunted. He grunts a lot, and it's rarely a pretty sound. Whether he was displeased by the young officer's interruption or the thought of a crime scene complicated by historical status, I couldn't guess.

Oliver rubbed the back of his neck.

"Not that I want you to take all day," Tracy said, dropping into a leather chair that groaned with his weight, "but if you're going to, I might as well sit."

Oliver perched on the couch opposite him, forearms on his thighs, hands tightly clasped. "I've always loved the hotel, though I never spent much time here. It belonged to my grandfather, on my dad's side. He died decades ago. The first-floor businesses all have separate street-front entrances." A lock of hair fell over one eye and he flipped it out of the way. "When I moved in—"

"What prompted that?" Tracy asked.

"I broke up with my girlfriend and needed a place." Oliver shot Seetha a quick look. "But it was time."

How much did she know of all this? We see each other most Tuesday evenings at Flick Chicks, a group of five woman who talk as much about our personal lives as about the movie of the week, but Seetha doesn't say a lot. She doesn't get much chance, chatty as the rest of us are. She had mentioned having lunch with a new employee at a downtown hotel where she sometimes works as a massage therapist, and her cheeks had gotten bright. But that was all she'd said, and it hadn't occurred to me until she recognized him during the lion dance that she, not by any means a foodie, had harbored an ulterior motive for joining my mother and me on the Lunar New Year food walk.

I sipped my tea and Oliver continued.

"The Changs were redoing their tearoom and ran into trouble with the plumbing. The access is through our basement, and when I took the plumber downstairs—"

Tracy made a twirling motion with one finger, telling him to speed it up.

"Turns out a couple of old doors had been blocked by false walls. One led to the passage with the plumbing access, and the other to the pharmacy. Clinic. Herb shop—whatever you want to call it."

That explained the piles of construction debris.

"When were these false walls put up?" Tracy said.

"No idea. I'd already hired Roxanne to inventory all this stuff"—he gestured toward the lobby cabinets—"and the things in the rooms upstairs, so I asked her to take a look. That's all I know about it."

How had the lion dancer gotten into the hotel? I was sure he'd been searching for something.

Had the killer found it, or was it still downstairs, hidden by the mystery of time?

AFTER THE ME's crew carried out the body, the crime scene detective came up to brief Tracy. Spencer was still in the basement. In Seattle, crime scene investigations are conducted by officers, not lay technicians. They focus on the physical evidence, freeing the major crimes detectives like Spencer and Tracy to focus on the victim and witnesses. The CSI detective explained their procedure. First, a structural engineer would be called, to ensure short-term safety. Then, they'd photograph the scene and use 3D scanners before evidentiary items were collected, so someone who hadn't been at the scene could see it in all its detail.

"It's old. It's been closed off," I said. "How can you tell what's evidence and what isn't?"

"Experience and professional judgment," the detective answered. "We use alternate light sources to identify stains and pick out hairs and fibers. Putting evidence together to help solve a major crime is, frankly, one of the coolest things in the world."

"It's not like on TV," Tracy said, "but it is pretty impressive."

Roxanne seemed mollified, at least for now. Oliver's parents hadn't arrived yet.

"Detective," I said to Tracy. "The victim was wearing a silver pendant." My fingers went to my throat.

"Shape of a fortune cookie. I saw it. Any luck, ME's office will find his name engraved on it, but I'm not holding my breath."

They hadn't found a wallet or other ID, then. John Doe, Lion Dancer.

After making sure she had our contact information, Officer Ohno escorted Seetha, Roxanne, and me to the door.

"I'll tell my grandmother I met you," the officer said. "She'll be pleased, despite the circumstances."

Outside, the crowd had thinned. I was starving—the har gow, memorable as they were, had been hours ago. Back we went to the Fortunate Sun, where the after-parade crowd nursed cups of tea, sake, and other comforts. We found a table upstairs and ordered the Lunar Special—a cabbage pancake with shrimp and a variety of sauces, sized to share, and a red bean cookie sampler. Roxanne protested that she was too upset to eat, but when the plates came, she dove in.

Me, I am rarely too upset to eat. Food is my comfort and joy, as well as my profession, and I was thrilled to see the café so busy on this special night. People in food service are the hardest-working people I know, from the produce sellers to the dishwashers to the line cooks. They do the work because they love food and feeding people, even though the job is hard, the hours long, the pay pitiful, and the people—well, people are difficult sometimes.

"I'm not sure the police understand how important that pharmacy is," Roxanne said. "Historically and culturally."

"What do you know about it?" I asked. No surprise that I didn't know the story, but neither did Paula Ohno, with her deep roots in the CID. Though her family was Japanese. But history is part of the air down here.

"Almost nothing," Roxanne said. "As Oliver said, it just came to light."

"Pepper can help," Seetha said. "She's great at asking questions and digging up the past."

Roxanne turned to me. "Would you? Please?"

"I don't know. I've got a full plate." I forestalled entreaties by excusing myself and headed for the restroom. Keith might know a few things about the Gold Rush, the pharmacy, and the Wu family, but he was far too busy for a pop quiz. On the narrow stairs to the basement, I stopped on the landing to let two women by, going up. The elderly woman in front used a cane, a burgundy version of Aki Ohno's purple stick, her slow progress made slower by her pauses to converse with the younger woman behind her.

"Shen-mo," the older woman said. *SHEE*-en moe, to my ears, not used to an inflected language.

"Seriously, Mom? Death by possession? Wandering ghosts? Where do you get these ideas?"

Mom moved up one step, talking over her shoulder. "That building knows. The Wus have not done right by it. They have dishonored the past."

She was talking about the body in the Gold Rush. I touched the brick wall next to me, the hotel basement on the other side.

"I know," she continued, and let go of the iron handrail long enough to tap her skull with one bony finger. "The spirits will get their revenge."

The daughter gave me a "what can you do?" look. I smiled in sympathy, though my bladder wasn't so understanding, and the moment they passed, I dashed down the last few steps. Oliver had said the Changs needed to upgrade the plumbing. Must have been for the kitchen, because the remodel had not touched the tiny restroom. Both sink and toilet were rust-stained, and the thick green paint on the walls was peeling in places, revealing shades of red and gold beneath. The effect was not unpleasant, stains aside. Back when faux finishes were the rage in interior design, trendsetters had paid good money for walls like this.

How had word spread so quickly? And what did the old lady mean, when she said the Wus had dishonored the past? Truth is, every community has its secrets, known only to those on the inside.

Which I was not. But I was intrigued. Enough to help Roxanne? Maybe. If I hoped to learn more about the secrets of the Gold Rush, I would have to hope fortune shone on me.

Four

> *Researchers have found that most people share
> similar preferences when it comes to smell, despite
> differing backgrounds and cultures, and consider
> vanilla the most pleasant aroma on the planet.
> Stinky feet come in last.*

THE UBER DROPPED ROXANNE AND ME OUTSIDE THE FRONT
door of my loft on Western, the street below Pike Place Market,
then sped off to deliver Seetha to her apartment in Eastlake. When
we left the CID, Roxanne had been so rattled that I'd invited her
to spend the night at my place. I showed her the bathroom and the
mezzanine that serves as my spare bedroom, then grabbed Arf's
leash and took him outside.

While Arf, a five-year-old Airedale, watered the nearest tree, I
checked my texts. One from Sandra, my assistant manager, saying
the afternoon had been slow but they'd wrapped up with a big sale
and I'd be pleased when I saw the day's take. I replied with a series
of hearts and happy emojis. Then Reed, saying no problem, his
sister had done great, video attached. I thanked him, promising
to watch. Finally, my mother, saying they'd seen a cluster of police
cars when they left the CID and hoped nothing had happened.

If you see a cluster of police cars, chances are something
happened. But I wasn't going to tell her tonight. Instead, I raved
about the food and the martial arts demos, and how good it was

to see Aki Ohno again. I did not mention meeting her grand-daughter.

I tucked the phone away and we got moving. Turned out I needed the walk as badly as Arf did. We strolled down to the waterfront, the bracing air coming off Elliott Bay strong enough to clear my head after the terrible discovery in the Gold Rush. Poor Roxanne. Most people never encounter violent death up close and personal.

But what if something else was going on, something she hadn't mentioned? She'd been slow to answer questions about the pharmacy and the victim, and I wondered if she recognized him but kept her mouth shut. Certainly Oliver Wu had given me that impression. Tracy would have picked up on it. At times, I swear, the man is a mind reader. Other times, he confuses tact with tactical training, swinging smart remarks like a night stick. Spencer kept him in check, most of the time, but she'd been downstairs with the forensics team when Tracy quizzed Oliver.

How much to tell Nate? After the walk, I'd tell him how his former sister-in-law had found a body and ended up sleeping in my loft. I'd managed to stay friends with Tag despite our divorce, and I adore his mother, who never hesitates to send me gifts she thinks I'll enjoy—for my birthday last June, Tag had delivered a vintage mint green Dr. Pepper cooler she'd found—but hanging out with Roxanne felt weird. I'd never met Rosalie, Nate's ex-wife, who still lived in their old house in North Seattle. He'd never said much about her, and neither had his friends. His brother Bron, whom I'd met a few weeks before Christmas and then saw earlier this month when he came through on the way to Alaska, said that Nate was honoring the old rule about keeping your mouth shut when you didn't have anything good to say. Despite the obvious invitation to beg for details, I'd resisted the temptation.

Who's sorry now?

Arf and I made our way home, entering the building through the lower-level garage. As we neared the first-floor landing, I heard keys rattle and a door open. The woman who lived in the loft next to the mailboxes, no doubt. Though she and I had passed each other countless times over the last three years, we'd rarely said more than "Hello" and "Good dog" and "Is the mail in yet?" Her door closed just as we reached the entry.

City life.

I grabbed the mail and we trotted up to the third floor. Inside, I unhooked Arf's leash and toed off my shoes. Hung up my coat and picked up Arf's bowls. An open bottle of red wine sat on the kitchen counter. Roxanne's voice drifted down from what my builder called the meditation room, though I view meditation the way others view cauliflower and the elliptical: I know it's good for me, but I can't be bothered. Who was Roxanne talking to? She lowered her voice to a level I couldn't decipher.

I filled Arf's bowls and in moments, he was lapping up the water. I poured myself a glass of wine and stood at the butcher block counter that divides the kitchen from the main living area. My loft is in an old warehouse, and outside the twelve-foot-high windows, the city lights glowed, reflecting double on the water. It's a magical scene, and I count my lucky stars every time I come home.

An object out of place caught my eye. *That's odd. I didn't leave that there, did I?*

Before he left a few weeks ago, Nate had given me a model ship made of cloves that he'd found, as a reminder of him. As if I needed one. He was everywhere in the loft, in my life, in my heart. I'd put it on the table behind the couch, visible from almost every corner. Now it sat on the butcher block, beside the wine bottle.

"Hope you don't mind," Roxanne said as she came down the steep wooden stairs, gesturing with the wine glass in her hand. "I was desperate for a drink. And a change in clothes."

She'd swapped her jeans and turtleneck for a pair of my leggings and my favorite sweatshirt. My boyfriend's ex-sister-in-law had been rummaging in my wine rack and dresser drawers. Of course, if I'd been here instead of dashing around with the dog, I'd have happily helped her out, so I couldn't be upset that she'd helped herself.

And it was certainly no stranger than anything else about the day.

"Not at all." I returned the clove ship to its place, its pungent, faintly peppery aroma hitting my nostrils, and sank onto the couch, wine glass in hand. Propped my feet on the old packing crate that serves as my coffee table. On it lay a book of Brother Cadfael novellas, a Christmas present from Kristen, my BFF. She'd found it while prowling the shops on Whidbey Island with her daughters over Christmas break. She knows I consider the old monk, a twelfth-century herbalist, my spirit guide, fictional though he is.

"So how did you become interested in Asian art and artifacts?" I asked.

"Came with the territory, I guess." Roxanne settled into one of the twin red leather chairs. Arf trotted over, a chew bone in his mouth, and stretched out on the floor next to the couch. "Our parents were teachers and international aid workers, and we lived all over the world. Mostly in Asia and the South Pacific, and a couple of years in Rome. Seattle was home base, but we never spent more than a year or two at a time stateside." She sipped her wine. This was all news. I'd known only that Rosalie, several years older, was a nurse who'd gone to school in Seattle and met Nate after graduation.

"When we were home," Roxanne continued, "we went to all the usual places. The zoo, the aquarium, Seattle Center. And the museums. Once I got tall enough to see into the displays at the Asian Art Museum without a boost, I was hooked. My parents had to bribe me to choose another place for a family outing."

"It was still the main art museum when I was a kid. We lived close by. But I'll admit, the camels were the only thing I cared about."

The old stone camels that sat outside the 1930s Art Deco building for decades had been moved safely inside and replaced by replicas when the new museum was built downtown. Kid magnets, then and now.

"It was the snuff boxes that hooked me," Roxanne said. "And the netsuke. Anything small and weird."

"Like the things we saw in the pharmacy. The bottles and tins and jars."

"Exactly. I studied art history, then got a double master's in Asian studies and museum management. Worked in San Francisco for a while, did a short stint in Tokyo, then this job at SAAM opened and I came home."

"What's a day in the life like?"

"Varies a lot, which is great. Altogether, the museum has more than twenty-five thousand items, from netsuke the size of a walnut to murals as long as this building. I don't deal with the paintings or textiles, or the big sculptures, but if we're organizing an exhibit, everyone's involved. First, we develop the focus. How does it fulfill our mission? What are the funding sources? All that can take years, literally. Then we choose the items, confirm what we think we know about them, and write the display cards and catalog copy. We work with the carpenters to design and build the displays. If we're borrowing pieces from other museums, that adds another layer of complexity."

"Wow. More involved than I ever imagined."

"Occasionally we're offered items for the collection, so we clean them, appraise them, do the research, and decide on acquisitions. We've got items that have never been fully researched or that need restoration, so we work on that, too."

Her tote bag lay tipped over on the floor and the embroidered silk pouch that held her loupe had slipped out. One of the tools of her trade. "Clearly you love it. How do you have time for side jobs?"

"Crazy, right? But consulting's great, because you never know what you'll find. Most of what I see is"—she lifted her glass but didn't sip, weighing her words. "Ordinary. Not significant historically, culturally, or artistically. But the Gold Rush has been closed up for so long. It was a residential hotel, and before that, temporary housing for immigrants and laborers. It wasn't unusual for families or individuals to come to Seattle, then go back to China. I thought that as a transitional space, there was a good chance I'd find something worthwhile."

"How did Oliver get your name?"

"I imagine he called the museum. Or the Wing Luke, the Asian Pacific museum in the CID. We work with them quite a bit, and they know I'm available."

"Oh, I love that place. We toured the old hotel—what's it called? The Kong Yick. The Gold Rush isn't anything like that, is it? Not with that nice lobby and all the polished woodwork."

She uncrossed and recrossed her legs. "No. The Kong Yick was more like a bunkhouse, with several men sleeping in a single room. They'd sleep in shifts, based on their work schedule, and eat or play cards in common rooms. I'm not sure when the Gold Rush was built, probably not long after the Great Fire, and it's been through several phases, most recently as SROs. Closed for ages."

Single room occupancy. Once a staple in the Market, too, though current housing there is a mix of senior, subsidized, and market-rate apartments ranging from studios to larger units. A few were set aside for working artists. I knew a good share of the five hundred residents, a varied cast of characters who make the community richer.

"What we've found in the hotel so far is interesting," she continued, "but not particularly valuable. Lots of jars and musical instruments. A set of figurines. Someone's prized collection of tiny stone pigs." She showed me a picture of the piglets.

"Adorable." I handed back her phone. "What are they planning to do with the place?"

"That, I don't know. I met Oliver's parents briefly, in passing. Bobby and—her name escapes me. Oliver works in one of the boutique hotels downtown, at the front desk. He gave me a key so I could work when I had time, without needing him to let me in."

Ah. I'd guessed right. Oliver was the man Seetha had met at work.

"Then, last week," she continued, "he took me into the basement. I hadn't been down there yet. I could hardly believe it. An intact, early twentieth-century Chinese pharmacy. There's one in eastern Oregon and another in Montana, but nothing like it in Seattle. I told him he needed to bring in real experts, but he hemmed and hawed. He is practically sitting on a museum, and ever since I saw it, I've been terrified that something would happen to it."

And now something had.

"He may not be able to keep it quiet much longer," I said. "Depending on what the police say. Reporters get wind of a history like that, he'll be flooded with calls."

"He's got to install a security system, as soon as possible."

"Not a bad idea." Another idea occurred to me, and it wasn't bad, either. "Meanwhile, if he wants someone local with knowledge of Chinese medicine to help identify what's down there, I might know who to call. I mentioned Reed, the college kid who works for me?"

"He was waiting for you. At a performance, I think."

"Right. He's a history major. His father and grandfather are doctors of Chinese medicine—acupuncture, herbs, all that stuff.

Dr. Locke the younger runs the clinic. It's in the Market, not far from my shop. Dr. Locke the grandfather is retired. He's got to be close to ninety and he grew up in Seattle, so he might know the history of the place. At the least, he could tell you about the herbs and medicines."

"That sounds ideal, though it's Oliver's call."

Oliver, or Oliver and his parents? Or if the Wus were like the Lockes, the whole fam-damily. Might be why Oliver hadn't wanted to reveal the secret of the cellar. How you ever got a clan to agree on anything, I couldn't imagine. My extended family couldn't agree on holiday dinner, and we were all reasonable people who got along. Mostly. My brother's wife goes through food fads like fish go through water, and my mother's sisters blow up at each other every few years, but it never lasts long. The diets or the spats.

"Great. Reed's working tomorrow. Come up to the shop and meet him then."

"Truth is," Roxanne said as she cradled her wine glass. "This isn't the first time something odd's happened since I've been working at the Gold Rush."

Arf raised his head and I rubbed behind his ear, waiting for her to elaborate.

"Doors left open. Strange sounds. At first, I assumed it was the street-level tenants, but Oliver said no, none of them had access to the hotel or the basement, although some have their own separate basements."

"Like the Changs' tea house."

"Yes. I even wondered if some kind of criminal activity was going on. People taking advantage of vacant spaces to—I don't know, do drug deals or hide stolen goods."

Not impossible, but the place had such an undisturbed air. As if the last tenant had left for the day and simply not returned. In 1960.

"When you work with antiquities," she continued, "you sometimes feel the presence of the person who owned the object. We all feel it; we talk about it. Among ourselves." She let out a strangled laugh. "Outsiders might think we were certifiable. But more than once, when I knew Oliver was at work, I was almost certain I wasn't alone. You know how that is."

I did.

"Anyway, when I mentioned it to Oliver, he said there was a rumor the hotel was haunted."

"There's rumors about every old building," I said. "You'd get nightmares from some of the stories people tell about the Market."

"He said Bruce Lee once lived there and I'd probably encountered his spirit."

"Whaaat?" I leaned forward.

"I thought he was joking, but he insisted. So maybe . . ."

Her words trailed off, but they stuck in my head. Bruce Lee? Seriously? One of Seattle's most famous residents, in life and death, though Lee had only spent a few years in the city. I'd grown up riding my bike through Lakeview Cemetery and often saw visitors at his grave, where his son Brandon was buried beside him. Lee's influence lingered, in a pub in the former mortuary that had handled his funeral, a walking tour in the CID, and the permanent exhibit at the Wing Luke. But I'd never heard talk, not a whisper, that his spirit lingered.

"Wait," I said. "Is that why you went in the basement? Did you hear something?"

"I thought so. I didn't see anybody, but I was so sure someone was down there."

What would Brother Cadfael say about that?

I didn't know, but Cadfael liked his ale and I liked my wine. I took a deep drink, letting the rich, fruity blend loll on my tongue.

"You think I'm crazy," she said.

Not crazy. Not quite. But the discovery in the hotel basement had cracked the polished Dr. Davidson's poised façade.

"I think it's been a long, difficult day," I said. "And there's a lot in this world that we can't explain."

She unfolded her legs, in my leggings, and put her feet on the floor. "Pepper, it was incredibly generous of you to invite me to stay overnight, and I'm truly grateful. I wasn't sure, you being my sister's ex-husband's girlfriend and all, but it's been exactly what I needed."

"Me, too." I liked Roxanne, but I wondered if she was more deeply involved than she was letting on. She was hiding something. Still, it was good to talk over what had happened at the Gold Rush, even if I wasn't convinced that she'd actually encountered the ghost of Bruce Lee. Ever since the night last December when I was attacked in the parking lot outside the Spice Shop's warehouse, I'd felt more vulnerable alone after dark. Arf is good company and reasonable protection, and my building is safe. With Nate gone, I was keenly aware that no one sat home waiting for me, ready to go searching or call out the cavalry if I didn't show up. Of course, it had been that way before we got together, but now, being alone felt different. And I didn't always like it.

After Roxanne climbed the stairs to the loft, I texted Nate, not sure he'd be awake for a phone call. *You won't believe what happened or who is here with me.* I relayed the evening's strange events. I didn't expect an answer until morning and was surprised when my phone dinged a reply. *Be careful.*

Was he talking about the murder, or my overnight guest?

I switched off the lights, and my dog and I went to bed, to sleep on that quandary.

Five

*The Market's iconic clock and three-story red sign,
lit up by neon, were created by architect Andrew
Willatsen and erected in 1937, the year the Market
turned thirty.*

I WOKE WITH THE FEELING THAT SOMETHING WAS DIFFERENT.
Stretched out an arm and touched an empty pillow.

Something different besides Nate not being here.

Then I remembered. Roxanne. Roxanne, and the off feeling she gave me.

Time for Arf's morning constitutional. No one else in this building owns a dog, but a man from the next block was out with his goldendoodle, Mishka, and we exchanged greetings while the dogs rubbed noses and exchanged gossip or whatever they do. Sometimes I'd like to know what's going through my dog's mind, and other times I'm glad I don't.

Back in the loft, I started coffee and unfolded the Sunday paper on my dining room table, a weathered cedar picnic table my former mother-in-law snatched right out from under the trash collector's nose because she knew I'd love it.

Family is as family does.

Though a picture of the children's dance troupe had made the front page, and other photos from the Lunar New Year celebration in the CID filled the arts and entertainment section, nary a peep about the death in the Gold Rush. My guess, the cops and courts reporter couldn't glean enough info before deadline. If I wanted an update, I'd have to get it myself. But I had a hunch my sources would come to me.

"Oh, that smells so good," Roxanne said as she came out of the bathroom, and I poured us both cups of my favorite Market brew, an Italian roast with the faintest hint of chocolate. Funny—funny–peculiar, not funny–haha—to see someone else wearing my clothes. "I can't thank you enough for taking me in last night. I was quite the mess."

"I'd be more worried about you if you hadn't been upset. You found a dead body. And that didn't look like an accidental death."

The shock of it settled over us.

"After coffee," I said, "we can go to the shop and talk to Reed."

"Oh. Yes. Sure. I don't know the Market very well." She was sitting in a pink wrought iron dining room chair—the table had come with two benches, not the customary four, so I'd supplemented with a pair of junk store finds that more than one visitor had called ice cream shop refugees. "I bet you know the best place for Sunday brunch."

"That I do. Sounds like a plan."

"I hope it's not too weird, hanging out with me. Nate's a terrific guy, and it's great to see him with someone who makes him so happy. Well, not *with*, since he's not here." Her tongue tangled and her cheeks flushed. I was seeing a different side of her this weekend.

"I know what you mean. And thanks." I hurried to change the subject. Her sister's loss was my gain, but no need for the details. "You live on Capitol Hill?"

"Yes, in a lovely old apartment. The previous tenant was retired from the museum and when she went to live with her daughter, she contacted the director before even giving notice. She wanted another museum staffer to have it, and I adore it."

While Roxanne showered, I texted my pal Laurel. We had a flexible Sunday morning date, with the understanding that either of us could cancel at any time. I asked her to check on Seetha, who lives up the hill from her and has an unfortunate history with sudden violent death. I didn't mention Oliver; Seetha could explain. Besides, we'd all see each other for Flick Chicks Tuesday evening, in the loft. I'd chosen the movie days ago and now wondered if I should reconsider. No, I decided. It was ultimately less about death and more about kick-ass women, and who doesn't always need a good dose of that?

A few minutes later, Roxanne and I headed up the hill, Arf between us. I planned to spend the afternoon in the shop, and Reed and Cayenne would happily keep an eye on him for a while. Another reason I love my staff.

"Nowhere quite like this, is there?" Roxanne said as we made our way through the Main Arcade.

"Don't suppose you know anyone in the hunt for a retail job," I said. "I've got a part-timer starting tomorrow. We need another full-time salesclerk, as well as a production manager and crew."

"No, but I'll keep my ears open."

I exchanged a few greetings as we walked past the flower sellers and the arts and crafts tables. Arf wagged his tail. My mother started bringing me to the Market on her weekly shopping trips back when the big thrill was dropping a penny in Rachel, the bronze piggy bank near the entrance, and I've loved it ever since. We lived in an old mansion on Capitol Hill called Grace House, home to a Catholic peace and justice community. Kristen's great-grandparents built the house and she lives there with her husband and two teenage daughters. It's all spiffed up now, barely recognizable as the former home to two young families—her parents, mine, and five kids between them—along with an assortment of strays who helped do the community's work. We'd moved to our own house in Montlake when I was twelve, but Kristen and I had never stopped being best friends. She even works for me part-time. One more reason I love my job.

When my life fell apart weeks after I turned forty—when I found my husband the cop and a meter maid practically plugging each other in a downtown restaurant when I went out for drinks with friends from the law firm where I worked, on an evening when Tag had said he was taking a late shift for a friend, then lost my job a few weeks later when the firm exploded in scandal . . . Well, when all that happened, the Market saved me. I'd never expected to find solace in bay leaves, or cinnamon and nutmeg, but it was clear the Spice Shop and I were destined for each other. And not just because of my name.

And I love watching people who don't know the shop see it for the first time. Roxanne's mouth practically hung open as she drank in the sights and smells. The air's got a semipermanent tang of oregano punctuated with the aromas of cinnamon and lemongrass. The jars that line the walls are filled with the tastes of the wide world, showing off the jewel tones of turmeric and paprika, cumin and sumac. It's the rare herb or spice that comes in tins these days, but the top shelves and a display case near the front counter hold a collection of brilliantly decorated specimens. Some date back to the shop's early days, right after the voters saved the Market from "urban removal" in 1971. Others came from customers or my junking jaunts.

"It's exquisite," Roxanne said, almost breathless with appreciation. "And here I've been content with the spice aisle at QFC."

"Perish the thought," I said, with a specialist's zeal.

The antique red apothecary in the back, the one I'd been reminded of in the old pharmacy, holds our teas and tea accessories. We don't sell coffee, despite my devotion to the stuff. Talk about the specialist's zeal. We do carry books, though—cookbooks, chef lit and food memoirs, and food-related fiction.

Arf stuck his nose in Reed's outstretched hand—his usual greeting—then took to his bed behind the front counter. The Market is his home ground. He'd lived here with Sam, a man who bounced between its streets and low-income housing before returning to his family in Memphis almost a year and a half ago. Man, dog, and I had all agreed that Arf would stay with me. And because the Market is a sort of paradise, I consider it a match made in heaven.

I introduced Roxanne to Reed and left them to chat while I checked on Cayenne, the other Sunday salesclerk. A thirtyish Black woman with long braids, today gathered in a high ponytail, and a talent for innovative flavor combinations, she'd upped our food game the day she walked in. We could get by with two employees on Sundays in winter, but not for long. Matt, who'd started the same time as Cayenne, had left the first of the year to team up with my pal Vinny at his shop, the Wine Merchant, and they were busy working on an expansion. My part-timer, Cody, had gone back to school, and I approved, though I missed his eagerness and his delivery skills. He works evenings tending bar for our good customer Edgar at Speziato, so I see him now and then. That left four staff and me. I'd hoped I could entice Reed to stay on after graduation in June to run the warehouse and production. But the odds were slim.

And growing slimmer. I knew he loved history and Seattle history in particular, but he practically glowed as he listened to Roxanne talk about what she'd found in the Gold Rush.

A few minutes later, Roxanne asked if I was ready to eat.

"I am always ready to eat," I told her, and we strolled out into the cool gray morning. The sidewalk in front of the Triangle Building, the next one south of mine, was busy but nothing like a summer Saturday. Built on produce, the Market has its seasonal rhythms.

I heard a shout and a squeal and a crash. A scrawny man in a denim jacket sprinted across Pike Place, the Market's cobbled main street, then disappeared into the Main Arcade. An aproned produce seller stood on the curb, shouting. In the street, a green Mazda had screeched to a halt to avoid the runner, stopping so suddenly that a white van smacked into its rear end.

The driver of the van jumped out and charged toward the Mazda, reaching for the handle of the driver's door. At the same time, the Mazda driver pushed the door open, hitting the van driver and knocking him backward. He staggered into a pedestrian, who let out a startled cry.

The shopkeeper was still yelling at the long-gone thief. The van driver had regained his feet and was aiming for the Mazda driver, fists raised. Four-letter insults flew.

"Stop it," I shouted, but no one stopped. I thrust my tote at Roxanne and dashed into the street. The shopkeeper, a barrel-chested man of about fifty, rushed into the fray at the same time and I was glad to have someone bigger and stronger on my side.

Not for long.

"He got away because of you, you moron," he yelled, though whether at the van driver or the other man wasn't clear. He was ready to swing at anyone in his path.

"Stop it," I bellowed, stretching out my arms and making stop signs of my hands. "Act like grown men. This is no time for a fist fight or a temper tantrum."

"Butt out, lady," the Mazda driver said. "This is nothing to do with you."

"Or with any of you," I said. "To your credit, you managed to avoid hitting someone." I turned to the van driver. "And yes, he made a sudden stop, but if you'd been paying attention, you could have avoided hitting him. You can't drive street speed down here. It's too narrow and there's too much going on."

I directed my next bit of wrath to the shopkeeper, a man I knew well. Or so I'd thought. "All this because of one smashed pineapple?" It lay in the street, the pulpy mess already emitting a sickly-sweet smell. The thief had gotten away, yes, but empty-handed.

In the brief, stunned silence, I heard the whiz of bike tires. Bike patrol tires. A blissful sound.

"All right, all right," a voice I knew well broke in, loud but firm. A voice used to calming the irate and controlling the out of hand. *Tag.*

It didn't take Tag and his partner long to separate the three men and sort things out. They took names, and Tag glanced at me, eyebrows raised, when he realized who Roxanne was. His partner oversaw the drivers' exchange of insurance info. They got the description of the would-be shoplifter, but he was long gone. Another merchant swept the smashed fruit off the stones and the crowd of onlookers moved on.

It was a wonder road rage didn't erupt down here more often. The combination of inattentive pedestrians spilling off the crowded sidewalks, impatient delivery drivers, and looky-loos using Google Maps to scout out the original Starbucks, not expecting a narrow, cobbled street built for another era, was a recipe for chaos and collision. Throw in a shoplifter and a fed-up shopkeeper and we were lucky insults were all that had been thrown. Frustration overload. People did stupid things and didn't want to blame themselves, so they blamed anyone in their way.

"I don't suppose you'll listen to me," Tag said as life around us returned to normal. "But I wish you wouldn't do that."

"Try to keep people from bashing each other's faces and get them to see reason? Hey, it worked. Well, the first part, anyway."

"I heard you were on the scene when the body was discovered in the CID," he said. "I was already off shift."

Word travels fast in the Seattle Police Department. Tag and I may be divorced, but other cops knew my name, passed along what they saw or heard, and kept an eye on me. Like a little family, the men and women in blue.

"Nice to meet Officer Ohno. Paula," I said. "Her grandparents worked with my parents years ago on antipoverty programs. Any idea what the theory is, about the man in the basement?"

"Ohno's a good young cop." He reached for his bike, propped against a pillar. "As for the body, not a clue, but your pals are on it. They'll nail the scumbag."

I hoped so. Whether the lion dancer's death was the result of spur of the moment rage, a long-simmering dispute that had boiled over, or something else entirely, I could only guess. The detectives' job was to find the killer. They didn't care about the mystery of the Gold Rush and the hidden clinic, and the secrets swirling around my friends.

But I did.

Six

Szechuan peppers, so popular in Chinese cooking, are not a true pepper but the dried rind of fruit from the prickly ash, native to China. Lively and peppery but not hot, they leave a tingle on the tongue that adds a nice surprise to a variety of dishes.

"WHAT AN AMAZING PLACE. I NEVER KNEW IT WAS HERE," Roxanne said as we sat at a table overlooking the water on the upper floor of Maximilien. The French bistro is tucked at the end of a narrow hallway near the fish market known for the crew tossing crab and salmon through the air, to the delight of the nearly constant crowd. Then, to the waiter in his white shirt and black apron, "How about a Bloody Mary?"

He turned to me. A mimosa is usually as strong a drink as I can manage at brunch, but after the road rage incident, stiffer measures were required.

We gave our attention to the windows and the world outside. From here, more than anywhere else in the Market, you feel like you're on the water, despite the hill and two busy streets between here and the waterfront. The Ferris Wheel, the giant harbor cranes to the south, the ferries gliding back and forth—the city in motion. On a sunny day, sparkle and magic, Seattle at its best. Even on a winter day like this, the water, clouds, and mountains, all in shades of blue and green, tug at the heart.

Our drinks came and at the first sip, I felt a layer of tension slide away. We chatted about the Market, Roxanne's Capitol Hill neighborhood, and her work at the museum. Then our food arrived—a salade niçoise for her, the tuna so fresh it was practically still swimming, and a goat cheese tart for me.

When our waiter offered dessert, Roxanne immediately said "No, thank you." But I contradicted her.

"The apple cake and two forks. And coffee."

One bite in and she was sold. "This is so good. How did you know it would be so good? It's like a spice cake, but better."

"You met Cayenne at the shop. She's a trained professional chef, super creative, and works with some of our commercial customers on recipe development." I picked up my coffee. "The chef here is French, classically trained. The result is this traditional French custard apple cake, with Chinese Five Spice."

"Cinnamon and something that's almost like licorice?"

"Very good. That hint of licorice comes from fennel seed and star anise." I ticked off the spices with my fingers. "The other spices are cinnamon, cloves, and Szechuan pepper, which isn't a true pepper but adds a little bite. The blend is traditionally used with duck and pork, which have a lot of fat, but it also goes well on roasted vegetables."

"And cake." She cut another bite. "Do the spices correspond to the five elements?"

I tilted my head in question, and she explained. "In Chinese philosophy, the cycle of creation is expressed as the balance of the five elements: fire, earth, wood, metal, and water. Everything—health, well-being, peace—stems from the harmony of the elements. If you're ill, if you're angry or short of money—whatever the problem, it's the result of imbalance."

"I can safely say, after this meal, my inner harmony and balance have been restored."

She cradled her coffee mug. "Do food people talk much about cultural appropriation?"

"Yes and no. Food has always borrowed from other cultures," I said. We'd had these conversations at Wednesday morning staff meetings. "Take tempura, the Japanese method of coating vegetables with flour or breadcrumbs, then frying it. They learned that from Portuguese missionaries. Portuguese food has had a huge influence on the world. Sponge cake. Vindaloo in India. Lots more."

"I love sponge cake."

"The influence went both ways, through trade. Cardamom is native to India, but every Swedish grandmother puts it in her Christmas buns. These days, advances in shipping and preservation mean we have a global pantry. A few celebrity chefs have gotten into hot water by claiming a heritage they don't have or passing off a recipe as theirs when it wasn't. It's a question of respect for the culture and heritage."

"Not that I want to get political over breakfast," she said.

"I don't think of it as politics. I think of it as people. You can't talk intelligently about food in this country without thinking about these things." My staff were curious and adaptive, and always appreciative. We learned from each other, one more reason I value diversity in the workplace.

The waiter topped off our coffee.

"Do you get questions," I asked, "because you're a white woman working with Asian artifacts?"

"Now and then. But as you say, if you work at understanding the culture and the heritage, that's what counts. Sometimes an outsider can see, or value, things an insider misses. I grew up around these objects, and I've always loved them. When I was a kid . . ." A shadow crossed her face and she let the words fade away.

"Says a lot that the Wu family trusts you. The hotel is their heritage."

She shot me a sharp look, eyes narrowed. Reached for the check the waiter had set on the table in a discreet black leather folder.

Her mood had shifted and I had no idea why. "Did I say something wrong?"

"No. No." She was already fumbling in her bag for her wallet. "You go. I know you have to get back to the shop. I'll take care of this. It's the least I can do in exchange for your hospitality."

I was walking out of Maximilien leaving a bite of Five Spice Apple Cake behind. Talk about the elements being out of balance.

THE damaged car was gone and the temperamental produce man was nowhere to be seen when I passed the site of this morning's confrontation. Fine by me.

The abrupt change in Roxanne's demeanor had left me rattled. That, and the road rage incident. And the murder, and the destruction of historic and heretofore hidden artifacts.

I took comfort in the sights around me. The celebration of the Lunar New Year wasn't confined to the Asian grocery, the hum bao bakery, and the sushi joint—many of the Market merchants had put up decorations or displays. Any excuse for a party, especially if it meant a chance to sell more merchandise? I wasn't that cynical. The Market saw itself as a celebration of the entire city, and I reveled in it.

In the Spice Shop's tiny back office, I stashed my bag. Traded my coat for my apron, a black bib-front number with our name and logo—a shaker sprinkling salt into the ocean—outlined in white. Up front, I crouched to mug my dog.

After I'd rubbed his ears and buried my face in his fur, getting a good licking in return, I gave Arf a treat and washed my hands in the sink behind the counter. Then I surveyed my territory.

For big holidays, especially those that coincide with signature Market events, we spice up the whole shop. For the Fall Festival, just before Halloween, we'd hung wreaths of colorful leaves and fall flowers, filled baskets with warty gourds and goblin eggs, and focused on the flavors that make pumpkins and poultry beg to be eaten. For Christmas, we'd gone all out, in a tasteful way, knowing our customers were eager to celebrate the season after the pain and loss of the pandemic. As always, the spices and recipes are as important as the decor, and we'd already started brainstorming recipes using floral flavors, seeds, and petals for Daffodil Day and the spring Flower Festival.

Lunar New Year meant a focus on Asian flavors. Our Chinese Five Spice took center stage because it's well-known and highly versatile. We'd also whipped up a batch of a Japanese pickle blend, stocked up on Thai ginger, chiles, and lemongrass, and put together a ramen seasoning kit that was a big hit. Inspired by our cocoa-paprika rub, Cayenne had created a tea rub using cinnamon, black pepper, and other spices. She and Sandra had identified several recipes from our collection that fit the theme, printing up a few for in-store distribution and highlighting others on our website. I straightened a stack of a popular new cookbook focused on the wok, and patted the star of the show, a stone rabbit.

Our goal was to shine a light on great flavors, showcase the spices, recipes, and cooks, and join in one of the city's major celebrations. And when shoppers want to know where to get rice noodles or gluten-free tamari, we know where to send them.

"What's up, boss?" Reed said, using the name Sandra had given me when I bought the joint. She hadn't been at all sure a woman without any experience in food or retail—me—could save the faltering shop, but it hadn't taken long for us to find a rhythm and develop a strong mutual respect. What began as a veiled barb had become an affectionate nickname the whole staff used. "You seem a bit low. I mean, you were on the scene of another murder, but besides that."

Cayenne had finished restoring a rack of foodie fiction to alphabetical order: Vivian Chien's terrific noodle shop mysteries came before Jennifer Chow's LA Night Market series, and Mia Manansala's Tita Rosie's Kitchen mysteries, set in a family-run Filipino restaurant, came before *The Last Chinese Chef* by Nicole Mones. A customer had recommended that last title, and we'd devoured it.

Concern filled her wide brown eyes. "Was it murder for sure?"

I checked for eavesdroppers. The only customers were a couple deep in consultation over French cookbooks, a full shopping bag from the map and travel bookstore on the floor next to them.

"Nothing's for sure until the ME makes a ruling. Last I knew, they hadn't identified the man." I glanced at Reed. "Unless the rumor mill's come up with a name."

"Not that I've heard. I texted my dad about the pharmacy and he's super jazzed to see it. He'll ask Granddad about it at dinner tonight."

"Did your dad have any idea it existed?" Easy to imagine oldtimers mentioning it to Ron Locke, who'd been practicing a good thirty years, or his father, Henry. "Boarded up in the basement of the Gold Rush?"

"Not a clue," Reed said. "The hotel's been closed practically forever."

"Why would you let valuable property like that sit empty?" Cayenne asked.

"Not completely empty. The street-front businesses and offices may be enough to pay the taxes and upkeep." Although the plumbing problems made me wonder. "By the way, we stopped at the Changs' tea house last night. It was packed, and Keith is thrilled with our spices."

"Yay!" Cayenne clapped her hands, then went to check on the cookbook browsers. They'd found one of my favorite authors, David Lebovitz. Cayenne steered them to another, Dorie Greenspan, and a shop favorite on French bistro classics.

Reed poured himself a mug of our signature spice tea. "Some of the old buildings in the CID belong to the Chinese family associations. A few were built as residential hotels and centers for the families—you can tell by the ceremonial balconies on the top floor, like at the Kong Yick. Over the years, the larger, better-financed families have bought up other property, to consolidate and solidify their business. Nobody in the CID has completely forgotten the Chinese Exclusion Act and the efforts to drive us out. Or the relocation of the Japanese during World War II. Owning property is a way to say we're here, we're staying, we're as American as the rest of you."

"That's part of the concern about the transit system proposal, isn't it?"

"Right. We need a new station if the system's going to serve the entire region, but not one that will destroy what's left of the Asian community."

I'd read about the debate and listened to my neighbor Glenn, a city council member, explain the issues. Transit planners had laid out two routes. The easiest—a relative term, as both would tear up streets and limit access for years—would have the greater impact on businesses in the CID. Many, like the tea house, had already suffered through closures related to the pandemic and been forced to reinvent themselves. They feared they could not survive another major disruption. The other route would wreak less havoc but take longer and cost more. And some questioned the choice to build a new station in the neighborhood at all.

"You're serious about this stuff," I said. "Local events and history."

"I did a summer internship at the Wing Luke in high school. Best job ever." He realized what he'd said and blushed.

"So, which gold rush was the hotel named for, do you think?" The Klondike and Yukon booms had put Seattle on the map and built a lot of fortunes.

But before Reed could answer, three women burst through the front door and we got back to work. Groups of women are great for business. Competitive shopping.

Half an hour later, all was calm again. I took my iPad and a notebook and sat in the nook, a booth in the back corner, reading resumes. Hiring was always a challenge, and it had gotten tougher. But I knew how to find good people, and I'd started the process before the Christmas bows were tucked away, when Matt and Cody told me their change in plans. I'd contacted the cooking school placement offices and reached out to my HR pals. Posted online. Told customers we were hiring. Garlic forbid the chefs or producers who are the backbone of this business think I was poaching. Good for eggs and salmon, bad for client relations. But you never know who knows exactly the right person.

And the response had been decent. Job seekers had the advantage, though, and I'd made three offers before landing the young woman joining us tomorrow. We still had openings to fill. We'd grown a lot—a good thing, but growth brings its challenges.

My must-haves were simple. Retail experience not required. A retail personality, on the other hand, was essential. Our staff had to be willing to actually talk with customers and remain calm despite the occasional dustup. Heavy lifting not needed, but we make deliveries daily, and that can be physically demanding. Cultural diversity mattered, too. It makes for a more interesting workplace and reassures customers who don't look like me—a standard-issue white woman a pinch past forty—that they are welcome. And it helps all of us better understand the social, economic, and cultural issues surrounding food. So many issues.

No need for cul school, though Cayenne was a graduate. I used to think knowledge of food an absolute until I'd hired Matt, whose natural talent for retail more than made up for initially not knowing the difference between basil and bay leaves.

What I needed was the person whose passion was pointing them toward food, toward adventure, toward doing something new and interesting that also happened to taste and smell great. I flagged a couple of prospects in the newest batch of applications.

At the production facility, on the other hand, food knowledge mattered. So did organization and precision. You can mess around with the amount of red pepper and oregano you toss on ribs you're grilling in the backyard, but not in the blend you're mixing for professional chefs and picky home cooks.

One new app had come from a Nate. My boyfriend's name. My neighbor's name. No way could I have a third Nate in my life. But he'd worked in the grocery business and had a degree in marketing. A definite maybe.

Reed was busy filling a customer's order and Cayenne was on the phone when a woman came in, a quizzical expression on her face. Our eyes met in that instant "just who I'm looking for" moment of recognition, though I knew we'd never met.

"Hi. Pepper Reece. I own the shop. How can I help you?"

"I was talking to Sandy Lynn over at Say Cheese! and she said you had the cutest aprons."

"We do." When her childcare situation forced the woman who made the aprons to give up her craft table in the Market, we'd offered to sell them for her. "They're cute and durable. Made by a young mother in Phinney Ridge."

A customer with a sense of humor had hung a pair on the outstretched arms of the Guardian, a found-object sculpture that keeps watch over the shop, and we'd left them there. The newcomer fingered one. "Good sturdy fabric."

"We've got stripes, florals, plaids. Food puns." I held up a bib-front apron printed with a parody of the Eurythmics song. *Sweet dreams are made of cheese. Who am I to dis a Brie?*

"Oh, what a hoot!" She flipped through a stack of folded aprons, and I noticed the bulging shopping bag at her feet.

"You scored with the cheese. I spy a chunk of brie and I'm getting a whiff of feta. Sheep's milk or goat?"

"Goat, but she's got both. Her smoked cheddar is to die for."

"Smoked cheddar. Yum." Sandy Lynn's shop filled a tiny corner of the Main Arcade, near the top of the steps leading to the lower levels collectively known as Down Under. It's a funky menagerie of shops that cater to all variety of hobbies and odd interests, along with a café or two and even a psychic. The cheese shop was new since the first of the year. I'd seen the owner at a merchants' meeting, but hadn't had a chance to chat with her or check out her wares.

My cell phone buzzed in my apron pocket and I snuck a peek while my customer browsed. My mother, who'd taken to texting like the proverbial fish to water. *We spent the afternoon house hunting. Cross your fingers!*

I hoped they found their dream house soon. Problem was, they didn't know what they wanted. Last summer, a cohousing community in the trendy Pike/Pine neighborhood turned them down. Snowbirds, the residents had agreed, didn't fit the model. After decades of community work, coalition building, and blah blah blah, my mother had been heartbroken. Now they were house-sitting a floating home, aka a houseboat, on Lake Union, and loving it, but prices were astronomical. They'd scoured virtually every neighborhood in the city, in the suburbs, and on the islands, but so far, the perfect fit eluded them. And time was running short.

You'll know it when you see it! I replied.

My customer chose three aprons, then moved on to spice blends. I love everything involved in running Seattle Spice, except the hiring and firing. But talking to customers? Finding out what they cook, how they cook, what flavors make the people they cook for swoon—that is the cat's meow.

Or, in my case, the dog's bark. Arf is an incredible gentleman who somewhere along the line was trained to give out one tiny little yip when he needs to pee. Cayenne took over for me and out we went.

We angled northish—directions are skewed in the Market, as in much of Seattle—to Victor Steinbrueck Park, a delightful patch of green named for the architect credited with saving the Market. While Arf did his thing, I wondered if Roxanne would still want me to help her solve the mysteries of the Gold Rush. Depended, I supposed, on Oliver Wu and his parents. What would they decide to do, now that the secret pharmacy had come to light? Would they be interested in Dr. Locke's assessment?

We wove our way back through the afternoon crowd. But before we turned left to the shop, we turned right in search of cheese.

"Say Cheese!" read a dark red sign with yellow lettering, an old-fashioned script outlined in white and black. Retro and immediately charming. The refrigerator cases gleamed, the cheese behind the glass so beautiful my mouth began to water.

"You must be Sandy Lynn," I said to the woman behind the counter, a turquoise streak in her snow-white hair. "I'm Pepper—"

"Oh, I know who you are! Pepper Reece, the Queen of Spice!"

I almost expected her to rush around the counter and throw her arms around me.

"Great to see a new face in the Market," I said. "Winter can be slow, but that will give you time to iron out the kinks before spring. When the fresh flowers and produce start coming on, the locals start flooding in. And then come the tourists."

"I can hardly wait." She handed me a toothpick stuck in a cube of deep gold cheese and held up a bone-shaped cookie. "Can your dog have a treat? Homemade. Cheese is canine-safe."

"Absolutely." I gave Arf the dog biscuit and it disappeared in one bite. I ate my treat more slowly, savoring the mild earthiness that complimented the cheddar. "Oh, gosh, this is good."

"From Wisconsin. The best."

Both Washington and Oregon have plenty of creameries and cheese makers, but I didn't mind her regional bias. The cheese was that good. Besides, I could see by the markers in her display case that she offered selections from around the country and the world.

The Market is a sort of incubator for entrepreneurs. But she was older than most. "What prompted you to open a cheese shop? And why here?"

"It's been my lifelong dream. I grew up in Wisconsin, where cheese is religion. Married a military man and everywhere we went, I made it my mission to learn about the cheese. We ate the most divine goat cheese in Spain. Hiked up a mountain to a cave in France for an intense, creamy blue. My husband says our vacations were dictated by one thing. Not the grand churches or great museums or beautiful beaches."

"Cheese," I said.

"Cheese," she echoed. "His last posting was Joint Base Lewis-McChord. The kids and grandkids are in Seattle. So we settled here. I decided if I was ever going to open my own cheese shop, now was the time and this was the place."

"Good for you."

"Everyone's been so welcoming. Including the other cheese shops, which surprised me."

"Not me. We've got our grumblers, for sure, but most merchants realize that there's room for all of us, and competition helps grow the market. Small m." I scanned the cases. So many choices. "Could I have half a pound of that smoked cheddar? Too good to resist."

"You bet." She slid open the cooler door, talking as she worked. "Well, people couldn't be more helpful. Though I couldn't do what you did yesterday. Stepping between angry men." She handed me a small brick wrapped in white cheese paper and waved me off when I tried to pay.

"Thanks. As for breaking up the fight, you do what you have to do, to protect your community," I said.

"See? That's why I knew this was the place to be. It's a community. That's what all of us want."

That, and good cheese.

Seven

The China Day parade in the 1909 Alaska-Yukon-Pacific Exhibition, Seattle's first World's Fair, included a 150-foot-long dragon carried by 50 people, and members of the Chinese community wearing ancient warrior costumes marching on foot and riding on horseback.

IT'S NOT EVERY DAY THAT YOU WALK BACK INTO YOUR HAPPY place to find homicide detectives waiting for you.

I sent Arf to his bed. Stashed the cheese and joined my friends—I use the word loosely—in the nook, where Spencer was scrolling on her phone and Tracy was scowling. Probably because no one had offered him any cookies, although they did have tea.

"You brought good news, right? It was all a mistake. The dead man's alive and well. The pharmacy's intact and everyone's playing nice."

Spencer raised her eyebrows and Tracy glared like I'd been smoking in the boys' room.

"Well, a girl can hope." I slid in across from them. "At least tell me you know who he is. You've found his family, and you're sure you know who killed him."

At the sight of their blank faces, I slumped against my seat.

"One thing we can usually be sure of in the Chinatown-

International District," Detective Spencer said, "is that everyone knows everyone."

"Doesn't mean they'll tell us," Tracy said. "But someone knows."

"Officer Ohno and another of our Asian officers are making the rounds." Spencer scrolled through her phone again. "They've got good community rapport. We'd hoped the Wus or a tenant could identify the victim, but so far, no luck. Take another look."

She held out her phone and showed me the morgue photo. The lion dancer's face had been cleaned up. No blood. Cuts and scrapes. Dark hair, cut short on one side. Sad brown eyes—or did they look that way to me because I knew he was dead? Because I was looking at him through my own sad brown eyes?

"No. I'm sorry. Not familiar at all." The truth of it made me even sadder and I wished I'd poured myself a cup of tea before joining the detectives. "The other dancers, the festival organizers?"

"No joy," Tracy said.

Why was the dead man in costume, if he hadn't been part of the entertainment? This wasn't one of those events where attendees dress up. When the annual Comic Con takes over the convention center downtown, superheroes and demon slayers flood the streets, and I remembered vividly the day Sandra and I stood on the sidewalk and watched the entire cast of Batman traipse down Pike Place.

"So what was he doing inside the hotel? The pharmacy in particular?" I asked.

"We were hoping you had some insight. From your new best friend, Dr. Davidson."

"She's hardly that." I was glad Tracy had said "doctor" this time, so I didn't have to correct him.

"You let a stranger spend the night at your place?"

How did he know?

"It's hard to explain." But I did, and then asked the question that had been bothering me all day. And all night. "You think this was murder, don't you?"

"Pepper, you know it's too soon to say." Spencer slid her phone into her jacket pocket. "We're gathering facts. Waiting for the ME and the forensics. Scouting out witnesses."

"Which brings us back to your friend–not friend," Tracy said.

"You pour a little wine in her, she spill a little gossip? Talk in her sleep and tell you all about it?"

"Seriously, Detective. You don't suspect Roxanne? She's an art historian. A museum curator. I can't fathom her killing a man, and she would never intentionally break historic artifacts, no matter how small." Like the tiny glass vials and bottles that had crunched beneath my feet when I checked on the dead man. I pushed the memory away.

Tracy grunted. "Ask your boyfriend." Then, to Spencer, "You were right. She doesn't know anything, and she doesn't have anything to eat. Let's get out of here."

He slid out of the booth and stalked to the door. Spencer put a hand on my arm. "You know how grumpy dead bodies make him."

"He should check his blood sugar," I said, and she fought off a smile.

They left, leaving me thinking about Roxanne. They'd implied something negative in her past, something I didn't know that Nate did. My phone was in my apron pocket, but now was not the time.

"Do they have any idea who he is?" I hadn't noticed Reed approach.

"The victim? Not yet."

"'Course, even if the locals know him, they might not want to say," he said, unconsciously echoing the detectives. "If they think he's not legal or might be in trouble."

"In trouble? He's dead."

"Yeah, but they might have their reasons."

"What? Why? What reason could you have for not identifying a dead man? For not helping the police find his family and get justice?"

Unless identifying the victim somehow pointed at the killer, someone they wanted to protect. Or there was some other secret that people in the know wanted to keep.

I knew the neighborhood was concerned about increasing violence, especially hate-driven crime. And that rising crime feels like both an attack on the community and a failure of it.

"You ever hear rumors about Bruce Lee haunting the Gold Rush? Or any place nearby?"

Reed snorted. "Everybody likes a good ghost story, but no. No

way anybody would ever have kept that quiet. Bruce Lee's practically a god in Seattle. Everything about his life here's been dug
up and documented. You served him tea once, you brag about it
forever."

I made a framing gesture with my hands, indicating a sign.
"'George Washington slept here'?"

"Exactly."

Hmm. My turn to grunt. Detective Michael Tracy had that
effect on me.

SMOKED cheddar, I'm happy to report, goes well with apples and
homemade seed crackers. And red wine. I took another sip and
stared out the windows of my loft. The evening skies were still
gray, the lights of the harbor and Alki barely piercing the mist
outside. Or the fog in my brain.

I was restless and not because of the mist and murder—I was
sure the death in the Gold Rush was murder, despite Spencer and
Tracy's noncommittal responses.

Quite simply, I did not know what to do with myself, and the
weekend trauma underscored that undeniable truth.

I worked. I walked the dog. I read a bit and watched a movie
with my friends every week or two. Occasionally, I hit up a festival
with a friend or my visiting parents.

But I was feeling stagnant. Like my life was missing something.

And it wasn't just Nate's absence that had brought this on.
My parents were looking for a place to live, yes, but part-time.
New digs or no, they'd be heading back to Costa Rica soon. I
see my brother regularly and talk to him often, but he has his
own life and family. It had been months since Kristen and I had
gone antiquing. It's great fun to come across a cool old chair or
quilt, find a match for the vintage wine glass that broke, or score
the perfect addition to the salt and pepper shaker collection my
grandmother Reece started for me not long after my grandfather
bestowed my nickname. My cupboards were crammed with
vintage kitchen wares—the brightly colored Fiestaware Tag and I
hunted down when we were first married, my Hungarian grandmother's wooden rolling pin, and the stack of Pyrex mixing bowls
from a second-hand shop on Whidbey Island. But it's not a collection if you use them, is it?

I loved seeing those reminders of other times around me now, and I missed my jaunts with girlfriends. Not that any of us needed more stuff. Our homes—and Kristen's house dwarfed my loft—were full.

Besides, her girls were young teenagers now and she took every chance they'd give her for an outing together, sometimes with their friends.

Heck, even Seetha had a friend I hadn't known about—Oliver Wu.

I needed a hobby. But what?

My melancholy was pierced by questions from the weekend. Who was the man in the basement rubble? Why had he been there? What was Oliver Wu hiding?

And what had Detective Tracy meant by his comments about Roxanne?

I texted Seetha to see how she was holding up. No reply. I didn't want to bother Laurel. Most weekdays, she's up before the crack of dawn to bake, and Sunday evenings were her quiet-before-the-storm time.

Nate and I talked almost every night and texted regularly. If I called him this early, he'd know something was up. Besides, it wouldn't be fair to inflict my sour mood on him. And I didn't want to ask him to dish dirt about Roxanne. I wasn't sure what I'd be asking, or if I really wanted to know.

While I was dithering, my phone pinged with a message from Reed. His grandfather knew nothing about a Chinese doctor who'd worked in the Gold Rush. But his interest was piqued. For a sight like that, he'd brave the steep stairs.

I'll tell Roxanne, I texted back. Maybe one of the other businesses had a service elevator Henry Locke could use. Although now that I thought about it, I hadn't noticed any doors other than the one to the pharmacy. Did the basement not run under the entire building? Is that why access to the plumbing had been so tricky?

I thumbed a note to Roxanne, not sure she would reply. Something had shifted in her attitude toward me over brunch, and it wasn't from the Bloody Mary or the apple cake. So then what?

To my surprise, she replied almost instantly saying she was thrilled and would tell Oliver that the Lockes were on board.

Great, I texted back. Not unusual for an adult child, especially a son, to take over a family business and manage property. If it was family property, wouldn't he consult them before making major decisions like letting an outsider see a room that had obviously been hidden intentionally? Of course, as I was learning, there was Family with a big F and family with a small f.

The Gold Rush, though, did not seem to fit the usual patterns in the CID, even aside from the historic horde in the basement. And the Lockes were part of the Chinese community, which Roxanne and I were not.

No matter how tasty, smoked cheddar and crackers do not a dinner make. I put together a chef's salad with hard-boiled eggs, sliced turkey and salami, and a few cubes of that yummy cheese. Gave Arf a chew bone he took to his bed in the corner. Sat at my dining table reading a *National Geographic* article about harvesting black cardamom in a Vietnamese national park. The cultural and historical impact of the spice trade was huge and complicated, and as I read, I replayed my conversation with Roxanne. Things had gotten strange after she'd asked about food and cultural appropriation. I wondered how the conversations went in the museum world. Certainly, I'd heard news reports of countries and tribes requesting the return of stolen artifacts. And it had been headlines when two Seattle carvers pled guilty to federal crimes for falsely claiming tribal heritage to sell their work.

In fact, some Seattleites wanted to remove the totem poles that have presided over Victor Steinbrueck Park for more than forty years. Totem poles are often associated with Seattle, but they don't represent the Native peoples of the Puget Sound. Historically, they're the work of tribes further up the coast, from Vancouver Island north into Alaska. No one doubted these poles had been planned and created in the spirit of compassion, and visitors love them. But were they a sign of the ties between the peoples of the larger region, or a failure to acknowledge the local culture? The issue was undecided. I'd managed to avoid being forced to take a stand. It wasn't up to the merchants, and I always try to see both sides, even when it gives me a crick in the neck.

Which, in a roundabout path that only the truly weary brain can take, brought me back to Roxanne and Nate, and Detective

Tracy's veiled suggestion that the curator wasn't all she seemed to be and that Nate knew all about it. He hadn't said a word.

Actually, he had, last night. He'd told me to be careful.

A lover's reflexive response to my proximity to crime, or a warning from the voice of experience?

Eight

*At First Avenue and Pike Street, the character of
the Market begins to be revealed. It is a hustling,
bustling scene of essential human activity. The life
of the city flows through here. It is not a lonesome
place.*

—Victor Steinbrueck, *Market Sketchbook* (1968)

ARF AND I TOOK THE LONG WAY AROUND TO WORK MONDAY
morning, so we could swing by the bank and slip yesterday's
deposit into the secret slot. We came to the Market through the
main entrance at First and Pike. This time of day, it's busy not
with shoppers and tourists but with merchants and daystallers and
delivery people. Working people.

My people.

We got coffee and a cinnamon roll at Three Girls Bakery,
one of the oldest businesses in the Market and the first in the city
licensed to a woman, way back in 1912.

"Tell Matt we miss him," I told Misty, the manager.

"Tell him yourself," she said, eyes brightening at someone
behind me. My former employee, a big grin on his face. Though
he's not a huggy-touchy guy, Matt pulled me close.

I gave him a motherly inspection. "New haircut, for the new
job? Looks good."

He smiled at Misty, then back at me. "Everything's going great,

with the banks, the wine distributors, the PDA," he said, referring to the Preservation and Development Authority, the nonprofit
created by the city to run the Market.

And with Misty, clearly. It had taken me a while to catch on
to their relationship, but I couldn't be more delighted. The only
shadow was the death of his sister two months ago.

"Heck," he said, "even Vinny's great."

I laughed. In a place thick with quirky eccentrics, Vinny
Delgado, aka Vinny the Wine Merchant, ranked high on the list.
The Market's holiday theme had been "A Dickens of a Christmas,"
and Vinny, like many others, had dressed the part. Thank goodness my staff had stuck to our usual black and white dress code,
adding a seasonal pop of color with Santa hats and festive scarves.
Vinny had enjoyed wearing a top hat and cravat so much that he'd
threatened to wear them every day. But he knows wine and he
knows the Market. And in Matt, he couldn't have found a better
business partner and future successor.

Arf nudged Matt, who held up a hand. Misty tossed him a
homemade dog biscuit.

"Sit," Matt said, and Arf obeyed. The treat disappeared so fast
he couldn't possibly have tasted it.

"I'd say you're spoiling him, but I'm afraid that ship sailed a
long time ago."

We said goodbye to Misty, and Matt walked up the street with
me.

"How's construction going?" I asked.

"Good. Almost on schedule. Darren Yardley is helping me
build the new shelving. He's got all the tools, and my dad taught
me a few things."

A pleasant surprise. Yardley was the biological father of Matt's
sister. Half-sister. Her killer and an accomplice had been charged
and were awaiting trial. I was a witness, though I hoped they'd
plead out. Hard enough for the living to recover without the delays
and uncertainty inherent in the justice system, let alone the constant
need to tell the story yet again. The Yardleys had embraced Matt,
making him and Misty their family.

"Biggest challenge," Matt continued, "might be hiring. Misty
says the bakery has never had so much trouble staffing."

"Don't I know it."

"I loved working with you and Sandra and Cayenne," he said. "I didn't have any plans to leave."

"I know. You were at the Spice Shop to learn about food and flavor, and to get to know the Market. So you could be ready when the right opportunity knocked."

"And I'm taking over where my sister left off." His pace slowed as he considered his words. "It's almost like she knew she was doing this for me, setting me up for a step—a leap—I never would have taken otherwise. If that doesn't sound too woo-woo."

"I'm not the one to ask about that." Not with the twists and turns my life had taken that brought me here, to the absolutely unexpected, absolutely perfect place for me.

"However it happened," he said, "I'm grateful. People come in, people who knew her, and they want to talk about her. But when they figure out that she was my sister, they get all weird. Like they don't know what to say."

"They don't. They're afraid talking about her will upset you."

He looked straight at me. "I like talking about her. Her death was—is—as painful as losing our mom. But remembering her is pure joy."

Now that's a life well-lived, even if it was too short.

We'd reached the shop and he held Arf's leash while I unlocked the door. "Thanks. And remember, if Vinny drives you nuts, you've always got a job here."

"I'll keep that in mind," he said, though the lift to his voice said "nice try" and "fat chance."

Inside, I followed my morning routine, getting the till ready, brewing the spice tea for customer samples, and generally making sure the shop was bright and shiny. That left me plenty of time to sit in the nook with my coffee, still hot, and the yeasty, yummy cinnamon roll. The body in the Gold Rush merited two paragraphs in the morning paper, paragraphs that didn't tell me anything I didn't already know. No name, no cause of death, no manner of death—accident, murder, random act of the fates or furies.

And no mention of the hidden pharmacy. I had almost as many questions about that as about the man we'd found there.

Not "we," I reminded myself. But who wouldn't be curious about the history boarded up in the hotel basement? That was a mystery I could help solve. If I could help name the victim or solve his murder while I was at it, all the better.

Heck, I had nothing else to do.

I found the crossword puzzle. Devotees claim they're good for the brain. The puzzles are supposed to be easier on Monday and get harder through the week.

Ten minutes later, I knew I would never find out.

And now I had a shop to run. Cayenne arrived, Kristen sweeping in behind her. Next hire, I told myself, can't have a name that starts with a "k" sound. When Cody worked here, I'd been like one of those mothers of ten who ticks off the names of all her kids before landing on the right one.

Then came a knock on the door. Our new part-timer, Vanessa Rivera, a friend of the Orchard Girls, two sisters who run a Market daystall selling jams and preserves made from fruit grown in their family orchard. They'd all grown up together in Wenatchee, the farm country east of the mountains. She was twenty-one, new to the city, and bilingual. If she stayed more than a year, I'd be surprised, but giving young people job experience is part of retail.

I introduced her to Arf and the human staff, then showed her where to stash her things and gave her an apron. I'd given her a quick tour the day of her interview, but now it was time for the nitty-gritty. We walked the shop together. Fortunately, she already knew how to work a basic point-of-sale system, so getting her up to speed on ours would be a breeze. Cayenne showed her how to weigh and measure spices, using the electronic scale and the old-fashioned eyeball.

"She's smart," Kristen said to me, her blond ponytail bobbing. "She'll catch on quick. And so cute."

"So young." We got to work, packing up the morning's deliveries.

"Oh, hey," I said. "I met the woman who opened the new cheese shop. She's a hoot. Gave me a brick of smoked cheddar to try. Smooth and mellow."

"You make it sound like elevator music."

"No, it's good. She bought one of our cheese joke aprons and sent a customer in. That woman bought three aprons and half a dozen spice blends."

"You showed her these, right?" When we were teenagers,

Kristen worked in a bookstore up on Broadway, and she manages our book section now. She pulled a couple of paperbacks off the shelf. Our customers love the word play in the titles of light-hearted mysteries, proving that bad jokes are always in good taste.

"I completely forgot, but you're right. If we're going to forge a working relationship, we need to feed it. *For Cheddar or Worse*," I said, quoting the title of a cheese shop mystery by Avery Aames.

"Take them both." She held out a book by Korina Moss. "Unless you think she'd be *Cheddar Off Dead*."

I added the books to a tub full of deliveries, then checked my route on the iPad, a staff innovation. Cheese shop first, my hand truck clattering on the cobbles and reminding me of the altercation Sunday morning. A tossup which was more absurd, a pineapple thief or grown men ready to punch each other over a traffic mishap.

"That cheese was terrific." I handed Sandy Lynn the books. "We thought you might enjoy a little light reading."

She cackled at the titles. "I'm expecting some hazelnut smoked cheddar from Oregon later this week. I'll bring some over."

"Gouda on you," I quipped. "I'm mulling over recipes using your cheeses and our spices." An ideal project for Sandra and Cayenne.

Then it was back to work. I hadn't done the full delivery route in ages, and it was good to reconnect with my customers. January is when we catch our breath after Christmas, and this past season had been particularly busy. Soon, chefs and restaurant managers would begin retooling their menus for spring, prompting fun conversations about spice and flavor combos.

Outside the Economy Building, near the entrance to the Market, I glanced up at the second-floor windows. A dance hall once occupied the space across from the office of Arthur Goodwin, nephew of one of the Market's first owners. A natty dresser, he often wore a top hat as he assigned farmers their spaces and checked on vendors. He loved to dance, and many claim to see him still, in his top hat and tails, waltzing away on a long-gone floor. Me, I've never seen him, but I always look.

What about ballroom dancing? An old college friend had taken it up. She and her husband even compete, on land and on international cruises. But no. I'd need a partner. And shoes with heels.

Everywhere I went, the talk was about the road rage incident.

Some favored cutting back vehicle access to make the Market more pedestrian-friendly, while others feared restrictions would interfere with deliveries. It is a working market, after all. Plus, we needed to maintain access for those with disabilities, both shoppers and vendors. The question was how to improve safety.

"Saw you in the CID Saturday," one of the butchers said as I handed over bags of fennel seed and chile pepper flakes for his signature sausage blend. "Dumplings to die for."

Much as I'd enjoyed the food, the image gave me an instant stomach cramp.

"I heard," he continued, "they found a body in the basement of some rathole. My guess, a homeless guy or a druggie looking for a place to crash and waking up dead."

I didn't correct him or mention the "m" word. Nothing stirs up a bout of verbal indigestion faster than mixing business and murder.

Back at the shop, I handed Cayenne the list of orders I'd picked up on my route—a short one, consistent with the season—and checked on Vanessa.

She was standing in front of the Wall O'Spice, her phone in hand. The screen showed the A-Z listing from our website.

"I've never heard of half of them. Amchur?"

"The powder of an unripe mango. It's used mainly in Indian food—soups and stews, pickles, or anywhere you'd use vinegar." I found a tasting spoon and offered her a tiny bit of the fine powder, the color of an unbaked pie crust. "I tracked down a source after a regular customer said she couldn't find it and had resorted to grinding a piece of dried mango in her food processor."

Vanessa took a careful taste, touching the tip of her tongue to the spoon. "Oooh." Her eyes squinched and her lips pursed. "Tart, and I grew up in an orchard. You wouldn't need much, would you?"

"A pinch or a dash, I'd say. It's a finishing spice." I grabbed more spoons and we made our way down the wall, Vanessa asking questions and commenting on the colors and textures as she tasted. Curry leaf baffled her, as it does many people—it's not related to curry powder at all, though it is Indian. She noticed its resemblance to the bay leaf, and the uses are similar.

"We'll save the blends for another day," I said. "You've got a good eye and a good palate."

She swiped her phone to sleep and dropped it in her apron pocket. "How do you come up with all the blends?"

"Some are traditional," I said, "like Chinese Five Spice. Each maker uses basically the same ingredients, though the proportions may vary, depending on the flavor profile you're after. Occasionally we'll tweak a classic. We add lavender to our herbes de Provence, for a hint of the French countryside. Other blends we've created ourselves, like our lemon seafood rub and cocoa-paprika steak rub. Some we carry year-round. Some are seasonal."

"I'll never remember all of this."

"No worries. Give yourself time."

I was sitting in the nook, lunching on piroshky, when a text came in from Keith Chang.

Weekend knocked us out. 2 more weeks of LNY. 5 Spice and Szechuan peppers, double our last order!

Running out of your main spicery on the opening weekend of Lunar New Year might cause a temporary freak-out, but it's a great sign that business is back. Good for us, too—if we had all the goods on hand. I mentally crossed my fingers and got up to check our supply.

Pooh. We did not. I had planned to spend the afternoon in the shop. Foot traffic might be slow, but I had a million orders to place and details to handle. But I'd take any chance I got to solidify my relationship with Keith and, if I could, develop more customers in the CID. What about the dim sum seller? I hadn't gotten her card. I tried to remember the name on her sign. No luck.

Wait. I'd taken a picture, hadn't I? I grabbed my phone and scrolled. There we were, the three of us smiling and happy in front of the booth, the woman and her assistant in the background. The string of red lanterns hung below the banner, but I couldn't see the name.

Keith would know. And while I was in his kitchen, I might get lucky and figure out where he bought his tea.

I found Cayenne. "Can you take charge for the afternoon? I need to run to the warehouse, then make a few deliveries." With Matt gone, I was doubly glad I'd taken the time to train her on opening and closing. She thrived on the extra responsibility, as well as the creative projects. I told her about my conversations with Sandy Lynn at Say Cheese!

"Smoked cheddar and ham biscuits. Apple-cheddar scones."
Ideas flew out of her brain. "It's going to be drier than other
cheese—any idea what its melting point is?"

I held up my hands. "All I know is that it was delicious paired
with fruit and crackers and the Cotes-du-Rhone red I've been
buying." At the employee discount Vinny insists on giving me. I
reciprocate by sending him as many customers as I can.

"That's a good start."

"Mind if I leave the dog?" Arf loves the car and in this weather,
he could safely wait on the backseat for a few minutes. But I'd be
gone too long.

She agreed. I kissed the dog goodbye on my way out. He barely
noticed.

Maybe it was time to consider doggy daycare, I thought as I
hurried to the loft to fetch my car. I'd heard of a place close by
that caters to downtown residents and workers. It had a safe,
supervised play area and a spa for those days when your tail is
dragging and your fur is in your eyes. My one concern about
signing Arf up was that he'd rather stay there than come home
with me.

A few minutes later, I was in the ancient Saab, zipping down
First Avenue South past the baseball and football stadiums. Stadia,
as my father insists on calling them. Back when the first, the unla-
mented gray concrete Kingdome, was built, International District
residents had protested the plans because of the impact on the
neighborhood, including the destruction of apartment buildings.
One of Aki Ohno's causes, if I remembered the stories.

In every neighborhood, there are places you drive by regularly
and never notice. They're not new. You can tell by the age and style
of the structure, the weeds at the edge of the parking lot, the air it
gives off, that it's been there all along.

But I swear, until I saw the giant inflatable Baby Cupid
anchored outside a nondescript building, bobbing and weaving in
the breeze like the dancers we'd watched on Saturday afternoon, I
had never noticed the costume and party shop on a side street off
First Avenue South.

I switched lanes, earning an angry beep from the car behind
me, then made a right and came around the block. Parked at the
curb. A converted car dealership, single story, low-slung, with huge

plate glass windows, each sporting a garish costume display. Every superhero you've ever heard of and a few more.

And in the window closest to the front of the building, hanging from the ceiling with velvet-covered ropes, was a giant lion, a good thirty feet long from the tip of its massive nose to the end of its feathery yellow tail.

Nine

Australian spice wizard Ian Hemphill says cloves are believed to have been introduced to China during the Han dynasty (206 BC–AD 220), when courtiers held them in their mouths to sweeten their breath while addressing the emperor. That makes cloves among the first reported breath fresheners.

CLOSED.

As if the dark interior hadn't been proof enough, the red-and-white sign in the window made it clear. The costume shop was not open. I should go mind my own business.

But first, I wanted a better look. What I hoped to see, I couldn't say. The shop was close enough to the CID to do a good business at the Lunar New Year, or so I imagined. I am not a costume girl. Not after the Halloween when I was ten and an older boy deliberately stepped on my sari, made from my grandmother's lace tablecloth, leaving me standing on the sidewalk, blocks from home, half-naked and crying while he and his bully buddies mocked my long skinny legs. Between them, my mother and grandmother had been able to repair the lace, but the damage was done. Thirty-three years ago, and I haven't worn a costume since.

I peered at the lions and dragons and other regalia. The lights came on and I stepped back, startled. Had I triggered a sensor? Summoned the Imperial Guard?

No. The shop was opening for the day.

"Hello, young lady." An older man, seventy and well-padded, stood in the doorway. The bushy white beard and ring of white hair around his pale pink skull, along with the belly, suggested he'd come to the costume business through his resemblance to the chief denizen of the North Pole. And yes, his eyes twinkled.

"Welcome to Central Casting, Seattle's oldest costume shop." He held the door and I walked in.

"I never knew this was here." Everywhere I turned, I spotted a different holiday, sports motif, or movie wardrobe. Center stage—quite literally, on a slowly rotating platform built to show off the latest, shiniest new car—was devoted to Valentine's Day. Long strings of hearts hung from overhead pipes and huge Mylar heart balloons fluttered as I walked by. And the costumes. Romeo and Juliet, Taylor and Burton. Han and Leia.

"People do that?" I said, tilting my head at a pair of male and female mannequins dressed—if you could call it that—in nothing but hearts, pasted in strategic places and combinations.

"Oh, pretty lady, you'd be surprised what people do." he said, and I saw that it was true. Animals of all kinds. Bob Ross get-ups, with wig and palette. Every *Star Wars* figure I could remember and some I couldn't. I stroked a Chewbacca costume, the fake fur remarkably like Arf's very real fur.

"Cosplay's booming," he continued, noticing my interest, "and costume parties for the New Year will never go out of style. Santa and the elves—my personal favorite—are always popular and we do a good business in Easter Bunnies. But a costume shop lives and dies for Halloween."

As I could see by the way Harry Potter, Dumbledore, and Professor Trelawney watched me from one corner of the showroom, next to a display of wands and other wizarding paraphernalia.

"Now, how can I help you?" he asked.

"I noticed the Lunar New Year display in your window."

"Ah, yes. 'Bout time for that to rotate out. Leprechaun season is approaching."

Never once in my life had I thought about leprechauns having a season. "What I'm hoping you can tell me . . ."

I hadn't planned to stop at the costume shop. Hadn't ever noticed the place and didn't have a good excuse worked up. Or even a bad one.

So I told Mr. S. Claus, retired, the truth. If he truly was the old man, he'd know it anyway, wouldn't he?

"Hmm," he said after hearing me out. "Not sure I can be much help. We do have the big critter in the window, for parties and school events. Dragons are more popular—we've got a few rented out right now. Most of the dancers belong to regular troupes so they've got their own kit. At my age, it pays to double-check my memory, but I'm thinking we haven't stocked those small masks for quite a while." He strode toward the back, me on his heels, passing racks of tableware, party favors, and assorted paper goods. I ducked underneath a bevy of brightly colored piñatas, and as the shopkeeper paused to open his office door, I peered into the vast storeroom. Rows and rows of shelves filled with wig-topped heads and all manner of hats and helmets. Racks of vintage uniforms, clown costumes, and Elvis's spangled jumpsuits.

"Here we are." he said, and I followed him into his office.

In this barn of a building crammed with a funky mix of new and vintage, I would not have been surprised to see my spirited guide open drawers of a wooden card catalog, sending puffs of mid-last-century dust into the air as he searched his records. Instead, he moved to a modern standing desk and began clicking keys on a shiny laptop.

He pressed his lips together and blew out a breath. "No luck, I'm afraid. Now, I'm not the only costume shop in town, though I think I'm the best." His pink cheeks glowed as he said this. "Another shop might carry the kind of gear you're talking about."

But those other shops weren't on my way to the warehouse, and I had to get going. I thanked him. He wished me luck and we walked back through the showroom.

"You remember me next time you need a mermaid outfit or a dress for a flapper party."

The world is such an odd and interesting place, I thought as I drove down First.

Since my attack in this very parking lot, outside the warehouse and production facility where the Spice Shop rents space, management had upgraded the lighting and installed exterior security cameras. I locked the car and gave the camera an automatic glance, though it was broad daylight. Well, what passes for daylight in Seattle in January. The early afternoon gray gloom is a touch paler than the late afternoon gray gloom, but not by much.

Inside, operations were in full swing. Thanks to great ventilation, I couldn't smell the salsas, pickles, and pastries being made here, but my imagination filled in. Most tenants sold their wares through retailers, mainly groceries and specialty shops like ours. Some sold to the trade, that is, other food and beverage producers. And a few were ghost kitchens, specializing in catering or ready-to-eat goods.

Was my dim sum seller one of those, operating a pop-up booth for the food walk?

A bouquet of scents and a thumping bass greeted me at our production space. Reed immediately silenced his phone, a guilty look on his face.

"Hey. Didn't mean to startle you. I need to pack up an order for the Changs and grab a few things for the shop."

"Roger that. I'm almost finished picking the weekend online orders."

The major package carriers make a daily pickup at the warehouse. All we had to do was get our shipments boxed and labeled, and haul them up front before the witching hour.

"I'll stay out of your way then. How's our Five Spice supply? I need a boatload."

"Good. Sandra mixed a couple of weeks' worth." Sandra and I did most of the mixing and blending, and kept the retail shop supplied. Reed handled the web traffic and the regular restaurant orders, though we all pitched in at busy times. The pandemic had done a serious number on the restaurant business, but the explosion of interest in home cooking had been a boon, with no signs of slowing. We needed a full-time manager and an employee or two to keep up, especially when better weather brought more customers to the Market.

I set up my station at the worktable, out of Reed's way. Printed out the orders, then got the supplies I needed. When I'm here by myself, I listen to the local jazz or classical stations, but we follow an unwritten rule not to force our favorite music on anyone else, and Reed left his playlist silent. A few minutes later, I'd packed up what I needed and carried the bucket of Szechuan pepper back to its shelf.

Where I found Reed slumped against a worktable, his face as grim as the weather.

"Reed, what's wrong?" It's always a judgment call, whether to ask an employee a personal question. But the clock was ticking and the shipments weren't finished, and that made his mood my business. Unless he told me to butt out, which he had every right to do.

"How do you decide? How did you decide what to do with your life?"

"Oh. That's big." And entirely understandable for a twenty-two-year-old about to finish school. "Let's get these orders boxed while we talk."

We each carried a gray rubber tray full of orders and packing slips to the shipping station. I grabbed a stack of small boxes and started packing.

I was taping my third box shut when he spoke.

"I'd pretty much decided to ask you to consider hiring me as the production and shipping manager. I can't work full-time until after graduation and I know you need somebody sooner, but I thought maybe . . ."

Wait, Pepper. Let the man finish before you jump in.

"And then, you introduced me to Roxanne, and it was like, here was the thing I'd been waiting for and I hadn't even known it. Jobs for history majors are hard to come by, and grad school is expensive. But her asking for my family's expertise on the secret pharmacy, it was a sign. I mean, it's my family that has personal knowledge, not me, but digging that stuff up, learning about it, sharing it—it's all so unbelievably cool."

I'd seen it often. People need to vent or think out loud, but they aren't necessarily asking for advice. Male people, in particular. I was almost twice his age, his boss as well as his friend. He knew I'd worked HR for years before buying the shop. I was happy to help, if he asked.

"What do I do?" he said after a long pause.

"Let me text Roxanne and ask if she's got time to talk. One on one. Not with me or your family. About what she does in a day, and what the options are. Graduate degrees, internships, volunteer work."

"Could you? Would you?"

I could, I would, and I did. I reached Roxanne at the Gold Rush, working on the inventory of the upstairs rooms. I pitched her my plan. She agreed and I relayed it to Reed.

"Let's focus on what we need to ship today. Then we'll go to the Gold Rush. One of us can come back later and finish up here."

He agreed. As we worked, he told me about last night's family dinner.

"My granddad always comes for Sunday dinner and Mom makes Chinese food."

I remembered how my Hungarian immigrant grandparents insisted on the traditional dishes for family gatherings. My mother had been influenced by the vegetarian and whole wheat movement of the 1970s, but on Sundays, she and my grandma made goulash and chicken paprikash and insanely good mushroom soup. Sour cream on everything. Once, when my brother was sick, Grandma brought over poppy seed bread pudding—her cure-all—but he couldn't keep anything down so Mom and I ate it ourselves. She made me promise not to tell and I never had.

The seeds of my obsession with food, and spice, had been sown early.

"Bobby Wu, Oliver's dad, is a few years older than my dad," Reed continued. "He lived with his mom on Beacon Hill, a couple of blocks from my grandparents. A lot of Chinese families lived there, when they moved out of Chinatown and bought their own houses."

The Lockes still lived on Beacon Hill. "What about his father? Did he have any brothers or sisters?"

"No, he's an only child. Mr. Wu was quite a bit older than Bobby's mother. Dad remembers seeing him walking from the bus to the house, probably on Sundays."

Sunday dinner, the family tradition even in the unconventional family.

"Granddad said the old man lived alone in the Gold Rush, long after the hotel closed. He kept the ground floor tenants—probably lived off the income. Granddad used to visit some of the family associations to pay his respects, and he doesn't remember Mr. Wu or Bobby being part of any of that."

I double-checked the label in my hand and pressed it on the

box. "Any idea what Bobby's involvement with the hotel is? Looks like Oliver's taken over now."

"Beyond cashing the rent checks, nothing. Far as they know."

Just because you inherited history doesn't mean you're interested in it.

"What is he interested in, then? Bobby, I mean."

"He runs a comic book shop in Kent."

"Seriously?" I stopped and stared. "Comic books?"

"Dad says in high school, everyone knew Bobby as the kid who liked to draw. Everybody wanted him to sign their yearbook, because he'd draw them instead of writing something stupid like other kids."

"Comics," I said, popping the last flat box into shape. Almost done, for now. "Wonder what the old man thought of that."

"Dad thinks Bobby moved to LA after high school to try to get a job in animation. Years later, the old man got sick. Bobby showed up with a wife no one knew he had."

"Abigail," I said.

Reed nodded and went on. "They moved into the house and Bobby opened his shop. Apparently, Abigail spent quite a bit of time at the hotel—doing what, no one knows. Then Oliver was born, the old man died, and life went on."

Until a dead body showed up in the basement of the hotel, in the pharmacy Bobby may never have known was there.

"So, who built the pharmacy? An ancestor? A tenant? Why wall it up?"

But that we could not answer.

Whatever the rift between old Mr. Wu and his son, the property had been the family legacy. I couldn't help thinking of my friend Maddie Petrosian. For years, I'd believed her family's business, managing small commercial properties scattered across the city, had been thrust upon her unwillingly, only to learn that Maddie herself did not see it that way. Keith Chang had left Seattle but when his parents decided their restaurant was too much, he'd come back to give it his own flavor. But the Wus' relationship to the Gold Rush baffled me.

"You come from a family of Chinese doctors. The Lockes have lived in Seattle for generations. Your grandfather grew up in the CID. Did they know anything about the pharmacy?"

"No, but the education system for Chinese medicine has changed." Reed stacked the empty trays on the shelf beneath the table. "It used to be a family thing. You trained as an apprentice, with your own father or grandfather, or an uncle. Men only, to protect the lineage. That's what Granddad did, up in Vancouver because there was no one here who could train him. By the time my dad graduated and switched gears from premed, acupuncture and herbalism had been combined, and there were regular schools for Oriental medicine. Now it's called Eastern medicine. So, they didn't necessarily know all the old-timers or hear the stories."

"Someone has to know."

"Right? I mean, that building must be worth millions."

We hauled the shipping up front. Then we pointed the Saab north.

Parking in the CID is almost as crazy as driving in the Market. The handful of free spots for delivery vehicles are good for thirty minutes, but the way my day had gone so far, I couldn't risk it and found a lot instead. Mortgaged my life at the meter, and we headed for the Gold Rush.

My plan was to take Reed inside to meet Roxanne, sneak another peek at the pharmacy if the crime scene tape was down, then swing by the Fortunate Sun.

I had not been prepared for the scene outside the hotel's front door. It had become a shrine, even though—according to Spencer and Tracy not twenty-four hours ago—no one professed to know the dead man. Flowers. Candles. Paper cranes and tiny stuffed animals. Red envelopes stuffed with good wishes.

Roxanne had been keeping an eye out for us. We picked our way around the memorial and entered the building.

"It's like a time capsule," Reed said. "Or a dumpling. You think you know what you're biting into, but inside, it's completely different."

I hadn't gotten a good look on Saturday, focused as I was on Roxanne and the tragedy downstairs. It really was an astonishing place. On the wall behind the desk, cubbies held leather key fobs, stamped with faded gold numbers. Yellow crime scene tape crisscrossed the basement door. So much for seeing the pharmacy again.

While Reed took it all in, Roxanne turned to me. Back in

professional dress today, she'd recovered her poise, unlike when we parted after brunch.

"I was a bit abrupt yesterday," she said. "You've been nothing but generous to me, and I apologize."

"No worries. You had a bad shock and it threw you off." But Detective Tracy had known something I didn't, and suggested I ask Nate. What can of worms might I be opening? "I'll leave the two of you to talk, while I go do some business."

On my way to the door, I heard Roxanne offer to give Reed a tour and his enthusiastic reply. No sign or sound of Oliver Wu.

Bobby Wu had apparently wanted nothing to do with the Gold Rush. His son had made the hotel business his profession, although an upscale downtown hotel was a whole different kettle of fish. Now he'd moved in upstairs. Curious. I frowned, remembering. I was sure he'd said *we* are making plans. Meaning the family, or he and someone else?

On the sidewalk next to the makeshift memorial, I glanced up at the dark brick facade. Reed's dumpling metaphor had been cute, but it wasn't too far off. The Gold Rush, one thing on the outside, and inside, a mystery.

Ten

Where there's tea there's hope.

—Arthur Wing Pinero, English actor and playwright

"PEPPER, YOU'RE A LIFESAVER," KEITH CHANG SAID AS I HANDED over the bag of goodies. An alt rock station played in the background. "We are so busy; I could never have run up to your shop to get this."

"You've got a good thing going," I said. "And I'm happy to be part of it."

"I wasn't anticipating such a busy day, not on a Monday. It's me and a cook and one server, so I had to close the upper level." He jerked a thumb toward the stairs, roped off by a pair of dish towels tied together, then his expression shifted. "I was afraid the death next door would scare people off. Now I wonder if it's the opposite. If it's bringing them in."

"Was it someone you knew?"

"No. The police have been asking around, but we don't have any idea who he was. Or how he got in the basement."

"You've been in it, though, right? When you had the plumbing problems?"

"No. I mean, I crawled around our space, trying to find the access. But the pipes run into the hotel basement." He drew one hand through the air, pointing. "Everything on that side of the wall, Oliver took care of. He handles all the property management."

Oliver. Not Bobby or Abigail.

Curious that the plumbing for the restaurant wasn't accessible from its own basement. That there was a wall. Old buildings. You never know.

"When the pandemic hit, my dad asked Bobby for a break on the rent," Keith continued. "But he refused. I never saw him during our renovation, which is what made it so weird when he started showing up."

"When was that?"

"Off and on, the last few weeks. After I saw the white guy in the suit taking pictures and making notes. That worried me. I mean, we have a five-year lease, but what's to say they can't sell for redevelopment and kick us out? I'm not sure we could survive another blow like that."

This was the first concrete detail I'd heard about the family's plans, and it was about as solid as cat litter.

"White guy, you said?"

"Yeah. Fortyish, balding. Not sure I'd know him again, frankly. After he took his pictures, he met up with an Asian guy and they came in. I was too busy to notice anything else."

The dead man?

"The neighborhood's changed since I was a kid bussing tables for my parents," he continued. "I don't know everybody anymore. And you see guys in suits."

I scanned the room. None at the moment, but I knew what he meant.

"In fact, I saw the Asian guy this morning," Keith added. "I got off the bus up on Jackson. He was going into that coffee shop up there."

Not the dead man, then. And vague as the description was, I knew the coffee shop he meant. On the border between the CID and Pioneer Square, popular with both artistic types and business folk.

In this part of town, men in suits could be developers, bankers, lawyers, or real estate agents, with any number of reasons for scouting out the building that held the Gold Rush. Did they know about the hidden pharmacy? The Changs had not, despite having leased the restaurant for ages.

Whatever secrets the Gold Rush held, it was clear the current generations were intent on keeping them.

"One more question, then I'll let you get back to work. Saturday on the food walk, we had some terrific dim sum. Traditional stuff." I described the woman and her booth.

"Sounds like the Red Lantern. Family-owned, but Rose Zhwang runs it and she might have set up a booth for the food walk. You know how things work down here, right? I mean, if you want to do business with them, you can't just walk in and say so. You have to eat their food. Drink their tea. Chat with no agenda. Then on your third visit, leave your card when you pay the bill. If they're interested, they'll call you."

"You didn't make me drink tea three times."

"I'm a modern man." He shrugged one shoulder. "Besides, Reed insisted your stuff was the best. And he was right."

Speaking of tea, I could use some, but every seat was taken and no one looked ready to leave. Time to try the Red Lantern. I texted Roxanne. *You ready for a cuppa?*

She replied almost instantly. *We're headed upstairs. I'll leave the door open.*

Great—on my way!

From the lobby, I followed the voices to the second floor. I found Reed and Roxanne in a small room, the plaster walls a faded light green. A single bed stood against one wall, a dresser against the other. One straight chair. Plain muslin curtains hung at the single window, the outlines of a long-gone rug faintly visible on the wood floor. A radiator for steam heat.

"Hey, Pepper," Roxanne said. "I was just telling Reed that in the late nineteenth century and early twentieth, these hotels served as temporary housing for single men, many of them Asian, but also some Italians and Norwegians. Most were on their way to jobs in the canneries or up in Alaska. These hotels were incredibly important to the community."

The room was plain and impersonal, and a bit musty from disuse.

"From what I've seen so far," she continued, "it appears that all the rooms looked like this originally. In the 1930s, when labor contracting slowed down, the hotel shifted to a mix of short-term lodging, like this room, and residential rooms, down the hall. During the Depression, the SROs provided a safety net. Single room occupancy."

"Oh, we know about SROs," Reed said. "There are still some in the Market, though they're nicer now. And bigger. Sam lived in one."

"Arf's former owner," I said to Roxanne.

"During World War II," she said, "many of the hotels housed men coming to Seattle for jobs in the shipyards. A good number were Black. The CID was quite diverse in many respects."

We followed her across the landing and down a longer hall, this one graced with a carpet runner, yellow and green vines on a dark red background.

She opened a door to a simple old-style hotel room, larger than the first room. Double bed, narrower than the modern version. Wrought iron bedstead, dresser, desk, table with hot plate, and two chairs. A sink in the corner. Plain cream-colored walls. "Most of the rooms on this wing are set up like this."

"My dad said Bobby Wu closed the hotel after his father died and walked away," Reed said, "but I didn't expect everything to be exactly the way he left it. You could almost move in."

"Not quite right," Roxanne said. "The laborers' rooms, like the one on the other hallway, were closed after the war. We think Francis Wu continued to run the SRO wing until around 1970, though demand had dropped well before then."

"So the hotel was already closed before Francis died," I said.

"Yes." She shut the door behind us. "There's one more room I want you to see."

At the end of the hallway, she twisted a porcelain doorknob, cracked and crazed with age, and opened the dark paneled door.

This room was larger than the others, though it too held an old double bed, a pale green coverlet on the mattress, a thin bath towel draped over the foot. The iron bedstead and radiator had been painted a creamy white, chipped from age. Along one wall stood a maple chest of drawers and a matching dressing table with a bench, upholstered in green silk brocade. On top of the lace dresser scarf lay an ivory comb, brush, and mirror set, and a quilted cosmetic bag. A small table held a hot plate and a few dishes. A white porcelain sink was mounted on metal legs.

And in the corner stood a crib, a mobile hung with tiny stuffed animals clamped to the rail, so the child inside could watch and play.

I caught my breath. "Who lives here? Lived here? How long has it been this way?"

"I don't know," Roxanne said. "I haven't had a chance to ask Oliver about it."

"Wow," I said. "Wow." The walls were papered in a floral print, pink and white peonies on a yellow background. A pair of gold slippers, adult-sized but small, poked out from under the bed. "Was this room occupied after the rest of the place was vacated?"

"I think so. There's one bathroom for every few rooms. Nothing personal in any of them. She, whoever she was, must have carried her things back and forth. You've got to see this." Roxanne crossed the room and opened the closet. I glanced out the window to the alley below, then in the closet. It was full.

"She didn't take her clothes?" I was astonished.

"Creepy weird," Reed said, and I had to agree. "Is this the room where you found the letters?"

"What? What letters?" I asked.

"In here." Roxanne opened a side drawer of the dressing table and lifted out a wooden box, a brass latch on the front. She lifted the lid to reveal a thick stack of papers. Then to Reed, "I'll scan you copies of two or three."

My confusion must have showed. Reed explained. "Roxanne found this box of documents, but they're all in Chinese. I called my grandfather and he'll try to translate them."

"My Mandarin is decent," Roxanne said to me. "But these letters are written in the old-style script, in a regional dialect, probably Taishanese. My usual translator, a prof at U Dub, is traveling right now. Any help Dr. Locke can provide will give us a jump-start."

She closed the door behind us and we followed her down the hall. "I haven't found personal items in any other rooms. I haven't been on the top floor. Not sure what's up there, besides Oliver's apartment."

"When did he move in?"

"Right around Christmas, I think. Shortly before he hired me."

I drifted down the stairs behind the other two, still deep in their conversation. How much did Seetha knew about this place? Had she been in Oliver's apartment? Doubtful. When Detective Tracy quizzed us in the lobby, she'd appeared as mystified by the hotel as the rest of us.

Back downstairs, Roxanne's phone rang and she frowned at the screen before answering. After a brief exchange, she clicked off and turned to me.

"Your buddy the detective is on his way. Even two minutes with him and I'll be desperate for that cup of tea."

Tracy must have called from the sidewalk outside because in literally no time, he was in the lobby, with the forensics detective we'd met Saturday.

"Roxanne—Dr. Davidson—was showing us the hotel rooms," I said, forestalling his demands to explain myself. "Reed is interested in historic preservation, particularly in the CID, and this place is—well, it's intriguing."

"Any theories?"

"Sorry. Have you identified the victim yet?"

"Nope."

A movement outside distracted me. Officer Ohno was photographing the memorial and picking up the red envelopes. Hunting for clues?

"Detective," I said, "the dead man was wearing a lion dancer costume. If he wasn't part of a regular dance troupe, he might have rented it. I stopped in a costume shop in SoDo, not far from here."

"And you make a habit of haunting these places, like you're haunting my crime scene?"

"No reason to get snippy, Detective. It's on my way to the warehouse. They don't rent that particular costume, but there are other costumers in town. You might find a label identifying the shop the victim's mask and clothing came from."

Tracy grunted, then pulled out his phone. Dictated a text, followed by the bwoop of the message being sent. Then he gave us a pointed look. Time to leave.

Reed jogged up to Jackson Street to catch the bus back to the warehouse. Roxanne and I ambled down the sidewalk. I stepped aside to let an older woman pass. Instead, she stopped and poked me in the chest.

"You. Leave the past alone."

Then she raised her face and though her eyes were hidden behind dark glasses, I got the point.

Not that I was going to listen to some stranger, five feet of attitude and fury bundled in a heavy coat, the collar turned up against the chill.

We watched the woman stomp away.

"Did that just happen?" I asked Roxanne. She looped her arm through mine and we went in search of tea.

THE RED LANTERN was a throwback, filled with hot, steamy smells. We took a chrome and linoleum table in the corner, sat on vinyl-covered straight-back chairs, and ordered a pot of dragon green tea. It came with a plate of sesame balls. The woman we'd met Saturday afternoon—Rose, according to Keith Chang—stood at the end of the lunch counter, by the cash register. She didn't acknowledge me, but she knew I was here.

We sipped, and I told Roxanne what Keith had said about the men inspecting the building.

"He's afraid they're potential buyers," I said, summing up.

"I might have seen them, with Bobby," she said. "A couple of weeks ago? Outside, as I was leaving. Bobby was scowling. His tone was pretty harsh. Maybe they didn't think it was worth what he wants."

"Could be." Property, I'd learned, meant different things to different people. Money, yes. Legacy. Security. Even, sometimes, love.

I got that prickly sense of eyes on me and though I knew I shouldn't look, I did. I caught a glimpse of an old woman, one of those women you can tell don't approve of you. My hair—short and spiky, prone to sticking out all over the place on damp days? Or because we were strangers?

"Back to work, Auntie," Rose said. The old woman muttered a reply in Chinese, and I wondered if Roxanne could translate it, but she hadn't been paying attention.

"A shame to let it sit empty all those years," she was saying. "Especially when the neighborhood needs more housing."

"The whole interior would have to be redone. Small rooms, bath down the hall—that doesn't cut it anymore. Not to mention smoke detectors and sprinkler systems and an elevator. On the other hand, if that's what they decide to do, the commercial tenants could stay put." I sipped my tea, then plucked a sesame ball off the plate. "First there was the pharmacy. And now—"

"The woman and the baby." Roxanne took the words right out

of my mouth.

That, we couldn't explain. We agreed that the clothes in the closet had been stylish, some quite trendy, for a young woman of twenty-five or thirty years ago. Why had she left them? Where had she gone?

And what about the baby? We'd scoured the dresser drawers and found nothing for a little one. Not a diaper or a onesie in sight.

We finished our tea and I left cash on the table, the tip generous but not too generous. I slid into my coat and saw Rose in the kitchen, stirring a wok. At the door, I resisted the urge to look back. I was just another customer who'd come in for a cup of tea.

BACK at the Gold Rush, the crime scene tape blocking the basement stairs fluttered loose. Voices drifted up. I edged my way down the stairs, too curious to resist the temptation.

Tracy and the forensics detective, whose name I'd forgotten, stood with a man in canvas work pants and a hard hat. The engineer or inspector, I guessed, though whether private or from the city, I had no idea.

"Bottom line, you're saying my crime scene's not at risk," the other detective said, his frustration clear, "but you can't tell me when this wall was closed up or why there's a pile of bricks in the corner. Or whether that's where the brick used in the crime came from." He gestured to a stack of bricks beside another closed door, one my brain hadn't registered Saturday. Access to wherever the plumbing was, as Oliver had said?

"Meaning you're no help at all," Tracy said, and I stifled a laugh. Not very well, and he spotted us standing at the bottom of the stairs. "Ms. Reece, this is a crime scene."

"The tape was down," I said.

"My fault," said the engineer, or whoever he was, and Tracy shot him a look I knew too well.

"Oh, come on in, Spice Girl," Tracy said. "And bring your friend. Maybe you two can be more help than this yahoo. Just don't touch anything."

Where was Detective Spencer? I missed her. Tracy was always nicer when she was around.

"I can tell you," the man in the hard hat said, "that it's no surprise to see boarded-up doorways in a building this old. Especially in this part of town. After the fire in 1889, a lot of basements became little more than storage spaces. This wood isn't that old, but it's a safe bet that this door was boarded up a good long time. Thirty or forty years."

"Why would someone have covered over a door that recently?" I asked. "Safety issue?"

"Good guess," hard hat replied. "Brick wall might have weakened in a tremor and someone took it down, then threw up a new wall. This building predates the turn of the century—the last century—so it's been through half a dozen major quakes, and scores of minor ones. Inspections were required of all commercial buildings after our last major quake in 2001. Those are soft bricks, used in interiors. You could almost sneeze and knock one out."

Inspections. One more reason Bobby Wu hadn't wanted to reopen the hotel? Ensuring earthquake safety would be a major expense in any renovation plan.

"But just where those bricks came from in this maze or might have been used originally," he continued, "I'd have to do a lot of prowling to venture a guess."

"I don't care where they came from," Detective Tracy said. "I just want to know who used one to bash a guy dolled up like a lion in his ever-lovin' head."

At that, even the remaining walls seemed to shudder.

Eleven

Know yourself and you will win all battles.

Sun Tzu, *The Art of War*

AN ELECTRONIC PING BOUNCED OFF THE BRICK WALLS. TRACY took his phone out of the pocket of his camel hair jacket and read the message.

"Officer Ohno's upstairs with the Wus." He pointed one finger toward the ceiling, then made a shooing gesture. I touched Roxanne's arm. Tracy and the engineer followed us up the stairs, leaving the forensics detective behind.

Bobby Wu stood in the hotel's compact lobby not like he owned the place, but like he'd rather be anywhere else. I didn't blame him, not with a murder on the premises. I glanced at his wife, her face filled with the fear and confusion you'd expect, then back at him.

Beneath his black leather jacket, Bobby appeared to be trim and in good shape for sixty-something. Did he work out? I wouldn't have been surprised. No reason the man couldn't be both an athlete and a comic book dealer. He was a couple of inches taller than I, about five nine. Like his son, he had a narrow face, his hair neatly cut in a style reminiscent of that of Bruce Lee—or maybe I just had the late martial artist on my mind.

Roxanne reminded him who she was and introduced me.

"The curator," Bobby said, then acknowledged me. "This is my wife, Abigail."

He gestured, not quite touching her. She smiled politely, pale despite her makeup. Her coat and pants hung loose on her frame. Behind them, Officer Ohno stood with her feet apart, her hands behind her back, as if waiting for her next assignment.

"Any chance," Tracy said, "now that the shock has worn off and you've had time to think, that you've come up with a name for the man in your basement?"

"No," Bobby said. "As we told you and your partner Saturday night, we have no idea who he was, or why he might have been in this old fire trap."

"You also claim you didn't know about the Chinese herb shop in the basement?"

"No," Bobby said. "No idea. I have no use for that kind of nonsense."

"Oh, but the pharmacy is a major find," Roxanne said. "Pepper's arranged for the Lockes, the acupuncturists, to inspect it. I've made some calls. There's a professor in San Francisco and a curator I know who are experts in Chinese medical artifacts. And the museum staff who look after the original herb shops in Oregon and Montana are very knowledgeable. Everyone is eager to see it."

"Wait a minute," Tracy said, firing his next words at me. "What did you arrange?"

"Nothing, not yet. I thought the Locke family might know the story, but they didn't have a clue that there's a hundred-year-old Chinese pharmacy here. Your builder guy said it was boarded up thirty or forty years ago. If Mr. Wu didn't know about it, sounds like it's been a hidden a lot longer than that."

"It's got to be preserved," Roxanne said. "You could make this whole place into a museum."

Bobby Wu looked horrified. Had the discovery stymied a possible sale?

"Or pick it up and move it," she continued. "Recreate it as part of the Wing Luke."

"You make all the long-term plans you want," Tracy said. "But nobody's moving anything right now."

I glanced at my watch. "I've got to get back to the shop. Rox, make sure you show Detective Tracy the room upstairs."

Abigail Wu sucked in her breath sharply, her eyes damp and

bright. Then she composed herself, and I wondered what nerve I'd touched.

A few minutes later, I ransomed my car from the parking lot. My plan was to drop off the spices stashed in the Saab's trunk, then park in the Market garage.

First, though, I had to wend my way through the CID. If the red gate was the ceremonial heart of the neighborhood, its stomach was Uwajimaya. The sprawling Asian grocery drew customers from across the region. The CID was growing—it's popular with newcomers and immigrants reminded of home by the sights and smells and sounds. At the same time, the continuing redevelopment of SoDo increased the pressure on the neighborhood. South of the Dome. Dumb name, in my opinion. Much as I love baseball, nobody missed the Kingdome. But with the two new stadiums, plus rapidly expanding office and residential development, the CID was being asked to do more in less space—more expensive space. If Oliver Wu did want to redevelop the Gold Rush into a mix of low-income and market-rate housing, it would be a popular project, especially if it was aimed at seniors.

I stopped for the light near King Street Station. Did I get to have an opinion? This wasn't my community.

But it was. Community is a series of circles, some concentric, some intersecting like Venn diagrams, one of the most useful concepts I remembered from the fourth grade.

An elderly woman crossed the street, her cane rising and falling with purpose. Aki Ohno, on a mission. The sight reminded me of the woman who'd warned Roxanne and me off.

Not on your life.

The light changed. Two more blocks and a right on First. I drove through Pioneer Square, then passed the Seattle Art Museum, the fifty-foot-tall Hammering Man who stood on the corner swinging his metal hammer at a steady clip. Even without the memory of Sunday's road rage altercation, I knew better than to tempt fate at the Market's main entrance. Instead, I drove an extra block and made a left on Pine, then parked on the steep slope next to the Spice Shop's side door. Unloaded the spice and uploaded the dog, who hopped in the back seat. Wound my way to the parking garage and trekked back to the shop on foot, stopping long enough for Arf to do his business.

Any other day, I'd have visited with the artists and craftspeople as I went. Customers, especially tourists, often ask me questions about Market vendors and merchants, and I like to know what's what.

But though I'd left the shop in Cayenne's capable hands, I wanted a few minutes to chat with Vanessa. Wouldn't do to send her home after her first day on a new job without at least a brief check-in.

Arf trotted to his bed and I greeted the staff. Kristen was ringing up a purchase, and Cayenne was helping a customer choose the right chile peppers. So many chiles, so little time. Vanessa stood at the end of the front counter, looking dazed.

"How about a cup of tea to perk you up?" I said.

She nodded, and we carried our cups to the nook.

"So, first day. You'll be back for another?"

"I love it. But my feet hurt."

She wore sturdy, low-heeled boots—not a bad choice. "Hazard of the trade. Customers behave?"

"Oh, yeah. And Kristen and Cayenne were so much help. Have you and Kristen really known each other since before you were born?"

"Yep. Our families shared a house until we were twelve. But don't listen to a thing she says about me, unless it's nice."

Vanessa laughed. "You all know so much about herbs and spices."

"Once spice at a time. Drink up and I'll show you how to clean the samovar and get it ready for tomorrow."

Together, we rolled the tea cart behind the front counter, emptied out the last of the day's brew, and rinsed the kettle. Dumped the tea leaves and spices—our custom blend—into the food waste bin and refilled the tea holder.

"Water, too?"

"No. We'll do that in the morning so it's fresh. When we're fresh."

The doors were locked now. Vanessa pitched in with cleaning and I readied the till for the next day. We paraded out the door, four women united by our love of food and the joy of sharing it.

In the doorway, Vanessa turned. "Goodnight, shop," she called, and I knew she'd fit right in.

* * *

NOTHING says comfort like soup, especially when you use your mother and grandmother's recipe. And while I don't often cook Hungarian dishes, they sing of family to me. I half-watched, half-listened to the local TV news as I chopped the onions, minced the garlic, and sliced the mushrooms. I'd made the roux and gotten all the ingredients into the stock pot—the recipe is quick enough for a weeknight—when I heard the anchor mention the CID.

"Police have now identified the thirty-two-year-old man found in the basement of a derelict hotel in the Chinatown-International District last Saturday, but have not yet released his name, pending notification of the next of kin. Anyone with information about the crime, which occurred during Lunar New Year festivities, is asked to call the Seattle Police Department."

"It's not derelict," I muttered to the soup as I gave it another stir. Bubbles began to appear, and I lowered the heat to a simmer. "Just not actively in use." Not recently, except for Oliver's apartment and Roxanne's research. Though someone had been dusting the lobby and running a vacuum over the carpets.

I spooned up a taste of the soup, then added a pinch of kosher salt and another sprinkling of dill. As good as my mother's. She and my dad would be heading south soon.

Dang, I was going to miss them.

I needed a hobby.

While the soup simmered, I got out salad stuff and called my mother. How could we multitask without speaker phones? And mothers who don't mind the sounds of rinsing and chopping in the background.

I told her what I knew about the murder in the basement of the Gold Rush, all the details I hadn't wanted to share by text or voice mail. She was horrified. Then I told her about the pharmacy and the room upstairs, and our speculation that a young mother had left in a hurry and never returned.

"What a captivating mystery," she said. "Like the Panama, where the Japanese stored their things when they were sent to the camps."

"But more recent," I said.

"Did you ever read *Hotel on the Corner of Bitter and Sweet?*" she continued. "About the young Chinese boy in Seattle who takes a bus to Idaho to find the Japanese girl he's got a crush on? They lose touch but he tracks her down when they're much older. I couldn't get the story out of my mind. The Chinese children had to wear buttons that read 'I am Chinese' so people wouldn't think they were Japanese. Of course, Japan had invaded China, so no love lost, but these were *children*."

That's how my mother's mind works.

"Sounds like a great book," I said. "Hey, we ran into Aki Ohno Saturday, then I met her granddaughter. She's a Seattle police officer on the beat in the CID. Good cop, Tag says."

"I'm not surprised. Aki is fiercely devoted to the community. She and Ernie worked hard to protect the CID. Taught us a lot. And we tried to support their work as well."

"Were they involved in the Kingdome protests?" I trimmed a fennel bulb and started slicing.

"Yes. The construction displaced a lot of people and businesses. The Ohnos helped get funding for low-income housing and social services as a concession. Mainly for the elderly. Early 1970s, not long after the fight to save the Market. Such crusaders we all were." She had me on speaker, too, and I heard my father cackle in the background.

Aki might know who had designs on the Gold Rush. I should ask her.

"Speaking of our crusader days, I ran into your second-grade teacher today, from the Montessori school. You and Carl both had her. She's been ill. Some sort of cancer. Pale and thin but doing well. Not a woman to give in."

Laurel and I had chatted with her last fall at a community meeting in Montlake, our old neighborhood, where the police shared information about an attack that seriously injured a childhood friend of mine. "Good to hear. Where did you see her?"

Had illness been what I'd witnessed in Abigail Wu? Combined with the shock of an intruder dead, likely murdered, in their building?

"Oh, we made a quick stop for lunch on our house hunt."

"Any luck?" I slid the sliced fennel into the serving bowl, on top of the arugula, and started to chop a few fronds.

"Maybe. I don't want to jinx it."

"What do the stars say? The tarot cards? The tea leaves?"

"Oh, stop. You sound like your father." Her woo-woo ways and his calculated logic were proof that opposites attract. The fiery little Hungarian and the tall, steady Midwesterner. The hippie chick and the vet who met at a war protest. Forty-five years and counting.

We chatted another minute or two, then it was dinner time. Soup, salad, a chunk of crusty bread. A glass of wine. Life was good. Pretty much perfect, if it weren't for my restlessness. And missing my guy.

I distracted myself with thoughts about the old hotel. If Abigail was ill, that might explain Bobby's seeming lack of concern about Saturday's events. Although by all accounts, he had never been much interested in the place.

Arf and I had just returned from a stroll when Nate called. I treated myself to a second glass of wine and curled up on the couch.

"How are the fish biting?" Metaphorically speaking. They use nets, not hooks.

"Good," Nate said. "The catch is good. Crew's working hard. Weather's been mild, for midwinter."

"And Bron?" I rubbed Arf's hip with my bare foot. He loved Nate, but he'd fallen hard for Bron.

I heard him hesitate. The brothers had been partners for years on the two boats, the *Thalassa* docked at Fisherman's Terminal and the larger *Kenai Princess* that plied the waters of the North Pacific. Nate, two years older, had taken up commercial fishing first, Bron joining him later.

"Restless," Nate finally said.

"I know the feeling."

Silence.

"New part-timer started today," I said after a long pause. "She's smart and eager. She'll catch on in no time. And Kristen and Cayenne both gave her the thumbs-up, which is a relief. I saw Roxanne again this afternoon." I told him about our tour of the hotel and Reed getting a chance to talk with Roxanne about her work. "Meeting her is sparking his interest in actually doing something with that history degree."

"You said yourself you didn't want him to take over the warehouse if it's not what he really wants. And you know it's not."

"Yeah. Easier for me if he stayed, but I know how hard it is to change direction once you get settled in any kind of work." I reached for my wine.

"But not impossible. You did it."

"I thought I had the perfect job until it ended. I never would have bought the Spice Shop if the law firm hadn't blown up." Although I had been offered other jobs, when the lawyers formed new firms.

But I had something else to ask him about.

"Nate, Saturday night, what did you mean when you told me to be careful? You weren't talking about the murder. You were talking about Roxanne, weren't you?"

When I first met her, last August, she'd implied pretty strongly that Nate's marriage to her sister had fallen apart because of his work, and warned me against pushing him to change. Not that pushing someone to change ever works. Was that a source of tension between them, even after all these years?

"I didn't want to tell you," he said after a long moment. "You liked her, and I didn't want to mess with that. I never imagined you'd see her again, after the vintage shop murder was solved."

I felt the itch of anxiety creeping in, like a spider under my skin.

"Rosalie and I were renting a house in Ravenna, and Rox was staying with us while their parents were away. She was still in high school. I'd been selling to the guys at Pike Place Fish, but never had time to hang out in the Market, so one Saturday, we all went downtown."

No reason Roxanne should have told me she'd come to the Market once with my boyfriend, if she even remembered.

"We were in an import shop Down Under. They both love all that stuff. I—I was sure I saw Rox slip something into her pocket. I was trying to figure out what to do when the owner started shouting. Not that I blamed her—she witnessed a teenage shop-lifter."

"What?"

"Rox denied it, but both the owner and I had seen her. And the statue, some animal if I remember right, was in her pocket. It couldn't have been expensive—all the good stuff was locked up—and she had money. Why she did it, I never knew. Anyway, things got a little wild."

"Roxanne?" I said rather foolishly. "Shoplifting?"

"Dust settled, she was arrested and charged in juvenile court. It got pretty tense."

"I bet."

"Far as I know, she's never been in a lick of trouble since. Scared straight."

"But you thought you needed to warn me."

"Yeah—no. It's not like I thought she was going to steal the silver when you weren't looking."

"I don't have any silver." A silly attempt to lighten the mood. She'd rummaged in my dresser drawers and used my bathroom. And she'd moved the model ship Nate gave me from the sofa table to the kitchen counter. I'd dismissed that as idle curiosity. Was it?

"I should have told you sooner."

"No. No reason to. Like you said, it's not like she and I are best buds or spend tons of time together." Until now. And now what? I'd promised to help her. I'd steered Reed to her as a potential professional mentor. A mistake? I'd thought I knew what she wanted from me—friendship, reassurance, help during a difficult time.

I could still do that. I could do that, and be careful.

Twelve

"I grow herbs, and dry them, and make remedies for all the ails that visit us. I physic a great many souls besides those of us within."

"And that satisfies you?" It was a muted cry of protest; it would not have satisfied him.

"To heal men? After years of injuring them? What could be more fitting? A man does what he must do," said Cadfael thoughtfully.

—Ellis Peters, *The Devil's Novice*

I'M NOT ONE OF THOSE PEOPLE WHO WAKE UP AND POP INTO action, ready to start the new day. It's like my mind's been working out the previous day's kinks while I've been sleeping and wants me to pay attention to them before I do anything else. Tuesday morning, I woke with an odd sensation that something big in my life had changed, but what was it?

It flooded back quickly. First, Nate's revelation about Roxanne and the uneasiness it triggered.

Second, the sense that there was something else Nate wasn't telling me. Nothing so painful or fraught, but unspoken nonetheless. Last Christmas, Vinny had suggested Nate was looking to make a change, then clammed up. I'd chalked his comment up to

stress and confusion over the incident that led to Nate working in
the wine shop for a few days. And to Vinny being Vinny, and the
effect wearing a top hat ten hours a day had to have on the brain.

Now I wondered.

Arf and I took a quick jaunt around the block. On our way
back, I saw my neighbor striding up the street. I should invite her
over for a cup of tea or glass of wine. Not tonight. Tonight was
Flick Chicks, at my place. The movie and food were chosen. I'd
gone Chinese to celebrate the season. At the moment, though, I
wanted nothing to do with longevity noodles or fortune cookies.
Clearly, I was thinking with my emotions instead of my mouth. Or
my brain.

It happens.

Too late to pick a different movie. Last-minute changes messed
up the traditional thematic potluck. Like the time Kristen chose
Chocolat only to discover that one of her girls had taken the DVD
to a friend's house and come back with the wrong movie, so we
devoured a decadent French spread while watching *Enola Holmes.*

I unlocked the door to the loft, as eager for a shower as Arf
was for his chew bone. I was toweling off when my phone buzzed
with a text from Nate.

*Morning, little darlin'! Don't worry about anything I said
about R. She's great and I'm glad you two are friends. Love you!
Miss you like crazy!*

"Hmph," I told the dog, who did not reply.

Time for work. Arf and I hiked up the Market steps, past the
shops and restaurants huddled there and the double doors leading
to the lower levels. A couple stood on the wide landing, pointing
at the metal figure of a man walking down the wall, a white globe
in hand, one of a dozen light-fixture sculptures. The Market is a
virtual gallery of public art. At the top, we stopped at the bakery
for a breakfast sandwich. I'd marveled at the mix of languages in
the CID, but the Market was a tower of Babel, too. You might hear
Greek, Italian, Farsi, or Russian. In the family-run Asian market,
the owners switched between Mandarin, Cantonese, and English,
depending on the customer. The Orchard Girls, Angie and Sylvie,
often spoke to each other and to customers in Spanish. I remembered enough from high school for a casual chat and to shop in the
street markets with my mother when I visited my parents in Costa

Rica, but the native speakers talked too fast for me to catch every word. What about brushing up with lessons online? My mother swore by Duolingo. Learning a foreign language from an animated owl? What a hoot!

The counterman handed me a white paper bag. I thanked him, then Arf and I wove our way through the preopening madness. I buy flowers for the shop on Tuesdays and Saturdays, alternating between the florist at the corner of First and Pike and the daystallers, mostly Hmong women. This time of year, choices are limited, but a few have greenhouses.

The words the Hmong flower seller at the first table flung at her neighbor may not have meant anything to me, but the tone was loud and clear.

"She-dog, good for nothing," the woman muttered to me in English. "Her chrysanthemums are brown and her roses don't stink."

I was pretty sure she meant "don't smell," but didn't correct her. "A dozen of your roses, then." She continued muttering as she added baby's breath and ferns to a bundle of long-stemmed pink and yellow roses, then cradled the stems in paper. Despite her grumbling, I had a hunch the tension had less to do with her competitor's blooms and more to do with her prices or the theft of a long-time customer. Comes with the retail territory, especially in close quarters.

Arf and I ate our breakfast and got the shop ready. Sandra was the first staffer to arrive.

"How'd the new girl do?" she asked as she tied her apron strings around her ample middle.

"Great. Love having that young energy around."

She flashed me a grin. "You're all young to me."

A spark of terror stabbed me in the throat. "Tell me you're not thinking about retirement."

"No. I like working." She bit her lower lip. "But after this summer, I'd like to cut back to four days, and work solely in the shop. The warehouse is pretty physical."

Nothing I hadn't expected. Though it gave finding the right warehouse manager an extra urgency.

"We'll make it work. Oh, here's fun for you. Have you met the new cheese shop owner?" I told her about Sandy Lynn, the possibility of collaboration, and Cayenne's ideas for using smoked cheddar.

"Yum." She slipped on her readers, leopard-print on a black-and-gold beaded chain, then pulled out her phone and flipped through the recipes on our blog. "How about a variation of those cheddar rosemary crackers? The slice-and-bake ones. What herbs and spices do you like with the cheese?"

"I keep thinking paprika, maybe because I'm half Hungarian and ate two bowls of Hungarian mushroom soup last night."

"Smoked or sweet? The paprika, I mean. Not the soup."

"The smoked will have a deeper, fuller flavor, though it could overwhelm a mild cheese. Let's try 'em both." Smoked paprika might just be my favorite spice, if I were playing favorites, but I'd never say so out loud, where the other herbs and spices might hear me.

Vanessa arrived, wearing thick-soled, high-top sneakers. We started the tea, then readied for the day.

When my ten-thirty interviewee hadn't shown by ten minutes to eleven, I crossed her off the list.

My mind kept drifting back to the mysteries of the Gold Rush—the closed-up hotel, the abandoned room upstairs, and the dead man in the hidden pharmacy. The cops had a name now. Would they share it? I retreated to my office, about the size of your average home shower, and punched a phone number I wasn't supposed to have.

"Pepper," Detective Spencer said. "I was just thinking about you."

"Should I be worried?"

"Actually, I was hoping you could help us. Thanks to your idea about the costume shops, we tracked our dead man. He's Terence Leong, thirty-two. He gave an address in an apartment building in the CID, but we haven't been able to talk to anyone there yet. We've also confirmed that he was not part of any dance group on the official schedule. Probably not a local man."

Anyone could stay anonymous in the city, but not completely. Not for long. And wouldn't people want to help find a killer? I remembered Reed's comment about the community protecting its own. "Maybe people know who he is, but don't want to admit it."

"Always a possibility," Spencer said. "We see it often in

drive-bys or gang disputes. Shootings with witnesses who fear becoming targets if they talk."

This, in contrast, was a more personal crime.

"I've heard rumors," I said, "from one of the tenants, that the building might have been for sale. Or, that someone was interested in buying it." A potential buyer was a mystery, but what could it have to do with the murder?

"We've heard that, too. We're looking into it." She paused, then continued. "You've been spending time with Dr. Davidson. She say anything helpful?"

First Tracy pushed me about Roxanne, now Spencer. What was up with that? "About what? The Wus? The building?"

"Oh, anything," she said. "You never know what might come up in casual conversation."

True enough. Roxanne might tell me something she wouldn't say in an official interview, particularly if she still bore the scars of that youthful encounter with the system. Then there was that business about the ghost of Bruce Lee, but I didn't take it seriously.

"I can't think of a thing," I said truthfully. We hung up and I clutched the silent phone in my hand. What would Brother Cadfael do?

Honestly, I had no idea.

Back out front, a customer was surveying our Lunar New Year display. "So many spices I've never heard of."

"Me, too," Vanessa said.

"She's so new, her apron isn't stained yet," I said.

"We used to take the kids to see the lion dancers for Chinese New Year." The customer reached for a book on Chinese home cooking. "When did they change the name?"

"Over time," I said. "The name Lunar New Year acknowledges that many Asian cultures celebrate the New Year at the new moon in late January or early February, not just the Chinese. With any luck, that's when we begin to shift from winter to spring, the season of renewal. Each country or culture has its own customs and food. Makes for a more colorful celebration. And a tastier one."

"Ahh. Thanks. The big drum scared my daughter when she was little." She mimed swinging the big mallet.

"Still scares me," I said.

We finished our chat about spices and cookbooks. Then I left Vanessa and Sandra to pack her order and grabbed my coat and the handcart.

After a delivery to the bistro on Lower Post Alley, I stopped at the PDA office to drop off my December sales report. The PDA handles all the administrative doodah involved in running the Market, our own version of city hall. With more than two hundred merchants, two hundred daystallers, and a hundred bars and restaurants, plus five hundred residents, the Market is like a small town—one that hosts ten million visitors a year in nine acres. Rents are a combination of a fixed monthly sum and a percentage of sales. That structure saved a lot of businesses during the pandemic, effectively slashing their rent when sales plummeted. This past December had been my best month since I bought the Market more than two years ago, making my rent check the biggest yet. I did not mind one bit.

Yolande Jenkins, the leasing manager, stood behind the front counter, pointing out something on the computer screen to the young man seated in front of it.

"Hi, Pepper," she said. "Training a new hire. Hey, I hear you broke up a fight the other day between a couple of hot-headed drivers."

"Tried, but the damage had already been done. Sometimes it seems like everyone's living on the edge of their tempers these days."

"We're setting up a task force to address vehicle traffic in the Market. I'm hoping you'll be one of the merchant representatives. We can use your people skills."

"Thanks, I think." It was true that I'd helped resolve a debate on the Tenant Review Committee between bringing in new blood or favoring an existing tenant's expansion when I'd solved a murder that eliminated one applicant, but hopefully the traffic task force wouldn't require that particular skill.

"Great. First meeting is noon Wednesday. We'll provide lunch."

"That's fast."

"We'd like to get a solution in place before the Flower Festival."

Mid-March, near the first day of spring. Could we fix a perennial issue with no obvious solution before the perennials began to bloom? I didn't see how, but we could at least plant the seeds.

On my way back to the shop, I wondered if anyone in the Market might have known Terence Leong or the secrets of the Gold Rush Hotel. I parked my cart outside the Asian grocery and popped in. My young pal Lily would be at school, but her mother and I had become friendly. I grabbed a bottle of my favorite toasted sesame oil and plucked a couple of bags of fortune cookies out of the basket on the front counter.

"Been to any Lunar New Year celebrations yet?" I fished in my pockets for cash.

"We took Lily to see the dancers Saturday after we closed here," Mei said. "And her class is having a party Friday afternoon. My mother is making two hundred spring rolls."

"The dancers were terrific, weren't they? You heard about the one who died." Terence Leong had dressed the part, even if he hadn't belonged to an official dance troupe.

"Died?" Mei's skin paled and her eyes went very wide. She pressed her fingers to her lips. "Brings bad luck for the new year."

Clearly she hadn't heard and knew nothing. All I'd done was upset her.

So much for my people skills.

Thirteen

The Pekin Noodle Parlor in Butte, Montana, established in 1911, is believed to be the oldest operating Chinese restaurant in America.

I PAID FOR MY OIL AND COOKIES AND FLED. STOPPED AT THE Chinese pastry shop down the block and ordered crispy buns and egg rolls for tonight. I'd pick them up on my way home. With this wealth of food around me, from so many cultures, I didn't need to cook everything myself to appreciate it. That's what taste buds are for.

Then I asked for a triple order of pot stickers and another batch of buns for staff lunch. This time, I kept my questions to myself.

The afternoon's interviews went smoothly. Both candidates showed up on time, dressed like suitably free spirits, and had good interpersonal skills. Sadly, one was allergic to dogs, a question I should have asked when we set up the appointment.

"No dogs at the warehouse and production facility," I said. "But I'm not sure yet what the hours will be. Can I keep you in mind and call you, see if you're available when we're ready?" I held up my hands, fingers crossed.

"I need something pretty soon," came the reply, and my heart sank.

Next came an applicant for the warehouse manager spot, a

response to my listing at an online hiring site for the food biz. Good food knowledge and work history, no experience in production, eager to learn. He said all the right things, but something wasn't right. Finally, I asked where else he was applying, and he admitted he had an offer to work as a private chef for a couple on San Juan Island.

"Why on earth would you want to work for a living instead of cooking in paradise?" I asked.

Turned out he was concerned about being a long ferry ride away from his friends. The islands are remote, sure, but hardly the outback. Was he steady enough for the job? I needed to make a few phone calls and hope his references were honest with me.

Mr. Private Chef left, and I leaned back, eyes closed. Had hiring always been this difficult, or was I just being crabby?

I kept thinking about Terence Leong and the Gold Rush. Who was he? If he wasn't local, as Spencer guessed, why had he come to Seattle? What was he doing in the pharmacy? Rummaging for valuables or ancient wisdom?

The image of that fortune cookie pendant flashed in my mind. A gift, I imagined. Who was missing him?

Then there was Roxanne. I was rethinking every conversation I'd had with her since she burst out of the hotel last Saturday afternoon. But nothing about the shoplifting incident affected her credibility as a witness. And it had no connection to the murder.

Or did it? It was clear now that the detectives had known about her juvenile record, hence Tracy's taunt that I should ask my boyfriend about her. What else did they know that I—and maybe Nate—didn't?

Could she be more than a witness? A suspect?

Ridiculous. The entire mess had been ages ago. Nate said he'd never had any reason to doubt her in the years since. She'd finished college, gotten a graduate degree, and worked steadily in her field. Surely the museum had done a full background check. The Wing Luke kept her on a list of trusted experts. All that ought to be good enough.

Normally I know when to trust my gut. That's what told me the last job applicant wasn't telling me everything.

And it told me Roxanne and I needed to have a serious talk.

Later. Tonight was all about food and fun and the Flick Chicks.

* * *

THE buzzer rang and Arf didn't even lift his head.

"Some alarm system you are," I said as I pushed the button to let my friends in.

They came bearing gifts, mostly Chinese takeout. We were never short on food at Flick Chicks.

"We saw your invisible neighbor at the mailboxes," Kristen said as she unwrapped a platter of fortune cookies she and her girls had made. "I almost invited her to join us. But what if we didn't like her? Awkward!"

"Isn't it funny?" Laurel popped the cork on a bottle of Pinot Gris, which she swears pairs beautifully with any Chinese food. "I have a neighbor like that. I see his lights on. His kayak comes and goes. He waters his planters. But I hardly ever see him. He gave me a big hello at the grocery store and I literally had no idea who he was."

"You see hundreds of people every day," Seetha said. "You can't know them all."

"Some customers, I know by their orders." Laurel handed Seetha a glass of wine, then pointed at imaginary people as she talked. "That guy is a turkey panino. That woman is tomato-basil soup and a side salad with champagne vinaigrette. Names don't matter."

"Like the neighborhood dogs." I put a mason jar filled with serving spoons and another holding my chopstick collection on the counter. "I know the goldendoodle and the corgi, and the yappy Pekinese, but the owners? Nah."

Seetha carried a plate of mini spring rolls and a bowl of peanut sauce into the living room and I followed her.

"So, how you doing? Any bhuts?" We hadn't talked or seen each other since the fateful food walk, and our texts had been the briefest of check-ins. Encountering death face-to-face was hard enough, but with Seetha's history, I'd been worried.

"Not a sign of them. I think we banished the nasty little devils."

After Seetha's grandmother in Delhi died years ago, both she and her mother had begun seeing bhuts, the strange Indian ghosts that sometimes appear wearing white, often with their feet pointing backward. When a woman died in Seetha's building, she feared they'd come back to haunt her. But then she confronted another fear, and it was as if proving her courage had satisfied the spirits.

"Good to hear. Hey," I said as we drifted back toward the kitchen. "Tell us more about Oliver. Have you talked to him since Saturday?"

Laurel was standing at my stove frying up a batch of crab rangoons in a wok she'd brought. The crab-and-cream cheese puffs are best served hot, and while I consider myself a reasonably fearless cook, frying in hot oil on the kitchen stove does ratchet up the nerves. But Laurel is a pro.

"I met him at the hotel where I've been filling in at the spa," Seetha said. "We had coffee a couple of times and talked about a real date. And yes, Pepper. I knew he was dancing Saturday and I was hoping to run into him."

When he'd been wearing the same costume as the dead man. Had the killer confused one lion dancer for another? Had Oliver been the target?

Kristen's green eyes sparkled. "You gonna see him again?"

"Friday night. Dinner and the symphony."

"Ooh," we all chorused.

"Now that's a serious date," Aimee said. While she and Kristen quizzed Seetha, I focused on dinner, mainly to hide my wariness. Something about Oliver Wu and his family bothered me, but I had no idea what or why.

You're full of the questions today, Pepper Reece. I got out a bowl and opened the jar of sweet-and-sour sauce. *Keep them in your mouth.*

"I should try to meet someone," Aimee mused. "But I wouldn't know where to start."

"Work, friends, friends of friends," I said.

"Work? When's the last time you heard of an unattached, straight man shopping in a vintage store?" she replied. "But if you or Nate have a guy in mind, I'm game."

I shook my head, unable to conjure any good options. I poured some of that Pinot Gris for myself and took a sip.

"What about you?" Kristen asked Laurel.

"I have no interest in dating." Laurel lifted the last wontons out of the oil and spread them on a plate lined with a paper towel. She's a few years older than Kristen and I, tall, with wild gray-brown curls and a wicked wit. "Besides, who'd be attracted to an old kitchen hag like me?"

"Oh, come on." Kristen said. "You're too young to live like a hermit. What about your neighbor, the one stalking you in the grocery store?"

"He wasn't stalking me. And I do not need a man to complete my life," Laurel said in a tone that brooked no protest.

They say it takes a year after a breakup to be ready for another relationship. A year from the end-end, when all his things are out of your house or the ink on the divorce decree is dry. They say a lot of things, but it had been true for me. I'd tried dating too soon and gotten nothing but heartache in exchange. What was the rule when a marriage ended in death? Patrick Halloran's murder had gone unsolved for three years, until last October. Would Laurel feel differently this fall than she did now? Or was she simply stating the truth? None of us needed a man to complete our lives.

But need had nothing to do with my feelings. I didn't love Nate because I needed him. I needed him because I loved him.

And I wondered again who needed Terence Leong. Who loved and missed him. I wiped away a tear. I was sure Kristen noticed, but bless her, she didn't say a thing.

We carried our chatter and our plates into the living room. I refilled wine glasses and started the movie.

"How do they do that?" Aimee asked. Neither she nor Seetha had ever seen *Crouching Tiger, Hidden Dragon*.

"Fly? Wires," I said. "And other magic." It's one of my favorite movies, lush and historic, though it has no connection to the Lunar New Year other than its setting in ancient China. The female characters are smart and independent, though one honors tradition, one defies it, and one subverts it. And can they swing a sword.

If we hadn't gotten lost on our way from the sword fight demo to the dance performance Saturday afternoon, I wouldn't be tangled up in the mystery of the Gold Rush Hotel. In the movie, young Jen was fighting off the men in the tea house, and I thought about all the men who'd stayed in the hotel over the years. About the woman who'd taken her baby and fled, leaving her things in the room at the end of the hall. About Terence Leong and the broken bottles that crunched beneath my feet when I checked his body, like the tea bowls shattered in the fight on screen, so perfectly choreographed that we were all entranced.

Now I wished I hadn't chosen a movie with such a tragic ending.

I got up to pee, then detoured into the kitchen. Kristen joined me, leaving the others in the living room to watch Shu Lien, Mu Bai, and Jen fly through the air.

"I need a hobby," I said.

"No, you don't." She bit into an orphaned rangoon, then perched on a bar stool. "Like what?"

"I don't know. The only thing I do is work and watch movies with you guys."

"You solve murders. You don't have a sudden urge to take up cross stitch. You're just worried that you won't know what to do with yourself now that Nate is gone."

Ouch. "He's been gone before. That's been part of the deal since the beginning."

"But it's different now. And your parents are about to leave."

Was that it? Was I afraid of loneliness? I'd been on my own for years before I met Nate. Truth was, I'd been lonely in my marriage, knowing Tag and I had grown apart and not knowing how to fix that. Was I afraid of a repeat romantic disaster? Nate's ex-wife had tried to change him and lost him, and that was a cautionary tale, but I wasn't her. And he'd changed too, no doubt.

No. I wasn't worried about Nate, or about Nate and me. I wasn't even worried about my parents. I was concerned about the shop, about hiring new staff and taking the business to the next level, but not worried.

I was worried about *me*.

We rejoined the others in time to see Mu Bai die in Shu Lien's arms, finally professing his love for her. Then she delivered the Green Destiny, the fateful sword, to his mentor and Jen rode off to join her lover. We watched Jen foolishly ask him to make a wish, and when he told her he wished they could spend their lives together in the desert, she jumped off the bridge into the mist.

"Ohh." Aimee sank back on the couch as the credits began to roll. "How could she do that?"

"Because she can't bear to live someone else's dream," Laurel said. "Even though she loves him."

Kristen set the plate of fortune cookies on my packing crate coffee table and plucked one from the pile. "The girls had a blast writing the fortunes." She broke open a cookie and read. "You are your own North Star."

Aimee opened hers. "Friendship is the spice of life. I'll drink to that."

We all raised our glasses in a toast.

"You're never too old to learn new tricks," Laurel read. "Did you plant these?" Kristen denied it, but Laurel wasn't convinced.

"Embrace your dreams with passion," Seetha's read. Classic teenage wisdom.

"I'd suggest we take a day and go antiquing," Kristen said to me a few minutes later as she put on her coat. "Since you're looking for something to do. But I'm working extra hours this week and next. My boss is kind of a grind."

I stuck out my tongue. Arf and I trotted down the stairs behind our friends. The night had turned chilly and a light mist was falling. They drove off, leaving us to take a quick spin around the block.

Back in the loft, I got into my pajamas and stuck the last few plates in the dishwasher. The bowl of fortune cookies I'd bought from Mei sat on the counter. I unwrapped one and broke open the cookie. Pried out the strip of pink paper. There was a reason these things were the butt of many jokes—bland and banal, broadly wise and deeply foolish.

Be careful, it read. *Both friends and enemies wear many disguises.*

Fourteen

From listening comes wisdom.
From speaking comes repentance.

—Fortune cookie wisdom

WEDNESDAY MORNING, WE GATHERED FOR THE WEEKLY staff meeting. We all fit in the nook now, though it was tight. Cozy. Intimate. One more thing that would change as we grew.

Coming to retail from HR, I knew the staff was the heart of the shop. The best ideas come from the people on the ground.

Cayenne had brought apple-cheddar scones made with Sandy Lynn's smoked cheddar. We all dove in, and she scribbled comments in her shop notebook as we oohed and ahhed and suggested spice combos.

"What about a berbere?" Sandra suggested. "Or Five Spice?"

"Cayenne?" Vanessa said, hesitating as if to make sure it was okay for the new girl to speak. "I mean, the pepper, not you. Or you." She glanced between us, embarrassed.

"We do have the perfect names for our jobs, don't we?" I said. "They're called aptonyms. And if a Ginger or Rosemary applies, I'll hire her on the spot."

"Chiles would be great in the ham and cheese biscuits," Cayenne told Vanessa. "We have several varieties. Why don't you and I taste a few after the meeting?"

We were heading into a rare weekend without a special Market event. After we hashed over a couple of recent customer questions, I gave an update on hiring. "I talked to a decent prospect for the warehouse yesterday, but he texted me last night to say he'd decided to take another offer. Private chef on an island."

"Rough life," Kristen said.

"Right? Not sure I'd trust the judgment of anyone who said no to a gig like that. Any suggestions, bring 'em on."

Knowledge and experience counted, but fit mattered most. As with the crew crammed into the nook. My throat got a little full as I contemplated what we'd done in my two and a half years, taking the shop from a stale operation with shaky supply lines and a lack of spark to a truly collaborative crew. Working together, sharing our love of the Market and good food to give the customer a worthwhile experience. Not everyone would fit; not everyone would stay. Cody and Matt had been what we'd needed at the time, and I hoped we'd been what they needed—stepping stones on their own paths.

Had Kristen been right when she suggested, before I posted the job announcement, that I was reluctant to hire a production manager because I would no longer be in charge of everything?

Bah. She also thought a floral print blouse went with a striped skirt, so what did she know?

But I took the point. If I wanted the Spice Shop to prosper, I had to make sure I stayed out of its way.

"Pepper," Reed said as we slid out of the nook, ready to tackle the opening tasks. "Today's my grandfather's clinic day. He still comes in once a week, though he doesn't see patients anymore. Do you have time to meet him for tea this afternoon?"

"I'll make time." My mother had taken me to see old Dr. Locke—Henry—when I was a kid, for knee pain after a gymnastics class I'd had no business taking. I'd been anxious about the acupuncture needles, but they hadn't hurt, and two treatments had done the trick. And the shelves of glass jars, bottles, and vials had fascinated me. Until I saw a jar of flying squirrel droppings and another holding dried geckos on sticks. Reed's dad had taken over the clinic years ago and didn't rely much on the old herbal formulas. "Will you and your dad be there?"

"I've got class, but Dad's planning on it, unless there's an emergency."

"It's a date."

I spent the rest of the morning in the shop. Called the third Nate for an interview and discovered he too had found another job. I was disappointed—he had good credentials—but glad to avoid forever having to clarify which Nate I was talking about. I gave Fabiola, our graphic designer, final approval on the labels for our spring and summer blends, then went over the supply list. It's a constant juggling act, projecting sales months in advance. Extra jars keep, and I can always find more uses for yellow mustard seed or push hibiscus flowers for tea, but leftover beet root powder is a hard sell.

Then I updated our social media pages. Contrary to popular myth, not every digital native has mad social media skills or is hot to develop them. Texting with your friends or posting videos of dance moves on TikTok is not quite the same as designing and carrying out a professional campaign for a retail and commercial food business. But when we were fully staffed and I wasn't running the production facility, I'd have more time for promotion.

Truth be told, there were all kinds of projects I could give more attention to once I was spread less thin.

That's the life of a small business owner, and I love it.

Then it was time for the traffic task force meeting. I had managed to steer clear of most Market committees since buying the shop. Time to do penance, or play a part in some serious problem-solving?

Two by two we filled the meeting room in the Economy Market. Two produce sellers, two restaurateurs, two arts and crafts folks. Reps from the service sector, the residents, and the public. Plus two actual farmers, who set up booths on the cobbles to sell their fresh-picked crops. I was here as a merchant, representing the "stores with doors."

My compatriot was Dave Hudson, the comic book dealer from Down Under, a tall bulky man with a red beard who could have stepped straight out of *The Lord of the Rings*.

Fate, right?

We greeted each other and shook hands. "I met one of your competitors over the weekend. Bobby Wu."

The corners of Dave's blue eyes crinkled. "Bobby's no competition."

"Please," Yolande called. "Get your lunch, then we'll get started."

I grabbed a plate and helped myself to falafel, stuffed grape leaves, and pita, along with a spoonful of hummus and a healthy drizzle of tzatziki, the cucumber-yogurt dressing speckled with dill from my shop.

"Decent lunch might be the best thing we get out of this," the leather worker ahead of me in line said. "We'll never agree on a fix."

"Gotta agree on the problem," I said, "before we can talk about solutions."

And that was where Yolande started, introducing a planner from the city Department of Transportation. We proudly tout our ten million visitors a year, and in that context, two hundred collisions in twenty years didn't sound too bad. But every one of them involved real people, not numbers, who suffered physical injuries and property damage. Every one tangled up traffic and interfered with business.

And every one had the potential to spark road rage of the type I'd witnessed.

Not to mention that today's trucks and SUVs could do a lot more damage than the cars of yesteryear, when the decision to keep Pike Place open had been made.

"Bring back horses and wagons," the leather worker said. "Problem solved."

"You volunteering to scoop the poop?" Dave piped up.

I nearly choked when the urban planner described the harmful effects of repeated exposure to air and noise pollution created by vehicles. Most Market businesses are at least partly open air, so we're all affected. Not to mention our life blood: the shoppers. And the Market residents, many elderly or disabled.

"Can't shut down deliveries," one man said.

"Limit the hours," said a restaurant owner. "And no public parking on the street."

"Fortunately, we have detailed traffic studies," the planner said. "We know who's driving through here, when, and why." He pointed a laser at charts projected on a giant screen. Pedestrians outnumbered private cars by nearly twenty to one. Another chart estimated the numbers and types of delivery vehicles and the time they spent on the streets.

Our Historical District coordinator spoke next, explaining the process for reviewing any proposed changes. "Keep in mind the mission of the district," she stressed. "The mission always comes first."

Then an expert in community dynamics discussed the causes of road rage and the effectiveness of potential responses, using phrases like "high-anger drivers" and the "intensity of aggressive responses hinges on perception."

"Psycho-babble mumbo jumbo," Herb the Herb Man groused, but my HR-loving heart ate it up.

"Don't pretend you've never driven stupid, Herb. We all have."

"Bottom line," the speaker said. "There's a lot we can't change about the built environment. But we can change human interaction."

"Yeah, but do we want to?" Dave Hudson asked. "I mean, sure, nobody wants a tire jack thrown through a windshield or anybody getting hurt, but people walking around, eating donuts, listening to a three-piece band playing upturned buckets—that's part of the Market."

Murmurs of truth rippled through the room.

Yolande thanked the presenters, then handed out packets. "Staff has put together lists of possible solutions. Everything that's been suggested over the years, with no judgment about whether it's workable. Please review the options, add your own, and think seriously about how we can address the problems, in light of the Market's mission."

I skimmed the list. Some measures were already in place. Market security regularly restricted general traffic during festivals and peak tourist days, while maintaining access for taxis and those with disabilities. But retail's a tough way to make a living, and I was sure many of my neighbors feared anything that might send their customers elsewhere.

How did you measure how many people *didn't* come down here because traffic was a mess? How many would hear about Sunday's altercation and stay home?

Then we were adjourned, same time next week.

"Too bad we can't ban jerks," Dave said on our way out. "Coulda solved Sunday's problem before it started."

"Remember the Market mission," I said. "Preserve authenticity."

His howl of laughter echoed off the cobblestones.

I barely had time to take Arf for a quick walk before meeting Ron and Henry Locke. My dog would appreciate more open space, for sure. Recent changes added more tables and benches, so you could sit to eat your takeout, rest your feet, or watch the world go by. But isolated incidents, like the one on Sunday, I thought as I swerved to avoid a car door that opened unexpectedly, didn't warrant extreme solutions. This was a working Market, after all, not a suburban mall.

Puzzling out the traffic problem almost made solving a murder look easy.

"SORRY I'm late," I told Ron Locke. "I broke up a fight between a couple of drivers last weekend and got myself recruited for the new traffic task force."

"I heard about it," he said. "Happily, Market traffic isn't a big problem for us. Most of our patients come in from First Avenue, and many take public transportation. No worries. The tea is still hot."

The clinic was tucked in a tiny upper-level spot in the Sanitary Market, a virtual rabbit warren that dates back almost a century. You pretty much have to know where you're going to find it. And though Ron kept a stash of herbs and tinctures and other remedies, his clinic looked nothing like the mysterious Gold Rush pharmacy.

He ushered me into a small, windowless office.

"Little Miss Pepper. Good to see you again." Henry Locke rose and took my hands in his. His hair was completely white, his glasses askew. But behind them, his eyes were bright, and his grip was strong. "Sit, sit. How is your knee? We treated Stomach 36 and Gall Bladder 34, if I remember correctly."

"That was thirty years ago. How can you possibly remember?" There was not a file in sight, though the same rubber anatomical figurine marked with the points and meridians that had fascinated me as a kid stood on the corner of the desk, next to a brass lamp. "And it's great, thanks."

"Dad remembers every treatment he's ever given and every herb he's ever prescribed." Ron gestured to a chair and slid behind the desk, where he poured three cups of tea. "Just don't ask what he had for breakfast."

"Eat the same thing every day," the old man said, "and you never have to remember."

Ron passed the tea around and we cradled the small porcelain cups in silence. The steam carried notes of jasmine, and I inhaled them happily. Once Henry, the oldest person in the room, had taken a sip, Ron and I were free to follow.

"Reed is very taken with Dr. Davidson," Ron said. "She's given him some good ideas about how to pursue his love of history and turn it into a career."

"I'm going to hate to lose him, but I've learned, never stand in the way of someone following their passion."

As this family knew well. Old Dr. Locke had trained in Vancouver, BC, eventually marrying his teacher's daughter.

"My father-in-law was old school, refusing to train a daughter to follow in his footsteps," Henry said. "He preferred to train a male outsider. Happily, she put aside her resentment and fell in love with me. And agreed to move back to Seattle with me after my training was complete."

"It's kind of sweet," I said, "painful as it must have been for you both."

He nodded slowly, then gestured to Ron. "We were deeply gratified that our son wanted to practice medicine as well. No matter what tradition he chose."

"You never pushed me," Ron said, "and that's how we learned not to push our own children." Then he laughed. "Very un-Chinese of us, but they're all good kids."

The letters Roxanne had scanned for Reed with her phone had been printed out and lay on the desk, the handwritten translations beside them.

"I'm no longer fully literate in the old calligraphy. I learned it as a child, forgot it, then relearned what I needed to know to grasp the essence of a few texts." Henry waved a hand at a book-lined wall. "I can understand why the young lady had trouble with it."

"When were they written?"

"Two were written in 1930, to Fong, whoever he was. Could be a first name or a last. The Exclusion Act was still in force—it wasn't repealed until 1943—but a citizen could bring over a wife or children. Seems Fong's wife made the journey to Seattle, but after she was released from immigration detention, she got very sick and died. Heart failure, I gather."

"Oh my gosh," I said. "That's terrible."

"He took her to a Chinese doctor, who was not able to save her. Fong must have written his friend and explained the situation. The friend tells him he cannot sue the American government because he can't prove she got sick in detention."

"They would have claimed either she was sick when she arrived, and it wasn't detectible," Ron said. "Or she was healthy when they had her in custody and she got sick afterward."

"The latter, according to the second letter. They said the Chinese doctor must have been a quack who didn't know what he was doing, or that he harmed her somehow." Henry took off his glasses and rubbed the bridge of his nose. "The friend told him he could not approve of any plan to take matters into his own hands. Let it go, he advised. Find a new wife—whether here or back in China—and build a new American life."

"Wow. What do you think he planned to do, this Fong?" I asked.

Ron refilled our cups. "He might have intended to expose the Chinese doctor and try to get him deported. The practice of Chinese medicine, which was primarily herbal at the time, was not legal, though it was tolerated. His friend feared that the attempt might backfire and make Fong a pariah. The doctor was popular and malpractice claims are always hard to prove."

"What about the third letter?"

"Earlier, to Fong from his wife." The old man cleared his throat, then began reading.

My dearest Fong,

I received your letter and money. Though we have now been apart many months, I think about you constantly. My love for you is as deep as the ocean that divides us. I am grateful for all you are doing to build our new life together in Seattle. Do not worry about me. We will be together soon.

Your loving wife,
Pearl

I was momentarily speechless. "To work so hard, wait so long, then lose her. The grief." I gripped the cup, too small for any warmth to reach the chill I felt. Then I pictured the drawer of the dressing table in the abandoned room. "Any idea why these letters were locked up in the Gold Rush?"

"None at all," Henry said. "Most of the old hotels closed in the early 1970s. They didn't meet code, the rooms were too small—a variety of reasons. Though Francis Wu lived upstairs, even after it closed. The boy never had any interest in it."

"Bobby." Strange to hear a man in his sixties described as a boy, but a man nearing ninety could get away with that.

"Yes. The Wu family always held themselves apart. One child, born of a late marriage. I can't say I ever knew the family well." Henry shook his head.

"So if Chinese medicine wasn't legal," I said, "the pharmacy was hard to find on purpose."

"Most likely," Henry said. "It was considered the practice of medicine without a license, but enforcement was inconsistent. Chinese doctors often claimed they simply sold herbs, which was legal, and didn't diagnose or prescribe. But of course, they were doing just that, covertly. And they did some physical manipulation, in a style similar to acupressure or massage, though most didn't use acupuncture back then. Occasionally there was a nominal crack-down and a doctor would pay a fine or spend a few days in jail—the cost of doing business."

I pictured the pharmacy and the tiny treatment room. "That's quite the price."

"Truth is," the old man continued, "everywhere there were Chinese people, there were Chinese doctors. But by the time I started practice, times had changed. There had been no herb shops for so long that the people forgot about it. I had to educate my patients."

Poor Pearl. She'd crossed the ocean to rejoin her husband only to be held in detention, get a taste of her new life, then die not much later. "I've been in the old INS building. A few Market artists have studios there and invited us to an open house." On the edge of the CID, near King Street Station. Five floors of studios and workshops, plus performance space. A permanent exhibit told the history of immigration in Seattle. I shuddered at the memory of the cells in the basement and the marks that told detainees where to stand and put their hands on the wall so they could be searched.

"Not that building," Ron said, his brow furrowed. "It opened later."

"That's right," his father said. "The original immigration center was a few blocks from here."

My chills returned.

I thanked the doctors, gathered up the documents, and left. Instead of taking the stairs down to Pike Place, I walked out onto First Avenue. It had rained overnight, and the skies were threatening. I walked slowly, thinking about all I'd learned and the gaps that remained in the story. Letters. We don't write letters anymore. We write texts and emails, fragments that disappear into the ether, the connections they represent no longer tangible, like pen and ink on paper. Though little good the words did, if no one could read them anymore.

At Union, I stopped and looked down the hill. How many times had I walked this block? The building was easy to spot. Dark red brick, the terra cotta trim a rich cream. When Henry was a boy, he'd said, it held offices for the canneries and unions and a hiring hall. By the time he moved back to Seattle and opened his clinic in the Market, it housed mainly pigeons. Later, the building was gutted and the interior completely redone. More recently, the offices had been converted to apartments. I hadn't looked at them when I was on the hunt, wanting a more industrial loft.

I paused outside the entrance. Fluted columns—Doric, if I remembered my art history. Dentil molding above the stone lintel. A glass door and two sidelights that reminded me of the entrances to the Gold Rush and the Fortunate Sun. The door was locked but I cupped my hands around my eyes and peered in. Small, uninspired lobby. On one wall, a bank of mailboxes. On another, a bland modern couch beneath a framed print, a pairing designed to discourage anyone from sitting longer than it took to flip through their mail.

No name carved in the terra cotta—it had not been built for the INS. Did the residents know the history? Had the ghosts been exorcised along with the cracked plaster and the warbled glass? Small apartments, big views. Rooftop planters and trees. My neighbor Glenn and I had toyed with the idea of creating a rooftop garden on our building—it was plenty strong—but he and his Nate were preoccupied with their remodel, and I was preoccupied with my work and my life.

Or rather, my work, which was my life. Maybe the garden project was the hobby I needed. Although my tendency to kill anything but the hardiest herbs might be a problem.

I walked up the alley and after a short distance, found myself on Lower Post Alley, not far from the Gum Wall and the Market offices.

Humans. So clueless. We walk by a thousand stories every day, and we have no idea.

Fifteen

During World War I, Airedales carried messages for the British military, stood watch on the front lines, and warned troops when the enemy was approaching.

WALKING AND TEXTING ARE A DANGEROUS COMBINATION, in my experience, so I paused outside the Market office to text Roxanne.

Dr. Locke gave me rough translations of the letters. I'll get them to you. Meanwhile, can you trace the ownership history of the Gold Rush?

The reply was nearly instant, and I guessed she was in her office at the Asian Art Museum. *Does this have something to do with the pharmacy?*

Maybe. Pure speculation on my part, but the letters relating complaints about a Chinese doctor had been found in the same building as a Chinese pharmacy. Logical to think it had been his. We knew nothing about the doctor. Had he committed malpractice, as Fong believed? Had he kept records in one of those cabinets? If he had, and Henry Locke or Roxanne's professor pal could decipher them, we might be able to tell.

Tell whom? Nearly a hundred years later, did it even matter?

I considered going Down Under to quiz Dave the comic book

dealer about Bobby Wu, but that would have to wait. My shop needed me.

I stashed my coat, kissed my dog, and got to work. Spices, jars, and labels are shipped directly to the warehouse, but books, teas, gadgets, and other spicenalia come to the shop. Everything we'd ordered to fill the after-Christmas gaps seemed to have arrived today. On the upside, that meant Sandra and Kristen had Vanessa unpacking boxes while they showed her where things went. On the downside, she was filthy. I rubbed a spot on my cheek to indicate the smudge on hers.

"Bathroom break," she said, and headed for the back of the shop.

"Don't kill her on her third day," I cautioned my bestie and my assistant boss. "We need her."

"She's a doll," Sandra said. "Hardest worker we've ever had. Does she have a twin?"

Tea at the clinic had not involved a snack, so I settled in the nook with my iPad and the last of Cayenne's scones. The smoked cheddar baked up beautifully. I scanned the recipe she'd printed out for me. Nothing went on our blog or on a recipe display without being thoroughly tested. Cayenne and Sandra were pros; they could make anything. But what about a decent home cook like me or eager newbies like Kristen's girls? Those were the results that counted. She'd combined smoked and regular cheddar, but hadn't specified the type of apples. I like to bake with a variety, for a more interesting flavor, but availability varies. Our customers are literally across the continent. So suggestions were always a good idea.

And what about a pinch of cayenne or sweet paprika? I'd give it a try.

I opened my email and skimmed a couple of applications that had come in online. Sadly, the trend toward wacky job titles, driven by Google and other tech companies, had not waned. Took me far too long to figure out that the man who described himself as a modern hunter-gatherer had been a kitchen supply officer for a small school district.

Then came a resume that stood out, not for the education or work history but for the applicant's current workplace, an Italian restaurant I knew well. I picked up the phone. After a brief chat with one Hayden Parker, I asked the question that was bugging me.

"Edgar know you're looking?"

"He suggested I apply. He and Cody both rave about you." His voice was deep, and tinged with a Southern accent.

Were Edgar and I about to trade employees? Too funny. He'd hired Cody on my referral, when the kid needed evening hours after going back to school.

"Good to hear. One more thing. You okay with dogs? I sign the paychecks, but my Airedale runs the show."

The bass laugh was answer enough. We scheduled an interview for Thursday afternoon.

Deliveries remained a hitch. They take a huge amount of time, and right now, the job fell to me. Reed worked mainly at the warehouse. Kristen didn't work every day, Vanessa was too new, and Sandra and Cayenne were more valuable in the shop. I'd already outsourced most deliveries outside the central part of the city, though I make a point of picking up the phone and calling every chef and producer—or hunter-gatherer—we supply for a chat each season. And if we have a new source or a special price on an item I suspect a particular client would like, I reach out. Retail is low-tech and high-touch. Personal contact is the best sales tool. That and good, consistent product.

Arf and I left early, though we weren't off work. I was pulling a wheeled tote full of spices for a restaurant in Ballard, a fairly new customer, so we took the elevator down to Western. Arf stretched out on the Saab's back seat and we made the drive in no time.

Delivery done, we stopped in Interbay. In working with every kind of food biz from hot dog carts to haute cuisine, I've learned you can't judge the food by the origins of the chef, or the exterior of the building. Edgar, a Salvadoran immigrant, makes a pasta Bolognese that is simply divine. The chef at the French bistro in Sammamish, a James Beard semifinalist, was born in Grays Harbor, a logging and fishing town on the Washington coast.

And Daria Nadeau had not one drop of Italian blood in her. But the line outside the door of her pizza place, formerly a gas station, at quarter to five on a damp Wednesday in January told the tale.

Last fall, the local paper declared her wood-fired pizza the best pizza in the county. Nate's brother Bron had met her when he stopped in Seattle for a few days and they'd been dating, in person and by phone, ever since. She and I had hit it off and I'd called ahead for a couple of pies, having been given Special Pizza Privileges.

With two tables, mainly for waiting in bad weather, most of her business is takeout. I stood at the counter beside the kitchen pass-through while Daria sliced fresh mozzarella, the air rich with the smells of tomato sauce and wood smoke. Bron had spent a couple of weeks in Seattle after Christmas, ostensibly to work with Nate on finalizing the crew and plans for the winter fishing season, but she was the real attraction.

"My parents are coming for a visit next month. Bron's flying down to meet them."

"Oh. Great. When they go back to harbor to offload." Which depended on the catch. Nate had flown home on short notice a couple of times. Quick trips, but so sweet.

Fish run, boats follow. Every business has its rhythms.

"I guess you're used to it," she said. "Nate being gone for months at a time. I'm not sure that's the life we want."

Nate's schedule was part of the deal. She was making me feel like some dull old married lady who didn't care if her husband came or went.

"Not months," I said. "We met last June, and the longest he's been gone is five weeks." Five weeks and three days. "Besides, your business keeps you crazy busy. So does mine."

The knife stopped its rhythmic motion and she met my gaze. "But life changes. You follow your path, and then the road forks. And you make new choices."

What choices was she talking about?

"Here you go, Pepper." The counter man handed me two boxes, and I said my thanks and goodbyes. Set the boxes on the floor of the front seat. Arf poked his nose over the back, sniffing noisily.

"Don't get any ideas, little buddy. Plenty of dog treats at mom and dad's."

Careful to avoid the Mercer Mess, I wound my way around the base of Queen Anne to the east side of Lake Union. Last summer, Nate had made more trips to Seattle than usual, leaving Bron in charge. Turnabout was fair play.

When a relationship is new, anything seems possible. Was Daria daydreaming, or were she and Bron making plans? Career-change plans? Vinny'd hinted at Nate rethinking his work and I'd brushed it off, but I'd never imagined that Bron might jump ship. He was smart and capable. He was a good mechanic, better than Nate, or so Nate said. Maybe he had job skills I didn't know about. Maybe he had other options in mind. Maybe it was none of my business.

But it was, because any change Bron made would affect Nate, and that would affect me. If Bron gave up the life, would Nate cash it in, too?

Lots of ifs. Forks in the road, as Daria had said.

I forked left and parked. Laurel had arranged for my parents to stay in a boat a dock over from hers for a few weeks while the owners basked in the warm dry air of another clime. I grabbed the pizzas and Arf's leash, and we passed through the gate into a magical world, scented by sea salt and a hint of diesel.

"Pepper, darling!" my mother cried, standing at the houseboat's open door. She brushed her cheek against mine.

"There's my girl," Dad said, and took the warm boxes from my hands.

Anybody who's seen *Sleepless in Seattle* thinks they know houseboats. That one is further up the lake, more mini mansion than boat, technically a floating home built on a dock. In contrast, a cluster of houseboats in the next bay are literal boats people live on, some more seaworthy than others.

My parents' temporary home, like Laurel's, is somewhere in between. Cozy, efficient, well-designed. We sat with our salad, pizza, and beer in the tiny dining booth, while Arf lay as close to my dad as caninely possible.

"How's the house hunt going?" I asked.

"Swimmingly," Mom said, and my dad's mouth twitched. "We're looking at houses. In the city."

"You said you didn't want a house. The yard, too much responsibility."

"Plans change," Dad said.

"Don't I know it?" I told them about my conversation with Daria.

"It would be nice for you to have Nate here full-time," Mom said.

"Yeah. But he hasn't worked on land in more than twenty

years. What would he do?" And part of the fun was rediscovering each other after weeks apart.

"He'll figure it out. Like you did when you lost your job."

On the heels of leaving my marriage. I wished that level of upheaval on no one.

"I had tea with the doctors Locke today. Henry asked about you and sends his greetings," I told my mother, then recapped his comments on the letters. "We don't know for sure that they have any connection to the pharmacy, except that they were found in the same building."

"If Oliver does intend to redevelop the Gold Rush, the pharmacy could throw a wrench in his plans," my dad said.

"No one seems to know what Oliver's plans are. Not even Roxanne."

"I'm sure that's the building Aki pushed to reopen years ago," Mom said. "Housing has always been especially important to her. She pestered the owners but didn't get anywhere."

"Hmm. Apparently there is a potential buyer, but what he—or they—have in mind, I have no idea."

"Want me to call Aki?" my mother asked. "She might know."

I shook my head. If anybody called her, it should be me.

My dad poured himself another beer. "You hear anything else about the victim?"

"They know his name and that he was staying in the CID, but that's all—or was, when I talked to Detective Spencer. He shouldn't be too hard to trace. There can't be many Terence Leongs around."

My dad left the table for a minute and came back with a VHS tape. "Found this in one of the boxes you've been storing for us. You should watch it."

Way of the Dragon, written, produced, directed by, and starring Bruce Lee. I knew my dad had studied aikido after he came back from Vietnam, but I didn't recall him staying up late to watch martial arts movies. "Might be interesting, after *Crouching Tiger*. Thanks. Hey, Roxanne said while she was working in the building, she sometimes heard odd noises or sensed that someone was there, though she didn't see anyone. When she told Oliver, he said it must be the ghost of Bruce Lee."

Dad's eyebrows rose. "I think he was pulling her leg. Or she was pulling yours."

"That's what Reed said. That Lee's life in Seattle was so well documented, any hint of a haunting and someone would have tried to exploit it."

"Besides, he died in Hong Kong. Why would he haunt a building in Seattle?"

"Oh, you never know about ghosts." As I'd had reason to discover. "They have their own logic."

We decided to take an evening stroll while the skies were dry. Porch lights glimmered on the dark water, and across the lake, we could see the lights of Queen Anne. We passed the tall rack of mailboxes at the entrance to the docks, many of the boxes painted to match their owners' boats.

"I'm going to miss this place," my mother said, looping her arm through mine. I pressed her arm close and blinked back tears I was glad she couldn't see.

A few steps down the sidewalk, my phone buzzed in my pocket. I fished it out.

"I need to take this," I said, falling back a few steps. Dad had Arf's leash fully in hand. "Hey, Rox. Find out anything useful about the Gold Rush?"

"Um, yeah." She sounded out of breath. "But what I called to tell you was—I'm okay, I'm not hurt, not really, but it was pretty scary."

"What? What happened?"

She'd been attacked as she walked home after work. As she walked past the Lakeview Cemetery. No serious injuries, thank God, but she was terrified. And not just because the most famous resident of Lakeview is the late Bruce Lee.

Sixteen

Started on June 6, 1889 when a glue pot in a woodworking shop boiled over, the Great Seattle Fire destroyed twenty-five city blocks, including wharves, mills, homes, and businesses. Thousands of people were displaced and jobs lost. Although no statistics were kept on the loss of human life, an estimated one million rats were killed.

ROXANNE LIVED IN A GRACEFUL OLD BUILDING ON CAPITOL Hill, with a spacious hex-tiled entry that was the polar opposite of the one I'd peeked into after tea at the clinic. I was glad I'd left Arf with my parents. She greeted me in bare feet, black leggings, and an oversized U Dub sweatshirt.

"Join me?" She raised the glass of bourbon in her hand. I declined. I was driving and I'd already had a beer with the pizza.

Built-in bookshelves lined the living room walls. A wrought-iron candelabra filled the fireplace, the hearth black marble, the mantle carved white stone. The decor was old books, gilt-framed paintings, and tasteful objects, likely souvenirs of her travels. The kind called artifacts, not knickknacks. I would have expected nothing less.

But the elegant Dr. Davidson herself was rattled. An angry red bruise was emerging on her cheekbone and the palms of her hands were cut and scraped from the rough cement sidewalk where she'd landed.

I accepted her offer of tea, my thirtieth or fortieth cup of the day, mostly to give her something to do while she steeled herself to tell me the story. The kitchen was small and tidy, and as she heated water and got out a cup and tea, I admired a sake set, an unfamiliar design painted on the pitcher. I turned to ask her about it.

"What is—"

The tip of a chef's knife was pointed at me, mere inches from my chest.

"Lemon?" Roxanne asked. Only then, as my heartbeat slowed, did I notice the lemon in her other hand. The one not holding the knife.

"Uh, no. Thanks."

When we were settled, she told me what had happened. Dusk, but the street was busy and well-lit, and she'd walked the few blocks home many times. A man rushed up behind her—she thought he'd been hiding behind a car—and shoved her to the ground.

"Did he touch you? Other than to push you down, I mean. Or grab your bag?"

"No. Nothing. I had my folding umbrella in my hand, but I didn't have time to swing at him. Everything happened so fast. But the weirdest part, the reason I called you—" She broke off and sipped her drink. I waited until she spoke.

"The weirdest part was what he said. He said, 'Leave the past alone.'"

The same words the old lady had hurled at us Monday afternoon near the Gold Rush. I'd been vaguely amused at the time, but there was nothing funny about them now.

"Did you tell the police about the woman in the CID?"

"No. I didn't report it. I'm okay, and they're busy. It couldn't be connected, could it? How would they—she—anybody?"

I hadn't a clue, but I did know what Detective Tracy always says. When odd things happen in or around the same circle of people, it always means something. And he always wants to know.

I called him. Got voicemail. Better luck with Detective Spencer. I gave her a brief rundown before handing my phone to Roxanne, who repeated the story in detail, including the man's few words, and described our earlier encounter with the woman.

"No. I have no idea who either one of them is. Or what they want. I mean, 'Leave the past alone'? I work with antiquities. I live in the past."

While Roxanne talked with the detective, I found the bathroom. More of those classic floor tiles and fixtures.

Had the attacker been referring to the letters? Who else knew about them? Or to the hotel and its secrets?

And how was the attack connected to the murder of Terence Leong?

I washed my hands in the white pedestal sink and stared at myself in the beveled, arch-top mirror. Knew what I was going to do even before telling myself it was an invasion of her privacy and a cliché to boot. In all my adventures, I had never done such a thing.

"There's always a first time," I muttered and swung the mirror open. The medicine cabinet shelves held all the usual suspects: toothbrush and toothpaste, floss, eye cream.

And in the center of the center shelf, a small bronze statue of the seated Buddha.

I closed the cabinet door and returned to the living room in time to hear Roxanne promise to meet the detectives at SPD headquarters in the morning to give a formal statement. Because Spencer agreed with Tracy, as I knew she would. Anything touching on a murder, however tangentially, mattered. Threats to witnesses most of all.

Roxanne gave me back my phone, then pulled a Moleskine notebook out of her black leather briefcase. "I looked up the ownership history of the Gold Rush. Just the abstracts—I didn't dig up the deeds yet. First title was issued in 1890, which is consistent with the cornerstone."

"Year after the fire. Great time to be a builder, or to own a brickyard."

"In 1906, it was sold to a man named Church, and in 1922, to one named Chen. Remember, Chinese names weren't always recorded correctly, because of the inverted order, with the family name coming first. And they weren't anglicized consistently. Chen was sometimes Chin, with one n or two, or Chien, an i before the e."

"That happened to a lot of immigrants. In my high school, there were two girls named Teresa Doherty, one spelled d-o-h and one d-o-u-g-h."

"Right? I have cousins named Schmidt with a d-t and Schmitt

with two ts." She tucked a foot beneath her and consulted her notes. "Then in 1931, it was sold to an F.H. Wu."

"Francis, Bobby Wu's dad. Oliver's grandfather." I sipped my tea. "Any idea what they plan to do with the building? Or planned, before Oliver found the pharmacy and you found a dead body? When did Bobby acquire it?"

"He didn't." Roxanne said. "I can't tell if F.H. sold it to her or left it to her when he died, but Abigail is the sole owner."

Now that put on an odd spin on things. Did Bobby lack interest in the building because he didn't own it? Or had his father passed him over because he knew his son saw the Gold Rush as an albatross, a distraction from his true love?

"Oh." A tiny light bulb flickered in my brain. "F.H. Chinese immigrants often took an American first name, right? Either legally or informally. Could F.H. Wu have been the same person, both Francis and Fong?" We'd been distracted by the attack and I hadn't told her about the letters.

"So this Fong blamed the doctor for his wife's death," Roxanne said when I finished my report. "A year later, F.H., aka Francis, acquires the building. What happened to the doctor? Is that when the pharmacy was sealed up?"

"No—way later. The building inspector said it was probably blocked off thirty or forty years ago. Too bad we don't know the doctor's name."

"There's got to be a way to find him." She put the back of her hand to her mouth, covering up a yawn.

Time to go. I reached for my bag and saw a wicker basket next to the couch, a piece of partially worked canvas poking out. "You do needlepoint?"

"My grandmother started that before she died; I keep thinking I'll finish it, but mostly it's there to remind me of her. I'm not like you, Pepper, with a balanced life. A shop and a dog and friends and a great guy. All I do is work."

Ha, I thought. If only you knew. I stood. "That's the shock talking. Take a hot bath and call it a night."

This time she couldn't hide the yawn. "I might skip the bath and go straight to bed. Pepper, thanks. Thanks for coming over when you got my call. Thanks for not telling me I'm an idiot. Thanks for knowing what to do. Nate was right about you."

What had the man said? I'd intended to confront her. To quiz her about Nate and Rosalie and the shoplifting incident, and now I was glad I hadn't.

I put a hand on her shoulder and leaned in for a quick hug. "That's what girlfriends do."

THOUGH it was full dark now, I detoured down to 23rd and zipped up to Montlake. You never forget the way to your childhood home. To my surprise, a FOR SALE sign stood in the yard. It had been a great place to grow up. I'd been happy at Grace House, and shocked to learn, last spring, the real reason we'd moved. Montlake was still a great place for families. Laurel had lived a few blocks away, moving to the houseboat after Patrick's murder, when their son Gabe was sixteen. My friend Maddie and her husband and tweens lived nearby.

My eyes swelled and I felt a fullness in my throat. I was never going to have a house spilling over with children or a yard brimming with azaleas. I wasn't going to set up a booth in an antique mall and sell ephemera and vintage quilts I scavenged from yard sales in small towns. I wasn't going to jet between a San Juan Island retreat and a jewel-box of an apartment in Paris.

Was this what midlife meant? I'd had the crisis, when I discovered that while Tag was sowing his wild oats, my biological clock had run out, and that the people I'd given sixty hours of my life blood every week for years had frittered away the human capital along with the firm's cash and reputation. When I decided to put my faith in the person I trusted most: myself.

That was the wreck. Now I was having the reckoning. The recognition of what you don't have, the consequences of the choices you've made and the forks taken. You can't go back and make trade-offs.

But that was okay, wasn't it? I liked my life. Loved it. My shop that supports the staff and the Market that feeds the city. The customers. My friends and my family. A dog who would do anything for me, and who knew in his bones that I would do the same.

And out there on the water, a terrific guy.

Who needs azaleas anyway?

* * *

I PASSED the neighbor's front door on my way up the stairs. There's a theory that a sense of community and well-being depends not just on the close bonds we form but also on the "weak ties"—our connections with the butcher, the baker, and the espresso maker. The neighbors you see at the mailboxes or in the parking garage. The dog owner you know as "the Irish setter's dad."

Strange to open my door to quiet. No dog nails ticking on the floor, no partner stirring up dinner in the kitchen.

Just the hum of the fridge and the questions rattling in my brain.

I kicked off my shoes and crawled into my jammies. Poured a glass of water and dug out my phone. I'd heard the beep of a message while I was driving, and now clicked it open.

Hey, little darlin'. Sorry I missed you. Calling it an early night.

Was it wrong of me to be a bit relieved? There was no way I could talk to Nate tonight and not be a blubbery mess. He'd know I was holding back. He always did.

I wanted desperately to ask him what he thought the future held, for himself, for his partnership with Bron, but most of all, for us. Part of that reckoning I'd mused about earlier was realizing that while being apart was part of my deal with Nate, it wasn't always easy, and I might want change. I wasn't going to be like Rosalie, making demands Nate could never meet. But I didn't want to be like Daria, either, assuming the future would bend itself into the perfect shape.

And I absolutely could not let on that Bron might be making plans Nate didn't know about. Not that Daria had spoken in confidence, but when to say what wasn't my call. The song from *White Christmas* about not coming between misters and sisters applied to girlfriends and brothers, too, even if it didn't rhyme.

I changed my water into wine and stuck my dad's video into the ancient player.

How would Nate know I might want more if I didn't tell him?

One more mystery to leave for another day.

Seventeen

*Spring rolls are traditionally served at New Year's,
the start of spring in the lunar calendar, and often
stacked to look like bars of gold.*

I WOKE UP THINKING ABOUT BRUCE LEE AND THE ATTACK ON
Roxanne. Who wanted her to stop—and stop what? As threats go,
"Leave the past alone" was annoyingly nonspecific.

It had to be connected to the woman who'd warned us off
outside the hotel. Who was she? I'd been her target that day. And
now? Would the man who'd gone after Roxanne come after me?

My parents were keeping Arf for the day. One more benefit of
having them close by. I decided to check out the doggy daycare on
my way to work.

I walked up Union, pausing at the entrance to the old INS
building. Any clues to the mystery of the letter writer's wife were
long remodeled away.

The doghouse—not its real name—was easy to find. The paw
prints painted on the pavers led me, like any good dog would, right
to the front door.

Where Yolande, the Market's leasing manager, crouched beside
a black-and-white French bulldog sporting a red collar.

"Be a good boy, Corker." She kissed the top of his head.
"Mama will be back before you know it."

"What a cutie," I said. "I didn't know you had a dog."

"Oh, hi, Pepper." We both watched as the staffer took Corker's leash and led him inside, the dog trotting happily toward a day with his puppy pals. "I used to bring him to the office, but I'm out and about so much, it wasn't fair to him."

Exactly what I'd begun to think. "You're happy with the place, then?"

We walked up the alley, Yolande giving me the scoop. "Best part is, I can drop in whenever I'm close, except during naptime. Theirs, not mine. I've been training a new employee while getting the new commercial tenants on board, and what I wouldn't give for a nap some days. This afternoon, I'm giving a tour to a group interested in combining residential and retail space, as we've done in the Market. It's a challenge, especially when you're talking about a historic building."

"What about one that isn't listed on the historic register, but has an interesting past?"

"Depends. If it's in a designated historic district, any major change has to go through the city. A redevelopment proposal can spark an outcry. Property rights versus preservation of a building with significance to the community. Passions can run high."

That, I knew. Emotions had flared in Montlake last fall, when residents thought a proposal out of sync with the neighborhood. And a plan a year or two back to demolish a historic theater a stone's throw from the Market had galvanized preservationists, music lovers, and downtown advocates alike.

"I got a tour of an old hotel in the CID the other day. It was like time travel, back to 1930."

"Oh, you must mean the Gold Rush," Yolande said. We'd passed the Gum Wall, too early for the throng of visitors who came to stick their chewed-up wads of Double Bubble to the pointillist display. Now we stopped outside her office. "The building is solid, though nothing special. Good potential for affordable or subsidized housing. Market-rate units, not so much."

"Why? Not enough room for amenities like a pool or parking?" Or a rooftop garden.

"That, and the size and location. No views. I used to consult on this stuff, before I came to the Market, so I know a lot of people, and there's talk that a group of investors made an offer but got rebuffed. No, I don't know who and I wouldn't tell you if I did."

Another staffer arrived for work and held the door for her. "Think about the doggy daycare. You could take Arf in for a few hours and try it out. I bet he'd love it."

I climbed the hidden steps up to Pike Place. Yolande had cut me off before I could ask more questions. She knew me well.

The Wus had several options. Renovate. Redevelop, a euphemism for scraping and replacing the existing buildings. Or sell.

I'd been assuming they'd decide as a family, but Abigail owned the building. Would she take Bobby's and Oliver's views into account? What if they didn't agree?

Keith Chang worried that any major change would mean the end of his family's business. Did the other tenants share those fears? How did the pharmacy and the dead man play into it all?

Little mysteries everywhere.

VANESSA had the day off—she'd told me she was going to spend the day with her feet up, her nose in a book, and a cup of spice tea close by—but the staff regulars were all on hand.

"What do you think?" Cayenne asked, as I took a bite of a biscuity baby quiche she'd made in a muffin tin, using smoked cheddar, ham, and chopped broccoli. And a healthy sprinkling of a mixed pepper and spice blend we'd created last fall.

"I think I want another. You've got a future customer favorite here."

I boxed up a pair of baby quiches and after we opened, carried them across the cobbles to Sandy Lynn.

"I admit," the cheese monger said, one bite in, "I've never seen the point of a crustless quiche. But this is terrific. It's like the crust is crumbled up inside."

"Any recipes we create using your products and ours will be credited to both shops." I made air quotes. "'Brought to you by Say Cheese! and Seattle Spice, in the Market.' We'll post them online and print up copies, and you can do the same. If we use a specific spice or blend, we can provide jars for you to sell. We don't have a cooler, so we'll send people to you for the cheese."

"That's perfect," she said. "Pepper, you asked me why I wanted to open my shop in the Market. This is why."

I said my goodbyes and stepped back into the fray of the Main Arcade. A gaggle of shoppers surged past me to the stairs leading to Down Under, a warm and cozy refuge on a drizzly day. I watched them descend and reach the wide hall, thinking about the surprising ties that seemed to bind everyone in the city to the Market.

And marching briskly down the hall, toward the far exit, Bobby Wu. Was it him? It had to be him. That black leather jacket. The hair and the walk.

I couldn't catch him. Didn't think I wanted to. What would I say? "Your family owns an amazing old hotel. A priceless pharmacy. There was a dead man in your basement. Don't you care?"

Not likely to get the most heart-warming response, was I?

So I switched gears and trotted down the steps in search of information. A Market fixture since its founding in the early 1960s, the comic book shop claims to be the oldest in the country. But no musty stacks of faded comics rummaged from attics or moldy storage sheds here. It was a riot of clean, well-organized color, its wire spinners and wooden shelves portals to worlds beyond this one, accessible through old-style comics and modern graphic novels. Dave Hudson and his staff were your travel guides.

Midmorning on a drizzly weekday in January, I was the only customer. Weekends, the place would be packed. I stopped to admire a rotating display case of early Wonder Woman memorabilia. Behind the counter, a staffer was sorting a cardboard box of comics while another unpacked a shipment of Baby Yoda dolls.

Not my enchilada, intriguing as it all was. I did remember dropping in a few times when my mother and Carl and I made our weekly trips to the Market. Carl went through a comic book phase, as many kids do, before settling his interests elsewhere. At Christmas, he and Mom brought Charlie down here in search of the latest volume in the Wings of Fire series of graphic novels. They'd found it, and a couple of classics Carl bought for himself.

"And they say there are no coincidences," Dave boomed as he emerged from the backroom. "First you and I were talking about Bobby Wu, then he shows up. Not five minutes later, you walk in."

I fessed up. "I spotted Bobby speed-walking toward the steps and figured he might have been here. Any chance you can say why?"

The law may not recognize a customer–shopkeeper privilege, but some shopkeepers do. Fortunately, Dave was not so persnickety.

"He's looking to sell a few things. I've got no need for any of it, but I promised to call a couple of my collectors. Guys with bucks."

"Can I ask, what are we talking about? What kind of money?"

Dave straightened a stack of jigsaw puzzles and picked up a card deck that wasn't where it belonged. "Depends on condition. Bobby says mint. And he does know his stuff. Problem is, everything he wants to sell is a partial. One series might bring a couple thousand, another four or five. He's missing a couple of the early volumes, though he thinks he can find them. If he does, twenty-five grand, easy. Forty, to the right buyer."

"Yikes. No wonder so many guys curse their mothers for tossing their collections."

"If it weren't for those mothers, nothing in here would be worth very much."

A customer entered, aiming for Dave, and I stepped back to give them space. Retail is the biz, after all. I glanced up at the high ceiling, dripping with all manner of space craft, and almost backed into a box of lightsabers. The customer now safely directed to the young adult section, Dave returned to me.

"Like I said, Bobby's got some good stuff, but that's not enough to build a successful business." He opened his arms and gestured. "Let's just say, I have every advantage and I've made the most of it."

"That you have. Location, location, location. Your theory, Dave, on the appeal of the comic book? Or the graphic novel?"

"On a physical level, they're fun, especially for those who are more visual or have trouble reading. They help kids visualize. They come every month, so they give you something to look forward to. And the superhero—well, ordinary people can be superheroes. You can see yourself in them, even if you don't see yourself in the world around you."

"Sounds pretty powerful, put that way."

"You're going to ask if Bobby told me why he's selling." The big man folded his arms across his chest. "He did not. And I did not ask."

Oops. Guilty. I gave him an apologetic smile. Must be important, though, if Bobby was going beyond his own clientele and approaching other dealers.

We talked about the traffic task force. Dave had been taking the temperature of his neighbors, as I had of mine, in the short time since the meeting.

"Lost in the talk about car counts and delivery hours is what set off that whole clusterfrack last Sunday," he said. "The problem you stumbled into."

"Shoplifting." I could still picture that smashed pineapple, so grateful it hadn't been a human head or foot. Market security did a good job, but they couldn't be everywhere.

Dave pointed a beefy finger to a model of the starship *Enterprise*, hanging above the cash register. "Got me some sophisticated spyware. And some very sharp-eyed clerks. But even Darth Vadar"—he nodded to the life-size statue guarding the front door—"can't stop 'em all."

"Truth. We get our share. Hey, thanks for the intel."

"Any time. Tell that ex of yours, he ever wants to sell his *Stars Wars* figures I can get him a pretty penny."

"Ha," I replied. "Pretty sure it's in his will, he wants to be buried with them."

I'D BEEN BACK in the shop less than a minute when Roxanne called.

"They're gone," she said.

I waited.

She blew out a breath so noisy it almost knocked the cell phone out of my hand. "I went to police headquarters, gave my statement, and answered the detectives' questions. Told them everything. Gave them copies of the letters and Dr. Locke's notes, and told them what he told you. I'm afraid the police will pay him a visit."

"I'll give Ron a heads-up."

"Then we went down to the Gold Rush. I've never ridden in a police car before. It's not as exciting as I thought it would be."

I could have told her that.

"I took them upstairs," she continued. "Opened the side drawer on the waterfall dressing table, where I found the box. It was gone."

"You're sure?"

"Absolutely certain. They talked about a warrant, but me saying the letters are missing isn't evidence of a crime. And there's no reason to connect them to the murder. I don't know what they're going to do."

"Without the letters," I said, "we may never know what happened to Fong's wife or the doctor. Or who was staying in that room and why she had the letters. If she did."

"As a historian, I always want the originals, and I hope they surface. But I have the next best thing. I scanned them all with my phone, not just the ones I sent Reed."

"You're brilliant."

"That's what Detective Spencer said. Detective Tracy grunted."

Figures. "Any signs of a break-in? Forced entry? Anything else missing?"

"None. The detectives went over all that. They made me look at all the cabinets, on the landing and downstairs. All the artwork, the old musical instruments hanging on the walls. Even the furniture. But the first thing I do on any project is take pictures, so we compared what's there now to my first day on the job. Not a ginger jar or an erhu out of place."

Whoever took the box hadn't known Roxanne photographed everything. Or didn't realize she'd found the box.

"They asked me again who had keys to the hotel," she continued. "I know they're intelligent people, but I find I have to repeat myself a lot with them."

"They're paid to be suspicious," I said. But of who? Beyond the Wu family. Roxanne herself?

I found myself repeating Nate's words from last weekend.

Careful, Pepper. Careful.

Eighteen

Fortune cookie baking changed dramatically in the 1960s with the invention of a machine to insert the fortune and fold the cookie, eliminating the need to quickly place the paper fortune in a hot cookie and fold it with chopsticks before it cooled.

CAYENNE'S BABY QUICHES HAD NOT LASTED THE MORNING, so Sandra ordered a sandwich platter for staff lunch. In the before times, I bought pastries for our Wednesday morning meeting and lunch on Saturdays, when the Market was so busy that I couldn't expect my employees to compete with shoppers for a table or takeout and manage to eat comfortably in the time allotted. But that had changed while we'd all been acting as a pod, spending most of our working time in the warehouse prepping mail orders and curbside delivery. Sure, the paid-lunch perk cost me, but ultimately, the cost-benefit analysis worked in my favor.

As it did right now. I sat in the nook with a turkey and Swiss on a ciabatta roll.

I'd already suspected the letters were connected to the murder, and the theft convinced me. Or at least, they were connected to the building, which might mean the same thing. But how? Who had taken them, and why?

Unlike Dave's comic book shop and my own place, the Gold

Rush had no security cameras. No motion sensor lights, no touch pad entry to record the user's code. Nothing but keys.

And keys could be copied, no questions asked.

I wondered why Bobby needed cash. Keith Chang had said Bobby refused to cut the rent during the shutdown. The Changs had paid for the recent upgrades to the café themselves. I assumed the other ground floor tenants had a similar arrangement. Clearly the Wus weren't investing the rent money back into the building, with its creaky plumbing and the pile of crumbled bricks in the basement.

If Abigail owned it, did Bobby have access to the revenue it brought in? Keith had linked his increased presence to the sighting of the men taking pictures and measurements, but Yolande thought the offer had been rejected. Who in the family wanted to sell and who didn't?

There are any number of reasons why a spouse needs money they can't get from the other. And most of them are bad news.

I had some year-end paperwork to drop off at our accountant's office, in the building where I'd worked for years at Fourth and Madison. Could I help it if my feet took me by Oliver Wu's workplace?

There's a trend in the hospitality industry to repurpose older buildings into boutique hotels, and this was a prime example. Another option for the Gold Rush. If you looked up, the rows of windows might hint that this place had once been an office building. At street level, though, it was polished to a shine, the American and Canadian flags flying above the brightly colored awning. I'd been here once for a wedding and reception, and both food and decor were hip and tasty. Seetha said the massage rooms were the most luxurious she'd ever worked in.

The lobby was equally trendy, the patterns on the upholstery and plentiful pillows perfectly mismatched. No one sat there at the moment. I was tempted.

Behind the front desk stood Oliver Wu, in a charcoal gray suit, his tie and pocket square the same soft yellow as the wallpaper behind him.

"So this is where you work," I said. "No wonder Seetha raves about the place. Pepper Reece. We met last weekend." I held out my hand.

"I remember." His grip was not very gripping. And his eyes—wary or worried?

"I was walking by and couldn't resist stopping in. You'd never imagine this hasn't always been a hotel. What a great place to work."

"It's an honor," he said, "to be able to help people create special moments and memories."

"And the Gold Rush. Oh my gosh. Despite the tragedy, I've loved getting to peek inside. What a gem. Your parents must be proud to have you take on the responsibility for keeping it going. And relieved."

He gave a noncommittal grunt that reminded me of Detective Tracy.

Might as well be bold. I wanted info about the building, and I wanted to know more about this man Seetha was so interested in. "How did it come to be in your family?"

"My grandfather bought the hotel in the 1930s, though it's older than that. He acquired the rest of the block piece by piece." The phone rang. Someone in the back office answered, the voice drifting through the half-closed doorway behind him.

"The Gold Rush would make a beautiful hotel like this," I said. "All that historic charm. Nothing like it in the CID, is there?"

"We—we haven't decided what to do with it."

When it came to plans, old buildings were expensive. Were those men in suits would-be buyers or potential financial backers? A modern hotel would require massive loans. On the other hand, subsidized housing would come with grants, low interest rates, and other assistance.

"Seetha might have mentioned that I run the Spice Shop in the Market. The old SROs have been rehabbed into modern apartments, and I can't tell you how much they've helped maintain the sense of community. Keeping it real. I imagine you're getting more of a feel for what the community needs and what it would support, now that you're living in the building." Where a man had been killed. Oliver's placid exterior reflected none of the inner turmoil I'd felt when a man died on my doorstep.

"Oh, yes," he said. "No shortage of opinions."

Was that why we'd been warned off? Though why attack Roxanne? I didn't know if Oliver knew about that, or the theft, though no doubt the detectives would quiz him about both. The front door swooshed open and I heard the chatter of guests arriving. I was running out of time.

"Tough decision," I said. "Lots of time and money either way. You could sell. But that would be hard, when it's meant so much to your family."

He gave me a sharp look, then greeted the new arrivals, a bellman pushing a wheeled luggage rack. I waved goodbye.

Back outside, I crossed the street to Ripe, Laurel's café, and popped in to see if she could take a break in five minutes. Then I rode the elevator to the accountant's office. Left my papers at the front desk and headed back down.

She was waiting with a cappuccino, a chocolate cherry biscotti on the saucer. About half the tables were full, and we took seats at the counter overlooking the street.

"Seetha stopped in during our lunch rush. I didn't have much time to talk." Laurel cradled her mug of dark roast, black, as always. "She'd just come from the hotel—they do a lot of weddings and she was part of a spa day team. She's all gushy-gushy about Oliver. I think she should back off until the police have a suspect."

"Tell me you didn't tell her that." I bit into the cookie and a dried cherry exploded on my tongue.

"I did." She raised the mug. "I know, I shouldn't have. It's the mother in me. I can't help remembering what a wreck she was when, well, you know."

"She swears, no bhuts. She said helping me solve the murder in the vintage shop banished them. Not that she helped much. But she stood up to her mother and confronted the racist creep on the street corner. Maybe bhuts cower at the sight of a strong woman."

"Like vampires vanquished by the sight of a crucifix?" Laurel was skeptical. "I may not have dated in the current century, but would it hurt her to be too busy to see him until all this is over?"

"Not that I disagree, but no way would she cancel their big date tomorrow night." I told her about the attack on Roxanne and the theft in the hotel.

"I don't like the sound of that," she said.

"Change the subject? I had the weirdest conversation with Daria last night, the woman Bron is dating, when I stopped to pick up pizza." I filled her in.

"So you're wondering what Nate knows, and if he knows, why he hasn't said anything to you, and what do you say without letting on that his brother might be making plans without telling him and without sounding like an insecure idiot."

"Nailed it."

"Pepper, listen. One of the things I admire about the two of you is, your relationship isn't that old, but it's so mature. Nate's an actual adult."

Unlike Tag. Or some of the men I'd dated since I left him.

"I know you," she continued. "You want to dive in and work stuff out. Hash it over. Talk talk talk."

"You sound like Tag."

She made a face. "But guys aren't like that."

"I want us to work together to plan our future."

"Pep, remember. Nate's been working on a boat in the middle of the ocean for the better part of twenty years. He's learned to work things out himself, as much as he can, at least until he knows his own mind. Not about you, that's clear. I mean, about himself." She picked up her coffee and swiveled her stool a few degrees. "Speaking of work. Gotta get back to it. Give him space to work this out. That's the way to show him you love him."

She gave me a quick hug and sped back to the kitchen, apron strings flying. I sipped my cappuccino and stared out the window. I wasn't good at giving people space. Space meant distance, and distance made time for the mind to spin scary thoughts. As Laurel said, I'm talk talk talk. Cards on the table. Everything in the open.

But she was right. This time was different. And if you want things to be different, you can't keep acting the same old way.

OLIVER Wu hadn't wanted to tell me his family's thinking about the future of the Gold Rush, and I couldn't blame him. But if Keith Chang was right, someone had been casing the place. And I couldn't discount Yolande's grapevine gossip.

I knew nothing about the ins and outs of this stuff. But it was a short walk to city hall, full of experts.

Seattle City Hall is a modern building, a blend of materials meant, I imagine, to reflect the vibrance and variety of the community. That variety was on full display as I aimed for the wide steps, passing clusters of people in all manner of dress conversing in half a dozen languages or more, some happily, some with the intensity that dealing with bureaucracy can trigger.

I stepped off the elevator on the fourth floor and almost ran into the coordinator of the Market Historical District.

"Pepper, hey! Don't see you in months, then twice in one week."

"Funny how that goes, isn't it?" The theme of my day. "Do you have a minute? I have questions. I promise they'll be easier than solving the traffic issues in the Market."

"Sorry—I'm running late." She held the elevator door open. "Talk to my assistant, Cathy. She's smarter than I am anyway." Then she got in the elevator and zipped away.

Moments later, Cathy and I were catching up across the counter. We'd always gotten along. I gave her the address of the Gold Rush.

"How do I find out if there have been any applications or inquiries for redevelopment? Or for historic status? That's all public information, isn't it?"

"Everything we do is public. Not my district, but I can check." A keyboard sat on a shelf below the counter and she clicked away. "I don't see any applications related to that building. Hold on."

She called to another woman and explained what I was after. "Nothing on file that I can see. Are you aware of any proposals in the works?"

"Any scuttle?" I asked. "Any info at all?"

The woman fixed me with a glare that would have withered a prison guard. "We don't deal in scuttle."

I felt a flush rise up my cheeks. "Poor choice of words. Sorry. I'm trying to help a friend make some decisions"—if you keep the excuses vague, they aren't lies—"and wanted to see what we could find out. But if there's nothing you can tell me . . ."

"Hold on," Cathy said. "That's the building the man asked about, isn't it?"

The stickler lowered her chin, looking over the tops of her glasses. "Men, and women, literally ask us about buildings dozens of times a day. That is what we do."

"I know, I know. You were on vacation, right around Christmas, and I had desk duty." Cathy shifted her focus from her coworker to me, and the other woman shook her head and turned away. "A man came in asking about an old hotel in the CID. Not a hotel in the modern sense—one of the semiresidential hotels from way back. If this wasn't the address, it was close. I specifically remember, he wanted the deeds and the architectural plans."

"Do you have records like that?" Might be interesting to see the plans for my loft—maybe unearth a clue why a warehouse built more than a century ago had twelve-foot high windows.

"People think the historic preservation office is the repository for all historic info, but it's not. The records are scattered all over the place, and most records that old are not online. It's frustrating. I sent him to the King County Archives, to the General Recordings Index for the deeds, and to the Department of Construction and Inspections for the plans. But I warned him not to get his hopes up. It's hit and miss, and it takes time."

"How can you remember all that?" I asked. "I barely remember what I had for breakfast. Or if I had breakfast."

"You remember what spices I buy every time I come in."

True enough.

She carried on. "Part of why it sticks in my mind is he said the building was built in 1890. That raises possibilities for historic designation and funding. I gave him our checklist."

That was the right date. "That limits what an owner can do, doesn't it?"

"Yes, but it's in a special review district, so we have to sign off on any major changes anyway. You remember."

My battles had been over exterior signage, which we'd solved by hanging our mock-neon saltshaker sign inside the front window rather than outside. Heaven help a business owner who wanted to put up an awning when historic photographs didn't show one.

"Did he say why he was asking? Do you remember anything about him?"

"No. He was pretty closed-mouthed. I'm good at details, but not so great with faces. I did tell him some requests trigger public hearings and input, and he didn't like the sound of that."

Afraid to tangle with Aki Ohno and her friends?

"Thanks. You've been a big help. I hope I didn't cause you any trouble with your coworker."

"Pooh." Cathy dismissed my concern with a wave of her hand.

"Let's say she and I have different views of what serving the public means."

I thanked her again and took my leave. Who was this mystery man? The more I thought about it, the more convinced I became that the Wu family had a secret they didn't want anyone to know. Bobby needed cash. And Abigail? Why had her father-in-law left the building to her? Good estate planning, or an indication that the old man had not trusted his only son?

And what about their only son? What did Oliver want? For Seetha's sake, for Roxanne, and Terence Leong, I desperately wanted to know.

Nineteen

*Traditionally, Lunar New Year celebrations include
extralong noodles to symbolize longevity.*

WHILE I'D BEEN FOLLOWING MY NOSE, TIME HAD BEEN
flying by. I texted Sandra to let her know I was on my way and
ask her to ply today's job applicant with tea and gush about
how much she loves her job. Crossed my metaphoric fingers that
he wouldn't mind a short delay. Says something if the applicant is late; says something else if the employer can't keep to a
schedule.

Luck was on my side. A cab drove up and deposited a well-
dressed couple in front of city hall. A couple dressed for a wedding,
if I guessed right. I slid in.

"First and Pine. I won't ask you to drive in the Market."

"For you, pretty lady, I'd do it."

Yeah, for me and the fare ticking away.

A Bruce Lee bobblehead perched on the dashboard, in strike
position with one arm bent, ready to punch, and one leg in a high
kick. I half expected the figurine to let out the high-pitched yell
burned in my brain from last night's video.

From the back seat, I texted a former law firm employee now
working in commercial real estate downtown. *Hey, Wynne! Heard
any scuttle about the old Gold Rush Hotel in the CID—listings,
offers? I know you keep your ear to the ground!*

At least talking to a real estate agent, I wouldn't get skewered for using the word "scuttle." Their business thrives on it.

I was watching the dots indicating a reply in progress when the cabbie pulled to the curb. I paid him and checked one more time before crossing First.

The reply appeared. *No, but I'll ask around. You investigating???* No surprise she'd connected the body and the building, though the news had only said "a derelict hotel." An example of scuttle in action.

Just have a few questions—thanks! Then I shoved my phone in my tote, hiked down the steep hill, and slipped in the shop's side door.

The applicant stood in front of the Wall O'Spice, a cup of tea in hand, deep in concentration. White man, maybe thirty, with close-cropped hair, in olive green pants and a brown tweed jacket.

"Pepper Reece. Thanks for waiting so patiently."

"Hayden Parker." He held out his hand. His grip was warm and firm, and I was sure I'd like him. "I'm drinking in the atmosphere. And the tea. Cardamom and allspice? They go good with the citrus."

"I'm impressed. Let's chat in the nook. Have we met somewhere?"

"Not formally, but I was all ears when you talked about spices at Changing Courses and showed us how you create blends."

"That's it." The program that trains disadvantaged adults to work in the food service industry. I'd given regular presentations in person for a good year. During the pandemic, I'd appeared by Zoom, to minimize in-person contacts and limit the risk to my staff. As a result, I hadn't gotten to know the students as well as I once had. Cayenne took over last fall and was doing a fabulous job.

Hayden had been a referral from a trusted source, so I hadn't looked at his resume closely, but I read it now. He'd finished the program a year ago, got the job with my buddy Edgar, and worked his way up the food chain.

The resume didn't reveal much about his personal history, and I didn't ask. It didn't matter. What mattered was he'd finished the course and came with a great reference from a man I knew to run a demanding operation.

"So why here, why now?"

"Getting married next month. Got a baby on the way, and I want a day job. But I still want to work with food."

"Congratulations." Good reason to make a change. His food safety certificate was up to date; he had a valid drivers' license. And I'd seen the way he studied the spices. Working for Edgar, he'd have learned a lot about consistency and quality, and balancing flavors.

"Tell me what you like to eat and cook."

Clearly the right question. His smile broke out and it was like the rain had stopped and the sun burst through the clouds. "Yes, ma'am. You're going to think because I'm from the south, I love barbecue and fried chicken and all that, and I do."

"So do I."

"Best thing about being in the Army was traveling and getting to eat what the locals ate. I got to eat real Korean food when I was stationed there. Love kimchi and Korean fried chicken, but that's the tip of the iceberg. And in the Middle East—" He broke off. "I mean, the work and the weather were hell, but the food was heaven. Pomegranates, olives, lemons."

"What was your favorite dish?"

"I loved it all but the thing I can still taste reminded me of shakshukah or menemen. You fry up onions and peppers and tomato, add herbs, and make a thick, rich stew. Then you add eggs and more herbs. Goat cheese or feta, if you have it." His hands darted and waved as he spoke, his passion infectious.

"You're making me hungry," I said. He'd named two trendy dishes with North African and Middle Eastern origins, great for breakfast or dinner. Or breakfast for dinner.

Then a shadow crossed his face. "Afghanistan was rough. The people there didn't have a lot, but they were so generous. On my way here, I passed the Greek restaurant. Caught a whiff of lamb. It sent me back before I even knew what I was smelling."

"There's a reason for that. The senses of taste and smell developed early, as humans evolved, and they're located in the same part of the brain as memory." I pointed to my own thick skull. "Smells alerted us to danger, and taste told us what was safe to eat. We had to remember in order to survive."

Hayden bowed his head and gripped his paper cup tightly.

"I need to tell you, I almost didn't make it. I was lucky—never got more than minor injuries, but it did a number on me anyway. Losing buddies, seeing the worst in people. And the best, too, but the worst sticks with you. I sunk pretty low when I got back to civilian life. Then I met my lady. A friend of hers suggested Changing Courses and"—he raised his face and gave me another grin—"it changed everything."

"Thank you for telling me that. You didn't have to."

He met my gaze. "If I want you to hire me, I want you to know."

"Sounds like your love of food helped you heal. Food can also be confusing. Tell me the difference between cilantro and coriander."

"Same plant. Cilantro is the leaves, so we call it an herb. Coriander is the seeds, which makes it a spice. To some people, cilantro tastes like soap, but the seeds have a different flavor entirely—floral, with a hint of citrus. They blend well with other spices."

"You have a good palate, or a good memory." He'd all but quoted me to myself. "How would you respond when a customer says she doesn't like spicy food?"

"Tough one. I'd ask her what she likes to eat, then talk about how herbs and spices enhance flavor. Lotsa times what people mean—and I don't know if I learned this from you or Edgar—is that they don't like hot food. Mouth hot, not temperature hot. I do, but . . ."

"You want to educate them, but not discourage anyone or make them feel bad."

"No. You want them to buy the stuff." He gestured to the shop, so full of stuff.

"Exactly. Let's talk salt." And we did. Hayden understood the differences between table and kosher salt, when to use salt during the cooking process, and what a finishing salt adds to a dish. All the rest—Celtic, Himalayan, fleur de sel—those were details I knew he'd pick up in a flash.

"Heart set on retail, or would you consider working in our warehouse?" I explained what we did and how the facility operates. "At the moment, we've got an experienced employee working afternoons, but he can't keep up. Demand is growing too much. You'd train with us, until you're ready to handle it yourself, along with another employee or two."

"You mean, manage the place?"

"Eventually, yes. If I hire you, you'd work in the shop for a few weeks to get to know the business." And to bond with the rest of the staff. This expansion wouldn't work if we didn't all work together. "You'll want to see the facility, and I'll want to chat with Edgar."

We talked job details, pay, and benefits, and arranged to meet at the warehouse Friday. Hayden made a point of introducing himself to all the staff, chatting a few minutes before he left. Cayenne caught my eye and nodded, and that was a relief.

I was mindful, though, of what he'd said about depression. Another reason to make sure the crew clicked and stayed connected.

A regular customer watched the interactions. "You're hiring. Too bad I'm happily retired. I loved working retail when I was young. And I ran the spice category on *Jeopardy!*"

All five answers—or rather, the questions. Even I hadn't managed that.

It was business as usual the rest of the day, if anything here is ever "usual." I helped customers, refilled displays, and tried not to think too much about the secrets of the Gold Rush Hotel. Fielded a call asking for an item we've never carried—today, it was scented candles. The woman was certain she'd bought them here; after all, they are herbal. It's a common occurrence in retail. Like the bookstore customer who can't remember the title or author but swears it was a paperback with an orange cover. Finally, the savvy staff extract enough clues from the customer's memory to find the book—a blue hardcover. All you can do is practice patience and remember that you've been that customer yourself at some point.

I flipped through the mail, sorting and recycling. Ogled a seed catalog. If we wanted to sell seedlings again this year, it was time to talk to Herb the Herb Man.

I found him in the Main Arcade.

"Great minds think alike," he said. "I was working on my seed order and wondered if you wanted to give it another go."

"You bet," I said. "April and May, the months when people are thinking about their gardens, even if their idea of gardening is a few pots on the deck. Those racks of tender baby plants are so tempting—they lure in people who might otherwise walk on by."

"A few pots is all most folks need."

We worked out a list: basil, parsley, thyme, oregano, and chives, along with an overlooked favorite of mine, tarragon. Plus a mint, which the savvy gardener keeps in a pot no matter how much space she has; it's a plant that simply does not know its place.

A customer arrived and I drifted down to the Orchard Girls' table.

"Vanessa is a dream," I said. "Thanks for sending her to me."

"She wouldn't even go out for a drink after work," Angie said. "She wanted to stay home and study the spice bible you lent her."

"Ooh. Sorry. Didn't mean to mess up your social life."

Herb's customer tucked her parsley and cilantro in her shopping bag, and he and I resumed our business.

"How about a flat of sage? And do you have a cilantro that won't bolt?"

He grunted. "I'll talk to my seed guy about that, but don't hold your breath. Lavender and rosemary? They're perennials, but not everybody's got them going."

"Great starter plants. And they smell so good. Yes on both, but no dill. It didn't sell last year, and Sandra took all the leggy leftovers."

We shook on it and I strolled up the arcade, past the arts and crafts tables. Goat milk soap and silk-screened dish towels, fused glass jewelry and stunning photos of the Pacific Northwest. Clocks made from old gears and scrap metal. Puppets. All the things people make and collect and do, each a potential hobby. But why spend months learning to make a lopsided pot when I could admire a perfectly made example right here? I picked up a celadon green vase, light and delicate, a spiral scribed into the clay like a vine. It was exquisite. I bought it. After all, art needs those who appreciate it every bit as much as it needs those who create it.

Sandra was ready to flip out the CLOSED sign when my dad arrived with Arf. I greeted them both with enthusiasm. Dad gave us a hand with the garbage and recycling, seeming to relish flattening the boxes from the day's deliveries.

"Want a job?" I teased. "If your references check out."

Then the floors were swept and the cash put away, and we turned off the lights. As I locked the door behind us, I remembered Vanessa's parting words her first day.

"Goodnight, shop," I said.

Dad had parked outside my loft and walked up the hill with the dog, so now we retraced their steps. The flower ladies were emptying their buckets into the street, but gave me a few leftover blossoms for my new vase.

In the loft, Dad happily accepted a glass of my new favorite wine, the light French red that had been Matt's first recommendation when he joined Vinny at the Wine Merchant. I arranged the flowers in the vase and set it on the picnic table.

"Fingers crossed for the new hires," I said as I joined him in the living room. "I think I've found a new warehouse manager. So tell me about this place you saw. Is it The One?"

"Could be," he said, gazing into his wine glass.

"Don't tell me you're going to start reading the future in wine dregs like Mom and her tea leaves."

"Well, after forty-five years, her ways have started to rub off on me."

The grandkids would be spending a couple of days on the houseboat with Mom and Dad while Carl and Andrea took a weekend getaway, and Dad asked my suggestions for activities.

"What about Lunar New Year stuff at Woodland Park Zoo?" I grabbed my phone and scrolled through the zoo's website. "Though the Year of the Rabbit isn't as dramatic as the Year of the Tiger. They've got talks and demonstrations and hands-on activities—"

"Paws on?" Dad said.

"Oh, look! They have an elderly English spot rabbit, whatever that is, and they're giving her acupuncture to help with aches and pains."

"Wonder if that might help me." He rolled his left shoulder, digging his fingers into the joint. "Sounds great. Charlie will love it. Lizzie, too, if she's not too cool to admit it. As long as the food carts don't swap the hot dogs for carrots, we're good."

"Speaking of Lunar New Year, I keep seeing Aki Ohno every time I go to the CID. No surprise, I guess. I don't know a lot of people there, so she stands out."

"Ernie was the firebrand. Aki was the eyes and ears. Together, they got things done."

Aki the observer. I was about to ask if he knew what this new cause of hers was when he continued.

"They were a good pair. Just as you and Nate are. I know

you're worried about keeping secrets from him, about Bron and the future."

I caught my lower lip between my teeth.

"It's not easy, when you're not sure you want the same things. Or when you know something you think might hurt the person you love." He leaned forward. "Nate's a good man, and he's been good for you. Whatever happens, make sure he knows he can count on you."

He made it sound so simple.

Maybe it was.

Twenty

Ancient Greeks regarded marjoram as a symbol of happiness and planted it on graves to ensure the departed rested in eternal peace.

"DID YOU KNOW," VANESSA SAID FRIDAY MORNING AS WE readied the shop for opening, "that oregano and marjoram actually increase in flavor when they're dried? And that oregano means joy of the mountain in Greek, because seeing the flowers growing on the hillsides and catching their fragrance is guaranteed to make you happy?"

I said a silent "thank you" for the heads-up Angie had given me. "Two of our most popular herbs. I'm glad you're getting to know them."

"The stories make the spices easier to remember."

"When someone buys an herb or spice I don't know well," Cayenne said, "I ask them how they use it. They think you're brilliant because you're interested in them, and you get to learn something new."

I headed for my office, knowing the shop was in good hands.

Though it was early, Edgar was already in the restaurant, and we had a long talk about Hayden Parker.

"Good worker. I hate to lose him, but better to lose him to a job where he can use his love of food," Edgar said. "And learn from a good boss."

"Thanks. He mentioned a struggle with depression. Did it ever affect his work?" I appreciated Hayden's honesty and had no intention of letting the disease influence my decision, unless it had interfered with his work. So easy to self-medicate in the bar and restaurant biz, but I knew Edgar tolerated no drugs or excessive alcohol.

"I know this struggle." Edgar's Salvadoran accent clung to the edges of his words. "It darkens too many lives. I tell him, find heart in the work. In serving people a plate of happiness. And he do that. I believe he will pack the taste of joy in every bag of spice. Your secret ingredient."

"Edgar, have I ever told you how much I love you?"

I'd barely clicked off the phone when it rang. I read the caller's name.

"Wynne Goodman, real estate agent to the stars," I said by way of greeting.

"In my dreams. Hey, it's not much, but I do have some news for you. The Gold Rush has never been listed for sale, as far back as the records show. An appraiser we work with got a call recently asking if he could put together a market value assessment. Sure, he said. Happy to. When could he see the property? And the man hung up."

"Who was it?"

"No idea. The appraiser assumed he'd get a call back, if the man was serious. But a month went by and crickets." Sounded like she was in her office, from the buzz and chatter in the background. "It's an underutilized property. All those connected buildings with street front commercial space, apartments, and the hotel. People have wanted to get their hands on it for eons. If you get a lead, a hint that the owners might be ready to list it . . ."

"I'll send them to you. Wynne, another question. Do you know a house in Montlake?" I gave her the address and heard her clicking keys, bringing up the listing.

"Oh, sweet house. Great price. It'll go fast."

"But no offers yet," I said, and she confirmed it, then asked if I wanted to schedule a showing. Did I? No. My life had gone another direction, a good one. "Tempting, but no. Thanks, Wynne. Let me know if you hear anything else about the Gold Rush."

So the property wasn't officially for sale, but someone had

considered putting it on the market. A man—Bobby or Oliver? And how did the unnamed buyer Yolande had mentioned, the suits who'd snared Keith Chang's eye, or the man who'd peppered my pal in the Historic Preservation office, figure into the equation?

The plot was thickening.

HAYDEN and Reed were waiting when I got to the warehouse after lunch, Arf left safely behind in the shop. They'd struck up a conversation about the Seahawks and whether the NBA would ever return to Seattle.

"Hey, guys. Glad you're getting acquainted." I showed Hayden around the facility, a converted marine supply warehouse that now held more than a dozen small food producers and kitchens. I waved at a woman I'd gotten to know last winter after her husband found me unconscious and bleeding in the parking lot, briefly becoming the top suspect in both my attack and a brutal assault in the Market. I'd never doubted his innocence, but Detective Tracy had.

Fresh from restaurant work, Hayden was intrigued by the ghost kitchens, cooking up takeout dishes for groceries and delis. Some also ran their own delivery services.

"A pandemic pivot," he mused.

"Here to stay."

Back in our space, Reed was packing last-minute orders for restaurant customers.

"Gonna need extra help in a week or two," he said, "for spice club."

I explained our quarterly spice club, shipping boxes of seasonal blends to members across the United States and Canada. "Last couple of years, it's exploded. Used to be, Sandra and I could fill the orders in one afternoon. Now it takes three or four of us twice that long."

Hayden's eyes widened when he saw the bags of black peppercorns and cardamom pods, and the giant plastic tubs of everything from Aleppo pepper to za'atar.

"Get a whiff of that curry," he said.

"State of the art ventilation," I said, "but spices smell. Be prepared. Even your hair will reek." He ran a hand over his scalp, the stubble not a quarter inch long. "Well, maybe not yours."

"Pepper," Reed said. "Labeler's balking. Would you take a look?"

I left Hayden to scout around and joined Reed. "What's the problem? You know it runs on sweet talk."

"No, it's fine. I just wanted to talk in private."

I raised my eyebrows.

"Roxanne wants me to apply for an internship to work with her on some projects. Paid."

"That's great. What projects? After graduation?"

"Or sooner. Depends how quickly the grant comes through. She's got a couple in mind, including cataloging the pharmacy. That would be so cool."

I placed my hands on his shoulders and looked my serious young employee straight in his serious young eyes. "This is what you've wanted. It's perfect for you. As for the timing, we'll make it work."

"Thanks. I knew you'd understand. But, Pepper. A man died there. How—you—"

"Yeah," I said. "It isn't easy, especially at first. The pharmacy was a place of healing for a long time. My guess, it will welcome you, because you respect what was done there. The medicine." Not the murder.

Especially if Terence Leong's killer had been brought to justice by then.

Maybe we should follow the lead of the ancient Greeks Vanessa had been quoting and add a few sprigs of marjoram to the offerings outside the Gold Rush's front door.

HAYDEN decided to shadow Reed for the afternoon, so we agreed he'd come in next week to complete the new-hire process, and I left the two young men to their work. Me, I had another shadowing in mind.

As I drove south on I-5, I thought about Roxanne. She was part of this mystery, and I didn't know how or why.

Nate's account of her teenage misdeeds, if that wasn't too nice a word, had me questioning her moves. Might she have taken the box of letters and claimed they were stolen? Why? What would she gain? And if she had taken them, why show me the photos? To follow up on the clues the letters contained without having to hand them over to their owner—or to the police if they proved to be evidence in the murder?

I'd seen her apartment. She was a collector, not a packrat or a hoarder.

Although there was that statue in the medicine cabinet. She liked small, curious objects. Was she trying to slow down the investigation while she searched for something in the wreckage—something the killer had been after?

She could have staged the attack. Dropped to the ground and scraped her hands and knees. Bruised her own cheek, though the thought made me wince. You'd have to be pretty seriously motivated to give yourself a black eye. No witnesses, no one to say it had or hadn't happened the way she claimed.

But she'd been with me when the woman warned us off using the same words. What would Roxanne have hoped to gain by falsely alleging a second confrontation?

Unless she'd arranged the first one, too.

Hard to fathom. And I couldn't honestly see her desecrating a historic place like the pharmacy. Unless Terence Leong had threatened it, or her. She would do a lot, I believed, to protect the objects she'd spent her career preserving, the antiquities she'd loved since she was a little girl. But if that had been the case, surely she'd have said so.

That I didn't want to believe her capable of such a complicated setup didn't mean it wasn't true.

I exited I-5 and wound through the maze of unfamiliar streets to a strip mall housing an Ethiopian grocery and a nail salon. And on the corner, Bobby's Comics and Collectibles.

After so many years shopping and working in the Market, I saw in an instant what the dealer Down Under meant when he said he had all the advantages. Not that a suburban strip mall can't be appealing, if done right. I'd visited one last month, making an unplanned condolence call, that was warm and welcoming. Part of the neighborhood.

But this one? Bleh. Only a few cars were parked on the cracked asphalt. I drove around the block, then parked on the side street. What I hoped to see or find, I couldn't say, but that was the point of snooping, wasn't it?

I stood on the sidewalk near the corner of the building, phone in hand for cover. The shop windows were coated in that reflective film that looks like sunglass lenses, to prevent damage to the inventory. That made it hard to identify the large cardboard figures stationed inside the door. Standees, if I remembered the word right.

The door opened and two teenage boys emerged, each carrying a comic book. That gave me a brief glimpse of the cutouts. Seriously? The Green Hornet and his sidekick Kato—as my dad had told me, Bruce Lee's first role on American TV.

The boys ignored me, crossing the lot to an older blue Ford Focus, and drove away.

In the ten minutes that I stood there pretending to be cool, no one entered or left the grocery. Two women came out of the salon and three went in. No one else entered or left Bobby's Comics and Collectibles.

I strolled past the front door, its glass front not covered by the reflective coating. No customers inside, at least not that I could see. Comics spilled out of spinners and leaned dangerously from wall racks. Stacks of comics and books were piled on the floor. Though I spied a few glass cases, probably for the more valuable items, it had none of the charm of the shop Down Under.

I retraced my steps, then walked along the side of the building. Peered around the back corner. Caught an overripe whiff from a large trash bin that partially blocked my view, but I could see that the shop's back door stood open, a red sedan parked on the other side. I crouched and crept forward, tucking myself behind the bin.

To my surprise, I heard voices.

"Blackmail, pure and simple," the male voice said. Bobby. Blackmail over what? Was this the reason he needed cash? "That building has dictated my entire life. No more. No more."

A second voice replied, lighter and harder to hear. Abigail, I was sure. Something about responsibility.

He had a responsibility? The building was a responsibility? It was all too vague to mean anything. I shifted position, hoping to see one of the Wus, but they remained out of sight, inside but near the back door. Something glinted and I noticed a small metal dish on the pavement.

"You were too innocent, trusting him like you trusted his mother." Bobby's reply was loud and clear. "I've given you a good life, but you've never gotten over your hard luck childhood. You're a sucker for every sad story."

I frowned. Who had she trusted that she shouldn't?

One thing was clear. Whether it had been Bobby or Oliver poking around at city hall and calling an appraiser with an eye to selling the Gold Rush, Abigail was not on board. And she held the title.

I didn't know how much Bobby's shop contributed to their livelihood, or whether the "good life" he referred to came from the rentals in the CID. Those had come from Francis, whom I'd started to think of as Fong. Had Bobby's father helped finance this place? Doubtful, if the Lockes' assessment of the old man's attitude was accurate. He'd had his ideas of what his son should do with his life, and comics were not among them.

The argument had died down but now the voices rose again.

"I'm doing this for us," Bobby said. "To give you the best. So we can have the life we wanted. The life we deserved. If you hadn't—"

A loud thunk echoed through the alley, and Bobby stopped. A stack of flattened cardboard boxes had fallen over, helped by a cat I hadn't seen until now, skinny and white with brown patches on her sides and brown rings around the tip of her tail. She skittered away, taking refuge next to the front tire of the red car. At the sound of footsteps, I scooted backward out of the alley and around the corner to safety.

"Damned cat," Bobby yelled. "Scat. Get out of here." A scuffle, then a yowl.

I'd only met Bobby Wu once, but I'd instinctively disliked him. He had just proved me right.

And while I'd fallen asleep before the end of the movie, I'd seen the cat working out with Bruce Lee in the Coliseum before his big fight with Chuck Norris, practicing their moves and their yells. I knew, no way would Bobby Wu's hero ever kick a cat.

Twenty-One

*Current status: Compassionately caffeinated.
That means I'm drinking coffee not just for myself,
but for the good of all. You're welcome.*

—Nanea Hoffman, *Sweatpants & Coffee* (blog)

I STAYED PUT WELL AFTER THE BACK DOOR TO THE COMIC shop slammed shut. The cat had disappeared. I put my shoulders back and strolled to my car with all the confidence I could muster, trying not to look as out of place as I felt. Then I drove to a coffee shop near Southcenter Mall and ordered a double espresso. Added a big fat piece of chocolate torte, for good medicine.

The coffee came and I inhaled the sweet perfume, what my artist pal Jamie calls the elixir of life. Roasted on site, dark and rich, like the cake. Funny how caffeine, with or without chocolate, can be both calming and energizing. I took a sip and let it do its work.

Though I didn't know just what I'd witnessed, I was reasonably sure it didn't warrant a call to my friends Spencer and Tracy. And I was reasonably sure Bobby Wu would not have hurt me, despite his mistreatment of the neighborhood stray. But that didn't mean I wanted him to know I was there. I believe a man capable of screaming at his wife and kicking a cat equally capable of murder, but that didn't prove he'd done it.

Did I really think he might have killed Terence Leong? Roxanne had heard sounds in the basement and her concern for the pharmacy had overcome any fear she might have had about going into a dark space alone. She'd met Bobby Wu. If she'd caught even a glimpse of him in the hotel that night, she'd have said so.

All the people you pass without realizing it. Who else might have been lurking around the Gold Rush last Saturday unnoticed?

I took a bite of cake. Perfection.

The comic book shop didn't look prosperous, but looks can be deceiving. Everyone knows someone who drives a beater and wears ratty jeans and T-shirts even though they have plenty of money, because cars and clothes aren't important to them. But, the shop. A visible lack of interest sends the wrong kind of message in retail, if you ask me.

Thinking of impressions, the one time I'd seen Abigail Wu, I'd gotten the sense of internal strength, despite her pale skin and loose clothing. As if she'd been ill. As if she were fighting. I wished I'd heard more of what she'd said to Bobby just now.

I cut another bite. Illness might explain the need to make a plan for the building. To estimate its value and lay out the options. The Wus weren't old—early 60s. They could run the shop and the rentals for years. Though at thirty-fiveish, Oliver might be itching to take over the property. You'd think a family would know the history of a place it had owned for almost a century. But the circumstances of the purchase were mysterious, and the stories of the Gold Rush's early years could easily have been lost. If Bobby had known about the walled-up pharmacy before Oliver discovered it a few weeks ago, he'd kept the secret. Why? After all this time, why did it matter now?

I sipped and ate, my sense of self slowly returning. Between bites, I scrolled the Spice Shop's social media on my phone, replying to a few comments. Cayenne's post discussing herbs, spices, and cheese would have had me salivating if my mouth hadn't been full of cake.

Long as I was snooping, I pulled up Roxanne's Instagram. Lots of shares from the museum and other places with great art, some Asian, some not. Scenes from Volunteer Park, home of the Asian Art Museum. And the Lunar New Year festivities last weekend.

I stopped scrolling at the shot of the lion dancers. Just what hackles are, I've never quite known, but I was sure mine were standing on their tippy toes. I used two fingers to enlarge the photo and scroll to the edges. I wasn't in it and neither were Seetha or my mother. But I recognized the angle, and the edge of the dumpling seller's lantern-festooned table where we'd been when the dancers came by. Whoever took this picture had been standing close to us, with the same view of the giant lions that we'd had. And with the same view of Oliver Wu and his dancing pals.

I hadn't seen Roxanne. Not only that, she'd said she'd been working late and was about to quit for the night when she heard the noise in the basement.

Why hadn't she called the police on the prowler? Simple, I'd thought. She wanted to protect the pharmacy, which meant keeping it quiet as long as she could. Not until she found the body did she go for help.

Now my hackles were jumping up and down, pointing their fingers. Any moment now, they'd start screaming and I'd have to either tell them to use their inside voices or skedaddle. And I still had cake.

I sat back, thinking this through. Had she said she'd never left the building, or had I made that assumption? I stared at the photo.

Now did I have something to tell the detectives?

Time to go. I dropped my phone in my tote and scooted back my chair. Saw that last lonely bite of cake on the plate and ate it.

After all, dumb as I may be at times, I'm not a complete idiot.

BACK in the car, I texted Seetha. No point asking if she'd seen Roxanne earlier in the afternoon; they hadn't met before Roxanne burst out of the Gold Rush, so Seetha wouldn't have recognized her. But I did wonder what she knew about Oliver's parents. I finally settled on saying I hoped they were okay—the discovery of the body must have been deeply upsetting.

Should I tell her I had my doubts about Oliver? That there was something strange going on? Laurel had tried to caution her, with no luck. I had no reason to worry about her physical safety. If I said anything now, she'd shut me out.

And by garlic, I couldn't blame her.

Traffic on I-5 is a nightmare on a good day, let alone snaking north through the bottleneck around downtown on a Friday afternoon. First chance, I exited and made my way to First for a straight, if slow, shot to the Market.

Just past the stadia, the old INS building, the replacement for the one barely a block from my loft, loomed large. Immigration loomed large over much of this city, not always casting the kindest of shadows. I tried to imagine Fong's wife, alone despite the crowded detention cells, frightened and possibly unwell. How long had she been held? Had he been able to visit? When had she realized she was seriously ill, possibly dying, in this terrifying new world? She and her husband had put their trust in a doctor from their own culture. Had he failed her, or had the situation been too dire?

And if Fong was Francis, what shadow did her death cast on the family?

The light changed and I drove on. My own grandparents left Hungary for the promise of freedom in the United States in the 1950s. Of course, they hadn't faced the changing winds of a country that first welcomed and then reviled them.

It was all too much to think about at the moment. So I didn't. I thought about Hayden and his enthusiasm, and what a relief it was to find promising young employees like him and Vanessa. I thought about scones and quiches with smoked cheddar and Five Spice apple cake and egg tarts and crab rangoons, about Pinot Gris and Pinot Noir. And all that raised my spirits so high that I didn't even mind the traffic near the Market. I zipped left on Virginia and left again into the parking garage.

In Post Alley, I stopped at the wine shop. My cellar—a rack for the reds and a mini wine fridge tucked under the kitchen counter for the whites—might runneth over, but I wanted to say hello and check on the guys.

Matt was helping a customer. Vinny insisted on showing me the progress of build-out. The opening between the existing shop and the new space had not yet been cut, so we walked outside and he unlocked the door. The workers were gone, but they'd left behind the smells of sawdust and promise. So much better than the stench of murder.

Vinny saw me hesitate on the threshold.

"At first, I could almost feel the girl's spirit, lingering. Kinda spooked me." Vinny rubbed his cheek. "Then it clicked. She's watching the place. Making sure we do it right."

"I like that."

"We're putting a special display right here." He stomped one foot on the pine plank floor. "'Beth's Picks.'"

"Speaking of wine," I said. I asked if they might like to get together after work, sample a glass of something yummy. But it was Date Night for Matt and Misty, and Vinny was hosting a garden club meeting. Naturally, there would be wine. He'd given up ghost hunting and was throwing himself into his perennials and his baseball cards.

Outside in the Alley—in reality, a narrow, paved street despite the name—I checked my phone for a reply from Seetha.

Seeing Oliver tonight, followed by a happy dance emoji. *I'll ask about his parents and let you know.*

Everybody, it seemed, had Friday night plans but me.

DETECTIVES, Tracy and Spencer like to remind me, do not work regular hours. They show up unannounced at five-thirty on a Friday afternoon when the proprietor of the shop—that would be me—is returning from a brisk walk with her faithful companion—that would be Arf—expecting to dive into the closing routine.

Instead, I found myself facing them in the nook while my staff swept the floors, wiped down the counters, and tackled other tasks essential to retail but invisible to the public.

Fine. I could run the till and count the cash later. I had no Friday night plans. Me and Arf and a bottle of red, and leftovers.

"Time to talk about your friend, Dr. Davidson," Detective Spencer said. "A few things in her past cause us some concern. We don't know how much you know, although your Mr. Seward is her brother-in-law."

"Former." I couldn't help myself.

"Former," Spencer repeated. "And he knows the full story."

"Which we assume you didn't," Tracy said. "Or you'd have told us about it."

My face betrayed me.

"Oh, for Pete's sake." Tracy tossed a hand in the air. "You of all people. You know we can't do our jobs if people don't tell us everything they know."

What did they mean, Nate knew the full story? There was an implication behind the words that I wasn't sure I liked.

"I just found out," I said. Monday. Four days ago. "It's not that big a deal, is it? A sixteen-year-old swiped a statue on the spur of the moment. Paid her dues—community service or whatever—and stayed clean. The system worked." Though my mind's eye did flash on that figurine in Roxanne's medicine cabinet.

Tracy snorted. "So he didn't tell you everything."

My chest tightened. What had Nate said? "He said things got kind of wild. But I didn't ask what he meant."

"When her brother-in-law tried to stop her, she took a swing at him. Hit him. The charges were shoplifting and assault."

A spasm of pain shot through my jaw and I rubbed it, stunned. "He—I—I didn't know that. He told me no one was hurt and she's never been in trouble again. Is that true?"

"Far as we know, yes," Spencer said. "Neither he or the shop owner wanted to press charges, but her sister was her legal guardian and she insisted. To teach Roxanne a lesson."

Holy crap.

Bless him, Detective Tracy gave me no grief, waiting until I found my tongue.

"I assume what you're after," I said, "is whether I know anything to suggest she might have violent or larcenous instincts. Whether she might have struck Terence Leong with the brick and taken the letters to throw you off."

They nodded but stayed silent.

"I don't, but I can't say it's impossible." I fished my phone out of my apron pocket and found the photo. "Have you seen this, on her Instagram feed?"

They leaned close, Tracy squinting.

"So she went to the parade. Lotsa people went to the parade."

"She didn't say she hadn't left the hotel that afternoon, but she clearly meant to give that impression." I scrolled back through my own photos, to the selfie with dumplings. "Same view, almost the exact same moment. She has to have been within fifteen feet of me. And that"—I pointed to a figure in yellow, dressed as Terence Leong had been when he died—"is Oliver Wu."

THE STAFF had left. The cops left. I locked the door behind them and turned off the lights. Taking that as a signal, my dog stood and gave himself a full-body shake, ready to "hook up" and walk home.

166 · *Between a Wok and a Dead Place*

Instead, I sat in the nook. He followed and after a long minute, sat on the floor beside me, his chin on my knee. I twined my fingers in the soft fur behind his ear.

"Why was Roxanne photo-stalking Oliver Wu?" I asked out loud. "Did she mistake Terence Leong for him?" Oliver had struck me as polished and pleasant, a loyal son unsure of his role in the family and his responsibility to it. Was he secretly up to something that would make someone—Roxanne, or persons unknown—want to kill to stop him?

Or was it the other way around? Had she been following Leong, and mistaken the two men?

And what about Nate? He knew the one thing I could not accept in a relationship was dishonesty. Not that he'd actually lied. He just hadn't told me the whole story, which amounted to the same thing. Or did it?

I sat for a long time. Finally, my bottom began to ache from the hard wooden bench. "Time to go," I told my faithful companion, and we walked out onto Pike Place. The shops were dark, the metal doors of the highstalls and street-front takeout joints rolled down and locked up. The vendor tables were bare. Lights glowed in the bars and restaurants, and clink and chatter spilled out, but it was subdued. Friday night, yes, but Friday night in January.

A few minutes later, I unlocked the door to the loft and shucked off my coat and boots. Fed Arf and wondered what I should eat, though my appetite had disappeared. My phone buzzed. Nate? What would I say to him?

But it wasn't Nate. It was Seetha. She'd had a date with Oliver, for dinner at the bistro inside Benaroya Hall before the concert.

And he was more than an hour late.

Twenty-Two

Never give away parsley if you are in love, or you'll give away your luck.

—European folklore

EVEN WITH THE DOORS TO THE CONCERT HALL ITSELF closed, the strains of something big and symphonic leaked out, highlighting the emptiness of the lobby. Seetha sat in the fancy food court where concert-goers could enjoy an unrushed dinner and a drink before the performance. Her phone lay on the table next to an empty wine glass, her coat draped over the back of the chair next to her. No one else was around, except for a small crew cleaning up behind the counters, the Caesar salads and quiches and berry-topped mousse no longer on display.

Seetha lifted her head at my approach, the glimmer of hope on her face vanishing.

"Why?" she said. "Why would he invite me, then stand me up?"

"I'm sure there was a good reason." I slid into the seat across from her.

"I texted." She held up her phone. "Nothing."

On my way here, I'd called Oliver's hotel to ask if he was working late. It was Friday night—were they hosting a big shindig that demanded all hands on deck? No, I'd been told; he'd left when his shift ended at four.

"Any chance one of you had the date wrong?"

She showed me his text from earlier in the week. The date and time of the invitation were clear. "I checked at the ticket counter. He bought the tickets online. They're still there. In his name so I couldn't go in, even if I wanted to, but don't you see, Pepper? Something must have happened."

"Why don't you go freshen up, then we'll find a place for a bite."

While Seetha was in the restroom, I called Detective Spencer. "I barely know the guy. But he sprang for symphony tickets to see a woman he's obviously hot for, then ghosted her. Something's not right."

"I'm on it," she replied. "I'll let you know when I've got news."

A few minutes later, Seetha and I walked into a favorite spot down the street. I'd briefly considered the restaurant in Oliver's hotel, then decided that was too much like stalking. Although not unwarranted, under the circumstances. And guaranteed to plunge Seetha deeper into the blues.

"You look great, by the way," I said as we settled into a romantic booth for two. After Seetha called, I'd managed to throw on a pair of pants and a tunic that didn't reek of oregano, but it was no match for her form-fitting sweater, narrow skirt, and kitten heels. A seriously uptown outfit.

We ordered drinks and a small charcuterie plate with bruschetta and herbed goat cheese. "They'll find him. Everything will be fine."

"It's probably his mom," she said, "though why not let me know? But he said her cancer is in remission."

The illness I'd guessed at. Was that what Bobby meant, when he talked about the life they deserved?

"What else do you know about her?"

"Not a lot. She came from a close family, but her parents struggled to support them all, including the grandfather who lived with them after her grandmother died. I guess he was pretty cranky." She paused while the server delivered our drinks, then drew her pear-tini toward her. Pear vodka accented with lemon, honey, thyme, and bitters. I'd been tempted but decided to stick with wine to stay in the vicinity of my wits.

"Or maybe I have the grandfathers mixed up," Seetha continued. "She wanted a big family, but it didn't work out that way. Oliver said she was always bringing home strays. Kids, not dogs."

I remembered the cat dish. "Is she very involved with the comic book shop?"

"Not according to Oliver. It's Bobby's baby." Her black hair swung as she shook her head. "He can't be involved in murder, Pepper. He can't be."

She was smitten.

"I'm sure he's not," I said, no longer sure at all. "Men are a mystery."

"I'll drink to that."

No word from Spencer by the time we'd finished our drinks and dinner, so we said good night. I was knackered. But before the dog and I took our walk, I had to call Nate.

The dilemma in having a serious discussion by phone: Do you lead with the "how was your day?" chit chat, or dive right in?

I dove right in. "You didn't tell me the truth about the incident with Roxanne. You said she pocketed a small statue, then when she got caught, things got wild. You didn't tell me she hit you. Or that her sister, your wife, insisted she be prosecuted. I had to find out from Detective Michael Tracy, of all people."

No reply.

"Why, Nate?" I continued. "Why not tell me? When you introduced us last fall, you said she was a sweet kid. Sweet kids don't shoplift, then punch their brother-in-law."

"I was embarrassed. I shouldn't have let it happen. And I wanted to protect her."

Now I was the quiet one.

"Besides, she was a sweet kid, except for that one time." We fell into an uncomfortable silence. "Listen, I know it sounds harsh. Rox is ten years younger and Rosalie was responsible for her. The parents—who knows where they were. And like I said, I've never been aware of any other problems."

Good garlic, Pep. Do you have to be hit in the head to get it? I'd been upset with Nate for not telling me the truth about something that happened twenty years ago and didn't involve me. For protecting someone he genuinely cared for. And here I was the one not being honest about what was happening right now.

"When I stopped for pizza the other night," I said, "Daria

hinted that Bron was thinking about staying down here instead of going back to Alaska after this season. I've debated telling you—you have a right to know, but should you hear it from me?"

"I do know. And likewise, I realized you'd want to know, which is only fair." I heard Nate shuffling around his on-board cabin as he spoke. "But Pep, Bron and I are different people. He thinks out loud. This isn't the first time he's talked about giving up fishing. Yes, there's usually a woman involved, and yes, this time could be different. He talks about Daria in a way I've never heard him talk about anyone. And that shoulder injury of his has been acting up again. Bottom line, I can't predict what he'll do. I didn't want to get your wheels turning if he was just spinning his."

That hadn't occurred to me. I barely knew Bron. But Nate knew us both, and I had to trust his judgment.

"Laurel was right. She said I always want to talk everything to death, in the guise of working it out, and that you want to know what you think before we talk. Or something like that."

"Laurel is a wise woman."

"I'll tell her you said that." Relief flooded through me. But I couldn't quite let the serious stuff go. "That's why you told me to be careful about Roxanne."

"Yes, and I see now that I should have told you the whole story right up front. But I'm serious, Pep. I don't have any reason to doubt her honesty now."

Neither did I, but the whole tangle of interconnected stories was proving pretty tricky to unravel. I told Nate about Seetha and Oliver, hiring Hayden, and the ongoing saga of my parents' house hunt. He talked about the catch, the balky engine Bron had whispered back to health, and the tentative schedule. It was a long conversation that could have gone on had my dog not been holding his pee far more patiently than I had a right to expect.

"Love you," I said.

"Love you more," he responded.

"I doubt that, but it's a nice thought."

Then my dog and I walked out into the mist.

SATURDAYS, families flood the Market. A pair of teenage girls came in with their dad. He handed Cayenne a shopping list and the girls browsed the foodie fiction.

Seeing them brought me back to Roxanne. The teenage slipup that could have derailed her but hadn't. Had her sister been right to insist on prosecution for the assault as well as the theft? Nate took the blame for getting hit—"I should have ducked"—but also because he'd been the adult. She'd been part of his household, and he hadn't wanted her lost in the juvenile justice system. Another good sign about the man.

I straightened the tea accessories—infusers, strainers, pots—pondering Roxanne's role in the mess at the Gold Rush. I'd wondered if she'd stolen the letters herself, or if she'd gone after Terence Leong to protect the pharmacy somehow. My speculation made less sense the more I thought about it.

And Oliver's disappearance blurred the picture further.

I snapped a few shots of our updated displays and settled in my office for some blatant shop promotion. We might appreciate winter's slower pace, but that didn't mean we could rest on our bay laurels.

But questions kept interfering. Why had Bobby and Abigail left the hotel empty? What was the blackmail he'd mentioned? Who was the woman who'd been staying in the second-floor room, and where had she and her baby gone?

As I edited the photos and created graphics, I recalled Roxanne's pictures of the lion dancers. Had she been spying on Oliver Wu or Terence Leong? Tracy would be wondering if she'd gotten the wrong man the first time and now gone after the other.

I couldn't believe that. I didn't know her well, but Nate did, and he was sure she'd trod the straight and narrow ever since that humiliating experience as a sixteen-year-old. He'd been married to her sister for another ten years, and he and Roxanne had stayed in touch despite the divorce. I thought about some of the girls I'd known in high school. Even if you'd lost contact. you knew the kind of women they'd become. Mostly—a few had done a one-eighty. Classmates might be surprised that I ran the Spice Shop in the Market, but not that I worked my tail off, or that Kristen and I were still joined at the hip.

How were Oliver and Terence connected, beyond their yellow costumes?

I retrained my focus on work. Sandra and Kristen had both tested Cayenne's scone recipe with fabulously tasty results, so I created a blog post, sent it to our newsletter subscribers, shared the photos on Insta, and all the other blah blah. So many business owners stumble because they don't like doing the business part of the job—they love books or wine or bicycles, but let the details they don't enjoy like HR and accounting and promotion pile up. I am grateful daily that there's very little about this job that I don't love.

One such thing is stepping in when a customer interaction goes awry.

I was back on the shop floor, intending to restock the recipe rack, when the customer at the front counter raised her voice.

"I specifically told you it's two separate orders. You've mixed them up and created a complete mess."

"I'm sorry about that," Kristen said. "I can void the transaction and start over. Just tell me which items you want rung up together." Vanessa had already bagged several items and stood frozen, a tin of grilling rub in one hand. No one likes a heated situation.

"No, no, no. It's too late for that. Just finish what you've started."

I slipped a stack of recipes for our Salty Oat Cookies into one rack and Pepper's Gingersnaps, starring my secret ingredient, in another. As I worked, I kept an eye on the front counter. Transaction completed, Vanessa came around the counter with the shopping bag. The woman snatched it from her hands and marched out of the shop.

"Oh, cardamom." On the floor lay a small brown leather coin purse stitched with a floral design. I'd seen it in the woman's hand but hadn't noticed her drop it. I scooped it up and dashed outside. Scanned the crowd on the sidewalk.

"Where did she go, where did she go?" I stood on the corner, muttering.

There, at the top of the hill, her teal coat standing out in a sea of black and tan. I sprinted up Pine. Stopped at the corner. Where had she gone? Had she stepped into the Bagel Bakery or the map store? Stopped for a milkshake or falafel? Down the street I went, glancing in the windows as I passed.

The cantankerous customer had disappeared. But inside the entrance to the upper level of the Sanitary Market, emerging from the Lockes' clinic, was Abigail Wu.

I shot one more glance up and down First Avenue. No sign of my target. I couldn't let two women get away from me within minutes. I opened the door and walked inside. Abigail had paused, fishing for something in her purse. Keys, phone, her Orca card for the transit system?

"Mrs. Wu," I said. "How nice to see you. Pepper Reece. We met at the Gold Rush a few days ago. I'm a friend of Seetha Sharma and Roxanne Davidson. I run the Spice Shop down on Pike Place."

"Yes," she said pleasantly, snapping her bag shut. "I see that."

My apron. "Oops. I ran out after a customer who dropped something and didn't have time to grab my coat." I held up the coin purse. "No luck, I'm afraid. Seetha is worried about your son."

"So I hear, from Detective Spencer. Lovely woman, considering what she does for a living. I'm sure Oliver's fine—just needed a day or two for himself. Ms. Sharma seems like a nice girl, but clearly, there's been a misunderstanding."

Granted, Oliver Wu was a grown man, but an odd reaction. There was no misunderstanding the text Oliver had sent Seetha, or the tickets he'd paid for and never collected.

"You came to see Dr. Locke?" I changed the subject. "I'm a big fan. His son works for me. His father translated a couple of the letters Roxanne found in the hotel, hoping to fill in some of the gaps in its history."

What had I said that stunned her? That I knew the doctors Locke, young and old? That Roxanne had found the letters and now had a rough idea what they said? Or that outsiders cared about the history of her family's building?

"Dr. Davidson has proven invaluable," Abigail said, a firm control on her voice. "We were fortunate to find her."

The words I'd overheard outside the comic shop popped into my mind, like one of those thought balloons in a comic strip. "You cleaned the hotel, didn't you? For the Lunar New Year. Clearing out the old, to make room for new. For good luck. I'd been wondering who dusted that beautiful woodwork and vacuumed those carpets. You even lit incense. You're the owner, and you've seen maintaining it as your responsibility. For your son?"

"And for—" She stopped herself. Ron Locke opened the clinic door and stuck his head out.

"Oh, Pepper. Hi. Didn't notice you. I saw Abigail standing here and wondered if something was wrong."

"I'm fine," she said. "See you next week." She pushed past me as if hurrying to escape without saying something she might regret.

"I wanted to reassure her," I said. "I'm sure the police will find her son safe and well in no time."

The expression on Ron Locke's face made clear she hadn't said a word.

And that convinced me that Oliver Wu wasn't missing at all.

Twenty-Three

Animals, says British science writer Ed Yong, experience the world in radically different ways than humans. A dog's world is full of smell, making a nondescript patch of pavement into a super-interesting corner of the world, crammed with new information.

I TEXTED SANDRA TO TELL HER I'D PICK UP LUNCH. WHILE I waited for our order at the Italian grocery, I debated the possibilities. Either Abigail Wu had harmed her son and stashed his body, which likely meant she'd harmed Terence Leong as well, and gone about her business, betraying nothing to her long-time acupuncturist, an astute observer.

Not in a million years.

Or she knew exactly where Oliver was.

While I know better than to underestimate the physical strength of an older woman, even one battling cancer, I also knew that it was impossible to overestimate the determination of a mother to protect her son.

Even if her mild-mannered, suit-and-tie wearing son was a killer.

One last question: Why was Oliver Wu's mother so carefully tending a hotel with no guests? Was she that committed to tradition, that bound by duty?

Out of the corner of my eye, I saw a blur of teal. I slipped off my stool and called out.

The woman's look of surprise turned to a scowl when she spotted me and my apron. I held up the coin purse.

"We found this on the floor after you left, but I couldn't catch you. Thank goodness you stopped for lunch."

She was speechless, unlike in the shop. Finally, she spoke. "Serves me right, the way I behaved. I just discovered it was gone. I had to use a card to buy a slice of pizza. I can't thank you enough." She paused, an idea forming. "Actually, I think I can. Let me buy your lunch."

"No." I waved her off. "It's for my whole staff. You don't need to."

"Even better," she said, and she did. Our goodbyes were heartfelt as we each went on our way.

Such is the restorative power of the Market.

MIDAFTERNOON, just after I'd finished with a customer, Detective Spencer called.

"Quick update. No sign of Oliver Wu. He's not at home. Not scheduled to work this weekend. Maybe his mother is right and he took some time to himself, though no one claims he makes a habit of that. We've interviewed your Ms. Sharma and several other friends. Officer Ohno and the rest of the patrol beat are asking around."

All stuff they wouldn't do for a missing adult—a man who got cold feet before a big date—if they didn't think they had good reason. Reason to fear he was a killer on the lam, or another victim?

I told her about running into Abigail Wu. "She's upset about something, but it's not Oliver going missing. I think she knows where he is and isn't telling you."

"That's obstruction of justice," Spencer said. "We'll follow up. You said you saw her coming out of Dr. Locke's clinic?"

"Yes. Seetha says she has cancer, in remission. Frail as she is, she's been cleaning the Gold Rush. By herself."

I heard a soft, musing "hmm," so unlike Detective Tracy's customary grunt.

"Pardon me telling you how to do your job, Detective," I went on, "but have you checked the hotel basement?"

"We have. Not much to see. Brick walls. A couple of store-rooms off the utility access passage. No more dead bodies, thank goodness."

"You can say that again."

"Thank goodness," the detective repeated, and it was nice to lighten the mood by a teaspoon or two.

A few minutes before closing, Seetha called. "Not hearing from him is driving me crazy. Aimee and I are going to Pioneer Square to hear a new band. Come with us."

So not my thing. "You two will have more fun without me. I'll live vicariously when you tell me all about it tomorrow."

And then it was home on a Saturday night with a good book. My mother had guessed right—I never had read Jamie Ford's *Hotel on the Corner of Bitter and Sweet*. I made a stir fry with snow peas, shiitake mushrooms, and flank steak I'd picked up on my way back to the shop after a dog walk, and settled in for a tour of the Seattle of the past through the author's loving but not uncritical eyes.

SUNDAY brunch is special time, whether it's at home, a neighbor-hood café, or a ritzy place like the Olympic Hotel—a once-a-year splurge with my girlfriends. It's a time to drink too much coffee, forget about a balanced meal, and talk, talk, talk. I love it.

Arf and I ducked under the weeping willow, passed through the gate, and strode down the dock. Laurel lived one dock over, but I was going to miss coming here so often when my parents left. More than the place, though, I was going to miss them.

"Comfort food," my mother said when I sniffed the air, detecting cinnamon and apples. "Morning Glory Baked Oatmeal. Did they find that boy? The one Seetha's dating?"

"No. And 'dating' might be overstating it."

We sat and ate, and I asked Charlie, my nephew, if he had any new comic books. He was caught up on the Wings of Fire graphic novels, eagerly awaiting the next volume, and told me all about Moonwatcher and the school for dragonets, formed to create a new future after the end of the terrible war.

"I've been reading them myself," my dad confessed. "They're a lot of fun."

"Dad, you were studying martial arts right around the time Bruce Lee was so influential. What was his appeal?"

"Never been anyone like him, before or since. I saw him give a demonstration once. He had physical skills you had to see to believe. He made your eyes pop. How he packed all that power in the one-inch punch . . ." Dad extended a fist and moved it ever so slightly. "But instead of making you feel like you could never do what he did, he made you want to try."

"Wasn't he a child actor in Hong Kong?" Mom topped off his coffee and he murmured thanks.

"Yes. Then he made martial arts movies there as an adult. Breaking into American film was harder. As I told you the other night, he played Kato, the Asian chauffeur and sidekick in *The Green Hornet* TV series. He auditioned for the lead in *Kung Fu*, but the role went to an American actor who wasn't Chinese."

"David Carradine?" I vaguely recalled the reruns.

"Yes. There was concern about Lee's accent, and whether he was enough of an actor—not just a fighter—to play the part of the Chinese American Shaolin monk. But he was so philosophical and had such presence. I'm sure he could have done it."

"Do you know anything about *The Green Hornet* comic books? Would they be valuable?"

"The classics, sure. They go way back, before my time, though the characters have been revived a few times, I think. Why so interested?"

"I saw a big cardboard cutout of the Green Hornet and Kato last week, and it got me wondering."

Wondering if that's the collection Bobby Wu had been trying to sell my friend in the Market.

"Can we walk Arf?" Charlie asked after he and Lizzie had cleared the table, and I agreed, though I was glad when my dad offered to go along. They're good kids and Arf adores them, but they don't have pets themselves, and anything can happen. Especially down here, where the smells that define a dog's world often involve water and motors and tight places where even an eleven-year-old boy might not go.

"So, what about the house hunt?" I asked my mother when we were alone. "You're both being so secretive."

"Oh, you'll know when we know." But there was a conspiratorial twinkle in her eyes.

I was not convinced. Dog and humans returned and we all

kissed, then climbed into our cars. "Have a blast at the zoo. I want a picture of the rabbit parade."

A few blocks up the hill, I parked in front of Rainy Day Vintage, closed now, and pushed the button for Seetha's second-floor apartment.

"Pepper, hi. Good boy, Arf." She greeted us wearing gray leggings and a flowing tunic pieced together from old saris. I'd only seen her in a sari once, on her way to the wedding of the daughter of a childhood friend of her mother's in India, but she did have several skirts and tunics made from the repurposed fabric.

She blinked, her eyes rimmed in red, and ran a hand through her unwashed hair. "Coffee? Or chai? My mother's special blend. I know you love it."

I followed her to the kitchen. After I'd pocketed a sample last summer, intending to create a copycat recipe, Sandra and I discovered that Mrs. Sharma did not in fact make her own version of the Indian spice and tea blend, as she'd led her daughter to believe, but bought it from a shop near the family's home in Boston. I know a few things about mothers and daughters and secrets. This one was safe with me.

"Thanks, no." I said. "I had brunch with my parents and if I have one more drop of caffeine, I won't sleep until next Thursday. Sparkling water, if you have it."

We sat at the kitchen table while her coffee brewed—like me, she's ambidrinksterous.

"There was something I was going to ask you, but I forget what it was." She blinked again, her skin pale, and refilled her water glass. "Too much fun last night. Or too much vodka, which seemed like the same thing at the time. And then, this."

She slid her phone toward me, open to a text. I read it, eyes widening.

"You call the detectives? They might be able to trace the message."

"Yeah, I called Spencer. But while I appreciate the apology for standing me up, it's about thirty-six hours too late. An out-of-town emergency, he'll explain everything? Dude, seriously? He works here, his whole family's here. He's never lived anywhere but Seattle."

"Could be legit. His mother might have family elsewhere.

Although she didn't mention an emergency." I told her about my conversation with Abigail outside Dr. Locke's clinic, when she'd brushed aside any concerns about her son.

"Ohh, I never thought to mention that. Abigail is seeing the Chinese doctor, along with chemo and all the regular stuff. According to Oliver, it's a big fight between his parents. Bobby doesn't believe in Chinese medicine. Calls it voodoo—"

"That's Caribbean, not Chinese."

"—snake oil, quackery. All the insults. But she's doing it anyway."

A true believer, or the cancer patient grasping for a cure? Not if she was in remission.

Was this why the pharmacy had been walled off and Bobby wanted so little to do with the building? Was his distrust of the old ways—nursed by his father, assuming Francis was in fact Fong—another part of the family legacy?

And what did any of it have to do with Oliver's disappearance or Terence Leong's death?

Arf and I were halfway down the stairs when Seetha called after me. "Pepper, wait."

We waited while she padded barefoot down the hall.

"I remembered what I was going to ask you. In Pioneer Square, in the sidewalks, there are these purple glass squares." She made lines and corners with her hands. "What are they? Aimee and I didn't have any idea."

"Oh, yeah. You see them all over down there. That whole area was basically a bog, constantly flooding. Sewage backups."

"Gross."

"After the Great Fire of 1889, the city raised the street level in Pioneer Square. That meant ground floor businesses became basements. So they installed skylights, sort of—cast iron panels that held small glass prisms, designed to magnify the light."

"How? They're purple." Seetha rubbed her hands up and down her arms.

"Not originally. They were clear, but the glass has some chemical—manganese maybe?—that darkened over time. Sun exposure. You can see them from below if you go on the Underground Tour. And from the lower level of the Grand Central Arcade. That's a historic district, so they're protected now. Replacements are pre-purpled. I read that somewhere."

"I knew you would know." She gripped her arms. "Thanks Pepper. For everything."

I blew her a kiss, and my dog and I headed out into what passes for sunlight in January in Seattle.

Arf and I made a quick stop at the shop to ensure all was well, but neither of us was quite ready to curl up at home for the day.

We took the secret staircase—it isn't a secret, just not obvious if you don't know it's there—from Pike Place down to Lower Post Alley. We passed the Market offices and detoured around a gaggle of teenagers gathered at the Gum Wall. When we reached the old INS building, I stopped, wishing for some kind of memorial to remind the thousands of people who passed by every day that lives had been lived and lost here. So many families' fates had been decided inside these walls.

Further down, we passed the doggy day care, closed on Sundays when downtown office workers were home with their dogs. "What do you think, Arf? Should we check it out, or do you like being a Spice Shop pup?"

He was too busy sniffing to answer, the scents of the canines who'd passed this way a carnival for his senses. They say dogs have more than a hundred million receptor sites in their noses, compared to six million for us, and watching him work the pavement, I believed it.

On we walked. Not that there was any question where we were going.

In Pioneer Square, I slowed to admire the purple vault lights. So much ingenuity and history.

We veered left at the venerable Smith Tower, built after the regrades, though I didn't remember the year. At thirty-eight stories, it was the city's first skyscraper and long the tallest building west of the Mississippi. We passed the ceremonial Chinatown Gate and my steps slowed. What if I was right? What then? I still wouldn't know who'd killed Terence Leong or why.

At Hing Hay Park, I passed the red metal sculptural arch that welcomes visitors to the festival area. Best, I decided, to ground truth my theory in a spot where I could act like a tourist without raising alarm.

In the next block, we passed Tai Tung, a landmark that calls itself the city's oldest Chinese restaurant. I'd never been in it.

Whichever spice and tea supplier had sewed up the trade down here had worked hard to keep and maintain it, and truthfully, much as I wanted to grow my business, I had no real desire to disrupt those relationships. Karma, as they say, can bite you in the dogma in a hurry.

A sign in the window registered a moment late and I backed up for a better look. "Bruce Lee's Favorite Restaurant!" it proclaimed. The menu was posted beneath it, proudly highlighting Lee's favorite dishes: beef with oyster sauce and garlic shrimp. In the back corner hung a nearly life-sized photo of the shirtless fighter, more photos plastered on the walls.

Dad and Reed were right. Bruce Lee had been gone fifty years, but he was still good for business. Any rumors that he haunted a building would have made banner headlines. And while Bobby Wu appeared to have no love of the Gold Rush, it was clear from the cardboard cutout of Lee in his shop that he idolized the man.

I walked on, to Maynard Alley, one of several Pioneer Square and CID alleys that had been brought back to life through a public–private collaboration. Where I'd meant to be a week ago, when Seetha and I got turned around. Utterly charming, even on a gray day, with its bricked streets and bright doors. I could picture the planters and pots now sitting empty on the metal fire escapes brimming with herbs and pansies in spring. The project had converted the CID's backsides into front doors, creating festival spaces and new storefronts just right for artisans and small businesses, much like Post Alley in the Market.

A chain of origami cranes hung in a window, delicate yet powerful. Popular hobby, and the papers were beautiful. Then I remembered how bad I am at wrapping gifts and folding maps and how I could never manage to get the tissue paper patterns back in their envelopes when my mother and grandmother tried to teach me to sew. No, no origami for me.

I moved down the alley.

There. That's what I was looking for. No prism skylights here. To limit flooding, the city had filled the streets and alleys with dirt from the regrades, leaving only the brick archways of the doors and windows of the past. Outside, they were ghosts of themselves.

But inside, life went on.

Or, in the case of the Gold Rush Hotel, murder.

Twenty-Four

How the Japanese tradition of tucking slips of paper with lines of poetry in "fortune crackers" led to the fortunes in modern cookies is a mystery, but no one can resist reading them —or being amused.

ANOTHER MONDAY, ANOTHER NEW EMPLOYEE. ARF AND I got to the shop early, taking a moment to relax and enjoy our double mocha (me) and doggy biscuit (him).

Hayden still had a couple of weeks to work at the restaurant, which was closed Mondays, but he'd wanted to get a jump start here, and arrived ahead of schedule. I got him settled in the nook and went over the paperwork. Issued him an apron and a pocket-sized notebook. Then training began. Vanessa was new enough to hover, listening in to catch what she might have missed, and experienced enough to pipe up now and then with her own newcomer's advice. I had a good feeling about the crew.

Teaching my new hires about the world of spice was a welcome antidote to yesterday's physical and mental exercise. After Arf and I took the bus home from the CID, I'd called Roxanne. I'd hauled out my Seattle history books and peppered my dad, the retired history teacher, with questions about the regrades. I was sure I was right about the Gold Rush and what I'd seen in the alleys. But I wanted to understand the lay of the land, literally and figuratively, before I shared my thoughts with the detectives. At this point, it was all very interesting, as Detective Tracy would say, but I had no proof that it meant anything.

For her part, Roxanne had contacted the genealogist and emailed her the documentation we'd gathered so far. The woman could see us this afternoon.

Genealogy. Now there's a hobby for you.

Meanwhile, spice beckoned. Two August brides, best friends, came in to sign up for our wedding registry. That gave me a chance to show Hayden and Vanessa how it worked.

"You're getting married soon," I said to him after the brides had left.

"She'd gobble this up," he replied. Food jokes come with the territory. I suggested he register, as much for practice as for the gifts, and left him and Vanessa to work their way through the form. Hayden would bring his fiancée in later to choose among the spice grinders, gift boxes, and other good things.

I kissed my dog and left him in the shop. The genealogist kept an office on Jackson Street, and I didn't want to be late.

But when I saw Rose from the Red Lantern at the bus stop, I had to say hello.

"Best thing on the food walk, your shrimp dumplings," I said. "Second best, your sesame balls."

"What I wouldn't give for a couple of sesame balls right now, and some tea." Her skin was drawn, the circles under her eyes a faint green. "I just brought my old auntie home from the hospital. I wish she'd come stay with us, but she's lived in the CID her entire life. She'll never leave."

"Isn't there an assisted living facility around here, one focused on the Asian community?" I was sure my mother had said Aki Ohno had been instrumental in developing one.

"She doesn't want to live with all those old people," Rose said, and we both burst out laughing. Then her bus came, and I rushed to meet Roxanne.

She was waiting for me on the sidewalk. Despite her makeup, a bruise bloomed on her cheek, her palms red and raw. I dismissed any suggestion that she'd thrown herself to the sidewalk on purpose to deflect attention from herself as a murder suspect. It was a long way from taking a swing at your brother-in-law when you were a pissed-off teenager nearly twenty years ago to bashing a man in the head with a brick and pretending you'd found him that way. Besides, nothing connected her to Terence Leong except the Gold Rush. Means and opportunity, but motivation? She'd been working in the building. Why had he been there?

Had you asked me what I expected a Chinese genealogist to look like, I would not have described Gloria Wong. A striking woman of seventy or so, she was slender and taller than I—at least five eight. Her salt-and-pepper bob brushed the turtleneck of her tomato-red sweater, the perfect shade for her coloring.

"What a fascinating mystery," she said, after Roxanne made introductions. "Thank you for calling me, Roxie. You and I haven't worked together for ages—not since you were tracing the provenance of that sword and wanted to confirm its history."

Roxie? I hid my surprise. Even Nate didn't call her that, and he'd known her since she was a kid.

"Right. The museum was offered a sword we suspected had been acquired during the Japanese occupation of Manchuria, though it was much older." Roxanne directed the explanation to me. "We wanted to make sure it hadn't been stolen. Gloria was able to use the identifying marks on the blade to track down the family it was made for, then helped us facilitate its return."

"We did a good deed," Gloria said.

Antique oak bookcases held books and objects. A carved stone Buddha seated on a corner table reminded me of the statue in Roxanne's bathroom. A poster identified the major dynasties of China, while another explained the Jia Pu system, the record of a clan's lineage and history, and noted the types of records and data commonly kept. A third listed the major immigration laws and events affecting the Chinese in the United States.

Gloria noticed my interest. "Traditionally, the Chinese kept detailed genealogies that go back at least to the 1600s, and in some families, much further. As you'd expect from a society that venerates its ancestors. Sit, sit." She gestured to a pair of modern black leather and chrome sling chairs across from her glass-topped desk.

"Sixteen hundred?" I said.

"Happily, I didn't have to dig nearly that far back to answer your questions. Clients often think genealogy requires spending hours in dusty catacombs, mixed with modern computer magic."

She pointed at the large monitor mounted on her desk but facing us, no doubt for showing clients documents and other findings. "And there is some truth to that. I could do more with more time, of course, but we can be pretty sure who sent these letters and who they were referring to. We start with the letters themselves. I understand enough of the old script to get the gist. Dr. Locke did a good job."

"I've sent them to a linguist for a more precise translation," Roxanne said. "Though I don't know when we'll have it."

"Good." Gloria rested her hands on the leather desk protector. I tried to remember the word for it. A blotter. "I cross-referenced the names on the deed abstracts you sent with other records. It would be helpful to inspect the deeds themselves, but that can wait. We don't need the full history of the Gold Rush block right now. We want to focus on one particular owner. Chen King Liu, in the traditional style of naming. Or King Liu Chen, in western style."

Not Wu Fong. No matter what style or name—F.H., Fong, or Francis Wu.

"Now, who was he?" she continued. "For that, let's look at the census records."

She inched her laptop closer and clicked a few keys. A hand-written census record popped up on the monitor, one name high-lighted.

"This is 1920. We see your man, King Lui Chen. Occupation: herbalist. Still there in the 1930 census."

She gave us the look of a parent watching a child beginning to unwrap a present and get an idea what's inside.

"There's more we can learn from the census, including when and where he was born, or where he says he was born, and the members of his household. We'll come back to Dr. Chen in a minute." Another record appeared on the screen. "Death certificate for Pearl Wu, in 1931. Her address is that of the Gold Rush. She's not listed as being under any doctor's care, which is interesting. The practice of Chinese medicine was not legal then, so the official record keepers would not have acknowledged a Chinese doctor."

"What did she die from? Do we know?"

"Beyond heart failure, no. That's all the record says. But see this?" Gloria pointed at the date. "She died not long after she was released from detention. It has to have come on quickly. If she'd been sick, they wouldn't have released her."

"If it came on that fast," Roxanne said, "could anyone have saved her?"

"That, I couldn't say. You'll need to consult a medical expert with knowledge of treatments at the time. But it's hard to blame Dr. Chen. The combination of the long voyage and detention might have weakened her. Detainees were subject to constant medical exams and interviews. The process could have made her reluctant to consult a western doctor."

"So Mr. Wu waits months for his wife, then loses her. Were there children?" I asked.

Gloria Wong opened her hands, her lips pressed together. She didn't know. "Many Chinese of that era believed that if there were no descendants, no one to tend the grave, the soul would wander, restless."

And haunt the Gold Rush?

"What happened to Dr. Chen? Don't tell us he sold the building and went back to China."

"Ah, now we're in luck. I found him in San Francisco, where he appears to have worked in an herb shop in Chinatown. You may know, herb shops were often fronts for clinics, until the laws changed. Lots of references to him in local records and the press, well into the 1960s."

Had Fong dropped his plans for revenge, as counseled by his friend, or had his efforts failed?

"When Dr. Chen died," the genealogist continued, "his obituary ran in both Chinese and English-speaking newspapers. He was well regarded."

"Family?" Roxanne said.

"Predeceased by his wife. Survived by his daughter and grand-daughter."

I peered at the screen. The newspaper page was old and yellowed, the print not easy to decipher.

"I sketched it out for you." The genealogist slid a neatly printed chart across the desktop.

And if I understood all the lines and squares and thises and thats, Gloria Wong believed the man who'd run the pharmacy in the basement of the Gold Rush, the man who'd been unable to save Pearl Wu, wife of Wu Fong who very likely became known as Francis Wu—that man had been Terence Leong's great-grand-father.

WE FOUND a table on the mezzanine at Fortunate Sun, away from prying ears. Keith brought a pot of green tea for Roxanne—I was still adderbabbled at the thought of anyone calling her Roxie—and his house-brewed chai for me, made with green cardamom I'd sourced from the monsoon forests of southern India. Someday, I'd get there in person. Then he set a small plate of egg tarts on the table and left.

"My head is swimming," Roxanne said, the steam from our drinks perfuming the air between us. "Wu Fong was Francis Wu, Bobby's father. We haven't documented that yet, but it seems pretty clear. Was he so unhinged by his wife's death that he—"

I held up both hands and she stopped. Gloria Wong had planted more questions than a farmer in springtime. But before we dove into the mysteries of the Wu family and Dr. Chen and Terence Leong, we had some air to clear.

"I know what happened when you were sixteen. Nate told me."

She set her tea on the table and slumped in her chair.

Finally, she opened her eyes and spoke. "You've done an amazing job of never letting on that the assistant curator of Asian antiquities at a major art museum was a juvenile delinquent."

"Considering what you do," I said, "and that you brought me into this mess involving small, possibly valuable objects that you're responsible for, and now the box of letters has gone missing, I think you owe me the story. The whole story."

"I swear to you, Pepper. I did not take the letters. I'm showing everybody the pictures I took. You. The cops. Gloria Wong, who looks like an elegant bookworm but puts up with nothing from nobody. Why would I do that, if I wanted to keep the originals hidden for my own gratification?"

I wondered, too. I said nothing.

She gazed over my shoulder, into the past. Folded one arm across her chest, her other fingering the pink-and-rose scarf shot with gold that I'd given her last summer as a thank you gift. Of all the accessories to wear today.

"I was an angry kid," she said. "My parents were in Thailand on an aid mission, and they parked me in Seattle with Rosie and Nate. Newlyweds, saddled with an angry teenager, though to their credit, they never treated me like a fifth wheel. Nate should have been resentful, but he wasn't."

"Not in his nature."

"I know that now, but then, I figured he just wasn't being honest with me. Nobody was. My parents, who said Southeast Asia wasn't safe for a teenage girl, and I'd be better off finishing high school stateside. Why was it safe for them? Why had the schools abroad been good enough for Rosie, but not me? It wasn't that I wanted to be in Lampang, necessarily, but they shouldn't have left me behind. They should have put me first, for a couple of years.

"That's how I felt then, and truth is, I still do. What they did wasn't fair to Rosie or me." She sighed and picked up her teacup. "Twenty years, and every detail of that day is burned into my brain. Nate had just bought the boat in Alaska and was home for a couple of weeks. They wanted to play tourist at the Market—eat, shop, poke around. I didn't want to go."

"Kristen and I loved hanging out there as teenagers."

"Would have been fun if I hadn't been such an idiot, dragging my feet, pouting." She refilled her cup. "We were Down Under, in the import shop. You know the one."

I nodded. The lamp with the red silk shade that sits on our tea armoire had come from there. So had the scarf around her neck, a fact I would never, ever reveal.

"They were ogling the jewelry. Opals, I think. I saw this cute little soapstone elephant. I'd always liked elephants. Rode one in India." The sounds of afternoon tea breaks rose from the main level. "I—I don't know what came over me. I had money. I didn't have to steal it. But I grabbed it and stuffed it in my pocket. The owner saw me and confronted me. I whirled around, fists flailing. And Nate . . ."

She stopped, still bewildered after all these years.

"He blames himself," I said. "Not for getting hit, though maybe for not reacting fast enough to grab your arm. For not keeping an eye on you. But mainly, I think, for not realizing how vulnerable you were."

"He wasn't responsible for me." She shook her head. "Nate has no reason to blame himself. He didn't want to prosecute the assault, and I think the shop owner would have dropped the matter if my sister hadn't gotten so uptight about it. Juvenile court. There is nothing so mortifying."

That, I believed.

"My parents didn't even come home, not until their mission finished months later. Nate went back to Alaska and it was me and Rosie. Good times." She shook off the memory and collected herself, almost resembling the self-possessed woman I'd come to know. "But I promise you, Pepper, I have never taken so much as a grape in a grocery store since then."

I believed that, too.

"The Market," I said, suddenly realizing. "When we went to the shop last Sunday, then out for lunch. That was the first time you'd been there in all those years, wasn't it?"

"But not the last."

I took a sip of chai, then dug in my tote for a notebook.

"So, Wu blamed Dr. Chen for his wife's death. Bought the building from him a year later—"

"For a pittance," she said, spitting out the word. "That much we know from the abstracts."

"The question, and the answer may be in the other letters, is whether Wu hounded Chen to abandon his practice and forced him to sign over the deed to the Gold Rush."

"One more question. Why would Francis or Fong leave the property to Abigail, not Bobby?"

"Dr. Locke—Henry—says Bobby's father was older when he was born and wanted a son who would follow in his footsteps. Not one whose ambition was to draw pictures. My guess, he saw the property as his legacy. He'd lost his first wife, but he'd extracted something valuable as payment." We stared at each other, thinking.

"What if—" we said at the same time, each of us breaking off.

"What if," I said, "the old man left the hotel to Abigail because he knew Bobby would sell it and spend the money on frivolous things. *Avengers* comics and *The Green Hornet*." I hadn't told Roxanne about the cardboard cutout in Bobby's shop or his offer to sell something valuable—I didn't know what—to the dealer Down Under. "But Abigail, with her impoverished childhood and her sense of duty to family, would hang on to it for Oliver. She as much as told me it would go to him, meaning she's made a will that bypasses her husband."

"So Oliver can carry on the family legacy, after her death," Roxanne said. "How do we prove any of this?"

"I have no idea." I pulled out my phone. "And that brings us to Terence Leong."

I brought up the morgue photo the police had given us and laid the phone on the table. I was about to ask Roxanne why she'd lied about leaving the hotel. Why she'd taken the pictures of a lion dancer at the food walk. Who she'd thought it was.

But I didn't get the chance.

"That's the man the police were asking about," Keith Chang said, standing at the side of our table with a fresh pot of tea. A young man was bussing the table behind us. "I didn't recognize him. But you were off the day they came in, weren't you? Take a look."

The busser set his tray down and wiped his hands on his apron. Poked the screen, bringing the picture back.

"Yeah, I know him," he said, glancing at his boss, then at me. "Well, I don't know-know him. But that's the man I ran into in the basement."

Twenty-Five

Fried sweet sesame balls, sometimes called smiling sesame balls, are often served at the New Year to represent happiness, good luck, and fortune.

"WAIT. YOU SAW HIM? IN THE BASEMENT? HERE?" I POINTED downward.

"Is this the guy who died? Was killed, or whatever?" the busser asked, his face ashen.

"In *our* basement?" Keith interjected.

"When?" I said. Bless him, the young man stayed calm despite the firestorm of questions. "Sorry. Let's slow down. Yes, this is the man who was killed, probably murdered, in the basement of the Gold Rush Hotel. His name was Terence Leong, and no one knows what he was doing in Seattle or in the building. Anything you remember could be important."

The four of us traipsed down the narrow stairs to the basement.

"It was about ten days ago, before the food walk," the busser said. "I'd have to check my work schedule to tell you what day for sure. I came down to get a bundle of clean towels and ran into this guy. It was raining, I remember that, and his hair and jacket were damp."

"What was he doing?" I asked. "Had you seen him in the café?"

"No, but I'm always on the move. I could easily not see a customer. I assumed he was waiting for the restroom, but a woman came out and he didn't go in. I opened the door to the storeroom, and he left."

Keith opened the door. Eight by ten, the wire shelving stacked with supplies, neatly organized. Boxes of paper goods sat on the floor.

"Does this lead anywhere?" I asked Keith. "Any doors or tunnels that connect with any other buildings? The Gold Rush, in particular."

"No. The plumber and I looked. We asked Bobby—"

"Bobby?"

"One of the rare days when he bothered to show up. If I owned all this"—he gestured, meaning not the cramped basement where we stood but the whole shebang—"I'd pay a lot more attention to it."

I didn't correct his assumption about the ownership. Instead, I turned to his young employee. "I'm going to relay all this to the police. They'll want to interview you, I'm sure. It's critical that you tell them everything you told us."

He nodded solemnly.

Then I spoke to Roxanne. "Meanwhile, you and I have some exploring to do."

WE HADN'T found what I'd expected. Maybe my theory was wrong.

Only one way to tell.

The rain had let up and the bricks in the alley behind the Gold Rush glistened in the light that filled the space between the shadows. Oil had left a palette of blue, gold, and purple on the pocked surfaces of the bricks and gathered between them in wraith-like shapes that shimmered, the way the past does when you peer into it too closely.

"What are we looking for?" Roxanne asked. Her boots had higher heels than I would have wanted to wear while traipsing uneven surfaces, but she didn't complain.

"This." She watched my screen as I scrolled for the pictures I'd taken in Maynard Alley Sunday afternoon. I pointed at the shot of a curved course of bricks inches above the alley surface, a narrow rectangle of glass visible below them, and explained how the alleys had been filled and rebricked to alleviate flooding, covering up doors and windows. "These buildings are all interconnected, whether they were built before the fill or after, on top of old foundations or new. If I'm right, there are hidden rooms all over this alley, accessible only from inside."

"Wow," she said, and we turned our attention back to the rear walls of the Gold Rush block.

"There." She pointed. "That's got to be a window."

She was right. A curved arch of old bricks was plainly visible, the glass below it hard to pick out, if you didn't know what you were looking for.

"The secret doorways," she said, turning to me. "What Terence Leong was searching for in the basement of the café."

"Searching for the door to his great-grandfather's pharmacy."

Above us, a window squeaked open and we glanced up. An elderly woman glared down at us, then jerked her head back and slammed the window shut.

"That's the woman," Roxanne said. "The one who threatened us. She was in your pictures."

"What?"

She grabbed my phone and scrolled back to my selfie of Seetha, my mother, and me mugging for the camera in front of the dim sum booth. Behind us, an unwitting photobomber, was the old lady that Rose had called Auntie when I'd seen her scowling at me in the Red Lantern. The woman she'd mentioned earlier at the bus stop. Above us, the window was closed and dark. I noticed the changes in construction where one building ended and another started. The upstairs window wasn't in the Gold Rush itself, but in the next building, all part of the block old Mr. Wu had pieced together after his first wife's tragic death.

Living well may be the best revenge, but doing so at your enemy's expense is even better. Or so the old man had thought.

"You might be right," I said. "But why? Why did she care if we poked around in the past?"

I scrolled backward. There. I'd taken a couple of shots of the lion dancers, as Roxanne had.

"She saw Seetha and me talking to Oliver, in his lion dancer costume. She must have seen you taking pictures, too." I held up a hand to stave off a protest. "I saw them on your Instagram. I wondered if you thought the dancer we were talking to was Oliver, or Terence. Maybe she wondered, too. But what's her connection to all this?"

"I saw Oliver leaving his apartment in the hotel, in costume," she said. "Later, I went out to get some pictures. I decided it would be a good addition to the story of the Gold Rush, if in fact we could establish that it had historical significance."

"Why not just ask him if you could take his picture? Why not tell me you'd left the hotel?"

"By then I knew Abigail was tending the building—I saw her cleaning it. But I didn't know she owned it. I thought if I could show her that Oliver, the family, and the hotel were an important part of the community, she might agree to try to save the hotel. And the pharmacy."

I didn't think Abigail needed convincing. But when it came to the hotel, would she go against her husband's wishes? Decision-making within a marriage can be complicated.

Despite the ominous shadows growing as the light faded, we picked our way through the alley, pointing out the brick arches of half a dozen old doors and windows buried by progress more than a century ago. The cold began to seep into my bones, and I grabbed Roxanne's arm to hurry us along. I didn't breathe easy until we reached the street. We rounded the corner and merged into the Friday evening bustle of people leaving their offices, rushing for the bus or the light rail, stopping for a drink with a friend, or grabbing takeout.

Then we arrived at the familiar double doors of the Gold Rush. The flowers and other offerings left in memoriam were starting to look bedraggled.

"You're sure," I said as we climbed the steps, "that you never saw Terence in the building?"

"I never saw him," she said, unlocking the door. "But now I wonder if he wasn't here. If he wasn't the presence Oliver had me half-convinced was the ghost of Bruce Lee."

INSIDE the lobby, I shoved my phone in my pants pocket and dropped my tote bag and coat on a chair, intent on searching the basement.

"Secret passages," Roxanne muttered. She was standing in front of the reception desk, coat on. A fine layer of dust lay on the counter, as if recent goings-on had stirred it up and it was only now settling back down.

As if the hotel itself had given up waiting for the guests' return.

"Secret doors, secret rooms." She darted around the end of the desk. Unhooked the velvet rope. Sat in the small chair and leaned over, out of my sight, but I could hear her opening and closing doors and drawers.

"The year we lived in Malaysia, the organization my parents worked for had taken over an old hotel. We kids had the run of the place and made a game of pretending we'd found hidden passages and secret chambers. But I'm not finding anything here."

I surveyed the tiny space. On the wall behind the desk, each of the cubbies held a key and a numbered fob. Except the top row, where each cubby held a small, lidded jar, just out of my reach.

"Hold that chair for me," I said. Roxanne stood and steadied the wheeled chair as I stepped on the seat. First jar, empty. Second, empty. I rattled the next.

"They're all empty," Roxanne said as I opened the third, a plain white ginger jar.

I turned over the lid. "Jackpot!" Inside, taped to the gleaming porcelain, was a small brass key. I pried it loose and held it up.

I climbed down and we scouted for a lock, me crawling on my hands and knees. Nothing. I leaned back against the paneled wall. I could almost see the gears churning behind Roxanne's eyes.

The gears clicked. She snatched the key from my hand, then charged past me. I pushed myself up, grabbing at the velvet rope for help, and followed her. Up the stairs she went, up the red carpet runner, past the displays of musical instruments and objects I couldn't identify. She picked up speed, running in heels, me on her tail. At the second floor, she tore down the long hallway to the room at the end. Turned the porcelain knob and entered. Sat on the bench in front of the dressing table and lifted the lace scarf.

There, beneath the rounded edge, was a recessed lap drawer. And in the middle, in the center of a small brass circlet, was a tiny keyhole.

"How did you know it was there?" I asked.

"I didn't. The dresser scarf hid it." She held up the key. "I'm almost afraid to open it."

"I'm not." I slipped the key into the lock. The same reluctance that had stopped Roxanne hit me like a warning. A lady of another era might have kept her rouge in such a drawer, her favorite earrings, or the locket her lover gave her. But the woman who had last lived in this room, the woman who had taken her baby and left everything else behind, that woman had hidden something in here. Who had she meant to find it?

I turned the key and slid the drawer open. Inside, underneath a stone chop, the kind once used in China to dip in a pot of thick ink and stamp a signature on a letter or a painting, lay a large piece of paper folded several times. I lifted it out. A tiny strip of paper drifted to the floor. Roxanne picked it up.

"'Fortunate is the son,'" she read, "'who knows his mother's love.'"

A shiver ran through me. A mother and son had lived in this room.

I laid the paper on top of the dressing table and unfolded it.

"Rice paper," Roxanne said.

At first the hand-drawn diagram meant nothing to me, squares and rectangles and lines, some labeled with tiny Chinese characters, as mysterious as the genealogist's charts. Roxanne pointed at the characters in the corner. A signature, stamped by the chop?

And then I thought I knew what we'd found.

A drawing of the rooms and passages beneath the Gold Rush. Made by Dr. Chen himself?

I'd have bet money on it.

Twenty-Six

A secret goal is in sight. Hang in there.

—Fortune cookie wisdom

"IS THIS WHAT TERENCE LEONG WAS SEARCHING FOR?" Roxanne asked. "When he was upstairs. To help him find the pharmacy."

"Maybe. Maybe his killer was after it, too."

"How did it get here? An educated man like an herbalist would have had a chop. But this couldn't have been Dr. Chen's room."

I sat on the side of the bed, thinking. "If Terence Leong is Dr. Chen's great-grandson, his mother was the granddaughter named in the obituary."

"Her name was Glee," Roxanne said. "I wonder where it came from. So hopeful."

"What if Glee Leong is the woman who lived in this room?" I pointed to the crib. "And Terence was the baby."

"She took what she needed for him but left her things behind."

"Along with the map." I pointed. "Does the signature match the chop?"

"Could be—I need my loupe to be sure. It's downstairs in my bag. But why was she here, and why did she leave in such a hurry?"

Forced to flee, like her grandfather?

"The man asking questions at city hall wanted the building plans. I suppose some city office keeps them on file, for fire safety, but how far back they go, who knows?" I stood and picked up the drawing. "What if it was Bobby? Wanting more facts about the building before putting it on the market? Though I doubt the plans would show the tunnels and secret rooms."

"Especially if they were used for illegal purposes, like gambling or opium. They built thick doors, and changed the configuration to avoid detection, resulting in blind passages and hidden rooms."

"Like the secret nightclubs during Prohibition," I said. "I doubt anything on file would be accurate anyway, after all these years. Especially since the rest of the block was cobbled together over time. Doors could have been opened or closed off. This drawing could be seriously outdated."

Roxanne closed the drawer and draped the dresser scarf over it, then slipped the key and chop in her pocket and followed me out of the room. "I can't see old Fong or whatever we're calling him disclosing anything he didn't have to. If he didn't tell his kid, he wouldn't tell the city."

"True enough. Okay, so Bobby didn't have the drawing. But he has to have known there were blocked-off rooms in the basement," I said as we walked down the hallway, the folded drawing in my hand. "The landing at the bottom of the stairs and the pharmacy don't account for the full footprint of the hotel."

"I doubt Bobby ever cared enough to ask questions about the building," Roxanne said, starting slowly down the stairs. "He was focused on his own business."

"So what changed? Why the sudden interest?"

"The potential buyer. Although we don't know who approached who. Or whom."

"I keep thinking about Abigail's cancer. Yes, it's in remission, but for how long? Maybe that's why he wanted to sell the hotel. But a sale could take a while, particularly in a special review district like this. So he decides to sell some of his more valuable inventory." The partial collections Dave, my dealer pal, had mentioned would have fetched a few thousand, but I was sure Bobby had other highly sought-after editions. You didn't offer your best pieces, or your favorites, first.

Abigail had all but admitted, outside the Locke clinic, that she was saving the hotel for her son.

My foot touched the bottom step and I turned to Roxanne, on

the step above me. Oliver had moved in, bringing his own ideas. And Terence had come poking around. "What if—"

And then it hit me.

MY HEAD hurt. My neck hurt, my back hurt, and I was one hundred percent certain that if I could feel the tips of my little fingers, they would hurt, too.

I blinked, trying to clear my vision. Not much luck. Gradually, the cobwebs in my brain gave way to the cobwebs in the room. The air was dank and mildewed, and through the thin fabric of my work T-shirt, I could feel the old brick wall behind me. The light was dim, almost nonexistent. I was in a basement. The basement of the Gold Rush, if I was not mistaken.

And I was not alone.

If you've never tried getting up off the floor with your feet tied together and your hands tied behind your back, with shoes on, take it from me: It's not easy. The darkness, and the unknown voice moaning from somewhere near my head—but not in my head; of that, I was reasonably sure—made it harder.

"Pepper? Is that you, Pepper?" The moans morphed into words, but not until she said my name the second time did I recognize the voice.

"Rox! Roxanne. I'm here. On the floor." I shimmied my way over to her, using my feet and backside. "What is this thing?" I groped the sturdy wooden legs and felt the hard wooden top. "Oh. We must be in the room off the pharmacy. You're on the doctor's treatment table. Are you okay?"

"Yeah, I will be." She moaned again. "We have to get out of here, before he decides to finish us off."

And then it came back to me. As we'd come down the stairs, Bobby had emerged from behind the basement door and hit me with the mallet for the giant gong I'd seen hanging above the stairs. He hit me over and over, and as I fell, I'd seen him swing at Roxanne. The memory of being half-dragged, half-pushed down the steps came in fits and starts. Somehow, he'd gotten me into this room and shoved me down, the back of my head scraping the brick wall, and tied me up. How he'd managed two of us, I didn't know.

But I knew I had to get us out of here. If I ever wanted to see

Nate, or Arf, or my parents or the shop, again. If I ever wanted to try a new hobby. A new recipe, a new café, a new anything. I had to get us out of here.

"Are your hands tied?" I asked. They were, but in front, not behind, and in between groans, she was able to untie her feet and slide off the table onto the floor, where she picked away at the thin velvet rope binding my wrists. Where had I last seen rope like that?

The rope between the reception desk and the lobby. And the matching ropes that held back the curtains.

"Oh, my god." I rolled my shoulders, gradually moving my arms and hands forward, back to where they should be, then untied her hands. "How can being free hurt more than being tied up? Where's my phone? Where's that light coming from?"

I did not have my phone. Either Bobby had taken it or it had fallen out of my pocket on the way down here. Roxanne had left hers in her bag, upstairs.

Roxanne tried the door. "It's locked. Or blocked. We're trapped."

"There! The light!" A beam of light flashed by, gone almost before I could tell where it was coming from. "Can we—? Can you—?"

How long it took us to drag the old treatment table over to the window, I have no idea. Minutes that felt like years, as our battered bodies balked and we bullied them into behaving. I sat on the edge of the table, pushed myself onto my knees, and managed to stand. Amazingly, the window had not been bricked over from inside or covered with an iron grate, like so many of the lower-level windows we'd seen from the alley.

"Give me your boot," I said. "Then stand in the corner and cover your face."

Rap, rap, rap. Smash. Crack. Another crack. The stacked heel of Roxanne's ankle boot wasn't the best hammer in the world, but it worked. The glass broke and splintered, some of it falling outside in the alley, the rest on the floor around us. I traded Roxanne her boot for her scarf and worked on breaking out the rest of the glass.

But the opening was too small for either of us to crawl out. We could call for help, though few people used the alley. Until another random stranger passed by, we were stuck.

And then I heard a sound. Footsteps, above us. Or closer?

"He's coming back," Roxanne said, in something between a panicked whisper and a shriek.

"Shhhh. Stand on that side of the door and don't make a sound." I took up my post and we waited.

Nothing happened. I put my ear close to the crack between door and jamb.

In the outer room, glass crunched underfoot. Bobby, searching? For what? Surely anything valuable had been found when the police investigated the crime scene. And they'd photographed it. So had Roxanne. Between them, they'd be able to tell if anything was taken.

But Bobby didn't know that. He'd paid no attention to Roxanne's work, letting his son oversee it. He hadn't known she'd taken pictures of everything in this building. Everything she'd found so far, that is.

I heard swearing, then the footsteps moved off. Heard knocking and rattling. A sound like a brick being thrown.

"He's gone," Roxanne said.

"Don't count on it." I grabbed the ropes we'd untied and tossed her one. Held another with both hands, fighting to keep the tension in my body down. A gust of cool air blew in through the broken window. *Don't let a rat come in, don't let a rat come in.*

I was so focused on warding off rats that I almost didn't hear Bobby come back until the key scraped in the lock. I raised the rope high.

The door burst open. "Where are they? What did the old man do with them?"

I brought my rope down in front of his face and jerked it back. Heard a wild, other-worldly yell. Bobby raised his arms to fend me off, but Roxanne dove in, grabbing one hand. I managed to loop one foot around his ankle and hold him while she snatched his other hand and tied them together behind his back. Together, we forced him to the floor and I put my knee on the base of his spine.

"Where's his phone? Get his phone."

Roxanne grabbed it from his hip pocket and pushed 911. I sent a silent prayer to the Wi-Fi gods that she'd get reception, down here in this brick-lined, bricked-in tangletown. Miraculously, she did, and was told help was already on the way.

How had that happened?

"Go let them in," I told Roxanne. "Hurry. I'll be okay."

Would I? Bobby had martial arts training and I was a wimp. But a wimp with a rope around the neck of a man whose hands were tied behind his back. A miracle, that—we'd had the advantage of surprise and his distraction.

Besides, I didn't think he would hurt me. Not until he found what he was searching for.

"You hate this building, don't you?" I said. "Your father forced it on you—you and Abigail—but to you, it's nothing but a burden."

"This stinking flophouse always meant more to him than we did. His own wife and son."

"Tell me about her. Your mother."

"She was everything to me, but nothing to him. When she got sick, he didn't care."

That was a twist I hadn't seen coming. Bobby strained against the rope and I pulled it tighter. Pressed my knee a little deeper, eliciting a pained moan. "Your father, Francis, was also called Fong, wasn't he?"

"Yes." He groaned.

"When were they married? What happened to her?"

"1960. Soon as I came along, he bought her the house on Beacon Hill, though he never lived there with us. Made sure I went to Chinese school. Learned the language and the rules he lived by. He didn't care what I loved. He wanted me to be a scholar or a property owner like he was. This building." Bobby spat. "He lived in it for more than sixty years, even after my mother died. Even when he was so decrepit he couldn't take a piss without help from my wife or that old lady. He loved these walls and bricks more than his own family."

One more reason Fong had left the hotel to Abigail? The hotel where he'd lived since coming to this country. Buying it had been his revenge, yes, but it had also been his community. His home.

That the family had not lived here might explain why Bobby hadn't known about the secret rooms in the basement. Francis aka Fong's late-in-life remarriage had been a means to secure his legacy, through a son. A son who did not love what meant the world to his father.

Bobby had said something puzzling.

"What old lady?" I asked.

"The one who lives above the café. He gave her an apartment

for life in exchange for taking care of him. She tells me what's going on around here."

He was raising more questions than he was answering, but I couldn't think about that now. "So along comes a potential buyer and offers you a chance to finally be free of this place, but your wife and son won't go along."

Bobby let out a strangled sound that might have been a laugh, or a cry of anguish. "Old man tied my hands. Put it in her name. Knew she'd never sell."

Why? Why was Abigail so committed to the Gold Rush? To hanging on to it, to helping Oliver plan for its future.

"Ohh. It was Abigail who helped Glee Leong. When she came to Seattle thirty years ago, with her little boy, trying to find out what had happened to her grandfather. What shame had forced Dr. Chen to give up his clinic and take refuge in San Francisco." Where he'd worked in another man's shop, despite his own reputation and following. "She gave Glee and Terence a place to stay, believing it was safe because the hotel was vacant, and you only came here to collect the rent." From the tenants in the rest of the block, in the buildings linked by secret passages.

He grunted again, telling me I was on the right track. But he was squirming. *Hold on, Pep.*

"When you found out what your wife had done, Glee was forced to leave with almost nothing. Like her grandfather."

"Her grandfather killed my father's first wife. Made him a bitter man."

Would we ever know for sure what had killed Pearl Wu? I doubted it. "If she'd lived, you'd never have been born."

"And that might not be so bad," a woman said behind me. Bobby stiffened. Not the police. *Abigail.*

"I have lived with your resentment for thirty-five years. I have played second fiddle to your anger and your obsession," she said. "I married an artist, or so I thought. A man with talent and ambition. But I was a fool. And poor Terence died because of it."

"He tried to blackmail me, like his mother did."

"He wanted to know the truth, just like she did," Abigail spat back. "About what your father did to Dr. Chen. If they discovered proof that your father acquired the hotel legally, they'd have gone away without a word. But I knew he hadn't."

"How did you know?" I asked.

"He told me, when he made his will leaving me the property. The hotel and all the buildings he snatched up over the years. He wanted to keep it out of your hands, his sorry legacy of a son. He knew you'd sell in a heartbeat if you ever got a chance to buy a copy of *Avengers* number one. But I knew what to do."

"How did you meet Glee?" I asked. Above us, I heard the creak of the wood floor. The police?

"Aki Ohno brought her to me. She knew I had a soft heart. Glee didn't want money or the deed to the hotel. To her, the goal was finding the pharmacy."

Aki, the woman my parents said knew everyone and saw everything. "You knew about the pharmacy?" I asked, and in the dim light, I saw Abigail nod.

But Bobby hadn't known. And now that it had been discovered, he didn't care. Which meant he'd been searching for some other gold.

Twenty-Seven

"Are you so eager to get rid of me?" Godith Adeney said to Cadfael, offended. "And just when I'm getting to know sage from marjoram! What would you do without me?"

—Ellis Peters, *One Corpse Too Many*

PROVING MY MOTHER RIGHT ABOUT HER EYES AND EARS, AKI Ohno had seen Roxanne and me on the sidewalk outside the Gold Rush. When she saw Bobby come by a few minutes later and go in, summoned by the old auntie upstairs, she'd been worried and called her granddaughter. But first, she'd called Abigail, who'd managed to beat Officer Ohno and the police to the hotel.

Bobby had been hauled away by the time the detectives arrived, as the EMTs finished checking us out. Even velvet ropes can leave marks, and Roxanne had a nasty gash on her temple that the EMTs thought warranted a trip to the ER for a scan.

"Not until I know Pepper's okay," she said, "and what Bobby was after."

"The clue's got to be in the drawing," I said. "A hidden room. A secret passage."

"I swear, she sounds like my ten year old," Detective Tracy said to his partner. "Reading too much Nancy Drew."

After knocking us out, Bobby had snatched up the drawing,

and we'd found it on the floor outside the treatment room where he'd dragged us. I explained as best I could, which left Spencer nodding her head, acknowledging the possibility, and Tracy shaking his.

"You mean to tell me there's another secret room? Filled with avengers and hornets? Do we need to call for backup?"

I looked at Abigail, sitting behind the hotel desk under Paula Ohno's watch. "He doesn't get it. Do you know which room? And where the key is?"

"Down this passage, I think." She pointed to a long hallway on the map, going the opposite direction from the hall to the plumbing access.

After all these years, and after what Bobby had done to Glee and Terence, Abigail was finally free of her promise to the old man, and it was a visible relief to unburden herself.

Detective Spencer got a text and left. Tracy, Roxanne, and I, along with two patrol officers, traipsed back down the stairs to the pharmacy.

"In an old jar," Tracy said, repeating Abigail's reference to the keys. "Does she know how many old jars there are in this rat's nest?"

Eventually, we found the right jar, and buried in the smelly old herbs, a ring of brass keys. Roxanne nearly bit her nails as the officers inched a cabinet filled with antique bottles and other mysterious items away from the wall to reveal a recessed doorway. Tracy stuck keys into the brass lock until he found the right one.

The latch squealed in protest and I held my breath. As Abigail had said, the door opened onto a hallway. Alas, she had not known which room we were looking for on the long, narrow passage. We used the drawing, and a powerful flashlight held by one of the officers, to follow the twists and turns through thick cobwebs that made Tracy shudder and cough, and we opened every door. As I'd suspected, each room mirrored the one where we'd been held. And each had a door or window that had once opened onto the alley, a connection to the outside world that was now just another eccentricity in a neighborhood packed with them.

Finally, we faced one last doorway.

"This had better pay off, Spice Girl." Tracy slipped the final key into the lock. I held my breath. The door opened and the flashlight beam picked out stacks of vintage fruit crates, the labels advertising Washington apples, cherries, and pears.

I could hardly believe my eyes. Beside me, Roxanne gasped.

"Wouldn't you know," Tracy said. "It's always in the last place you look."

The room held no furniture. Just boxes. Boxes and boxes of old comic books. The collection young Bobby had acquired, ten cents or a quarter at a time. I imagined old man Wu thinking at first that his young son's interest was nothing more than a hobby, something boys did. American boys. Maybe brought the boy comics. Gave him an allowance, then cut it off, knowing it wasn't going to bikes and bubble gum and movies, as with other boys, but to sketch pads and thick graphite pencils. And comics and more comics.

Then, when the boy dropped out of college to try his hand in animation, the old man had stashed his treasures where he could never find them. Told him so, all but daring him to fight back, to fight for what he loved.

Much as Bobby wanted to be rid of the building, he couldn't sell it. Not until his collection had been found. The collection his bitter old father had withheld from him, the collection he'd been trying to recreate, all these years, with his own shop. Had he been trying to sell lesser valuables not to pay for his wife's medical treatment, but to buy what he'd lost when the old man had hidden the boxes?

Dave Down Under had given me the clue. What Bobby was offering to sell was interesting, he'd said, but incomplete. Whether it was *Archie*, *The Green Hornet*, or *Spider-Man*, serious collectors wanted a complete set, and without those first few issues, the value was minimal.

My guess, the value lay in thin, colored paper hidden somewhere in this room.

WE RETURNED to the lobby covered in dust, the basement doors closed behind us, Bobby Wu's collection once more tucked away in safety. But this time, Detective Tracy had photographs and keys, and the evidence would be safe.

The outside door opened, and Detective Spencer entered, her long black raincoat glistening from the early evening mist. Oliver held the door for a man and woman I did not know.

Behind the hotel desk, Abigail shrieked. At a gesture from Spencer, Officer Ohno stepped aside and Abigail rushed forward. The newcomer opened her arms and they embraced.

A moment later, Abigail took a step back, gripping the woman's shoulders, then raised her hands to the woman's cheeks.

"Glee," she said, her voice cracking. "Glee. I never thought I'd see you again. I am so sorry about Terence. About what my—what Bobby did."

The man put a supportive hand on Glee's back, and Oliver moved close to his mother.

"It's not your fault, Abby," Glee said. I put her in her midfifties, gracious and attractive. "You did everything you could back then, to help us and keep us safe. Terence knew the risk. I warned him. But he wanted to know our family history."

I glanced at Detective Tracy, watching this reunion with interest. Abigail Wu had suspected her husband was a killer but hadn't told the police. How he'd deal with that, I didn't know, but I had a hunch she'd be facing some pretty uncomfortable questioning.

"You knew Oliver had gone to find Glee, Terence Leong's mother," I said to him. "You knew where he'd gone, and you never let on."

"Allow me some secrets, Spice Girl. Professional courtesy."

I didn't let him see me smile.

The police had not known exactly where to find Glee Leong, now Glee Webster, here with her husband, John. They had finally spoken with Terence's temporary landlord, a friend of Aki Ohno's who rented rooms, and traced him back to San Francisco. Abigail had begun searching for Glee when she became ill, telling her son about her quest. But they got nowhere until Oliver started his new job and saw a list of management for properties owned by the same company. There, on the roster for a hotel in Oakland, was a woman named Glee. With the unusual name, across the bay from the city where her grandfather had fled when old Fong hounded him away, Oliver and Abigail believed they'd finally found her. Last Friday, when he should have been at the symphony with Seetha, Oliver had been on a plane. Thanks to his text Sunday afternoon, the police had located him and helped persuade Glee to return to Seattle.

While Tracy and I had been battling spider webs the size of

Elliott Bay, Detective Spencer had gone to meet the Websters and Oliver at the hotel where he worked.

"I don't blame you," Glee said. She and Abigail were sitting together now on the small couch, holding each other's hands.

"How did you two connect in the first place?" I asked. "Back when Terence was a baby and you took refuge here? And how did Terence get into the Gold Rush?"

"I was widowed young," Glee said, her tone calm and steady. "Before Terence was born. My grandfather had died years earlier, and my mother told me what she knew about the Gold Rush. How Wu Fong had blamed him for his wife's death and cheated him out of the building. That was her word—he was never angry or bitter, despite knowing he'd been blamed unfairly. There was nothing he could have done to save the poor woman."

"Pearl," I said quietly, wanting her name to be honored.

"Part of the delay in getting up here," John Webster said, "was sorting through his files. It wasn't easy—they're in Chinese—but we think we found them."

"Dr. Locke could translate them," I said. "Old Dr. Locke, Henry."

"We've already called him," Detective Spencer said.

"Back then," Glee said, "I was desperate to learn anything I could about my family, since I had so few people left. I came to Seattle knowing no one. Or who to ask."

"Aki Ohno," I said.

"She knows everyone," Glee said, "and most of their secrets. She introduced me to Abigail, who told me what she knew and let me stay here."

"It should have been yours," Abigail said. "The Gold Rush should have been yours."

Glee squeezed her old friend's hand. "I was never after the building, my friend. And I am not after it now. I only wanted the story. The truth. But not at your expense."

"I promised you you'd be safe here. I told you Bobby never came into the Gold Rush. But that day, he did, and he found you. And—" Abigail choked back sobs. "We've found you, thank God."

"I've never known for sure," Glee said, "but I think the woman who worked for Wu Fong told Bobby I was here. I bought dumplings from her and let her play with Terence. Loyalty is a good thing, but not when it's to a bad man."

The woman who lived upstairs in an adjacent building, with a window overlooking the alley. The old auntie, as Rose the dim sum seller at the Red Lantern called her, who'd seen Roxanne and me at the food walk. Had she seen Oliver, and mistaken him for Terence?

I'd thought of Aki as one of those people, like my neighbor at the lofts, who are simply so present that you forget to truly see them. In my blindness, I had not recognized the woman who'd been watching me while I'd been searching for her.

And while I'd kept telling myself I should call Aki and hadn't, she'd been keeping her eye on me.

Why the old auntie had done what she did, telling Bobby about Glee's presence in the hotel he hated all those years ago, I could not say. Telling him about Terence. Had she known that Abigail had helped Glee, and was helping her son too, because Abigail believed Fong had cheated the Chen-Leong family?

Didn't matter. Glee was right. The old auntie had misused her loyalties.

"I begged Terence to put me in touch with you," Abigail told Glee, "but he didn't trust me enough yet. Then, when it became clear, when I figured out that my own husband had killed your son, I knew we had to find you."

"My little cookie." Glee's voice broke. "My little cookie."

Roxanne and I exchanged a glance. The pendant Terence wore.

"That's what I called him," Glee said. "We were in a car accident, driving home after dinner with friends. I was pregnant. My husband was killed, but I barely got a scratch. After dinner, I'd tucked my fortune cookie in my purse and it didn't break, so . . ."

I told her about the slip of paper we'd found in the drawer upstairs.

"'Fortunate is the son,'" she said, reciting from memory, "'who knows his mother's love.'"

Even Detective Tracy seemed momentarily stunned.

"I'd still like to know," Roxanne said after a pause, "who took the letters. And how Terence got in the hotel. I'm fairly sure he was watching me. I led him to the pharmacy, though I didn't know it. That's what led to his death. To Bobby following him and killing him."

"It was Bobby who attacked you," I said. "On your way home last week."

One mystery solved.

"Francis—Fong—kept the letters. I gave them to Glee," Abigail said, answering Roxanne. "When you started working on the upper hallway, I took them, not realizing you'd already seen them. And I gave Terence a key. So he could see what should have been his. You did nothing wrong. You love this place as Glee and I do, as Terence did. As I hope my son does."

Oliver nodded. Had he resented his father's devotion to *The Green Hornet* and the other comics Bobby collected, the way Bobby had resented his father's dedication to the Gold Rush? Certainly Bobby had dismissed Oliver's interest in the hotel. Neither had known the reason for their fathers' single-minded sternness, and in the way of sons everywhere, had seen it as a rejection of himself. Bobby had turned defiant. But Abigail had understood, and she'd done her best to nurture in her son a healthy independence.

Try as we might, the past doesn't always leave us alone.

Twenty-Eight

You put water into a cup; it becomes the cup.
You put water into a teapot; it becomes the teapot.
Now water can flow, or it can crash!
Be water, my friend.

—Bruce Lee

ROXANNE HAD WANTED TO SHOW GLEE AND HER HUSBAND the pharmacy, but the detectives said no, the entire basement was now a crime scene and they'd make arrangements for the Websters to see it after the crime scene investigation was complete. Bobby would face assault and kidnaping charges for his attacks on Roxanne and me, along with murder.

The patrol car dropped me off in front of my loft. When I hadn't returned to the shop, Sandra had called my neighbor Glenn, who'd come up to the Market to collect my dog. The chain of texts had been pinging like mad when I emerged from the hotel basement and found my phone, chiming like a clock stuck on the hour.

Now I crouched in the doorway to Glenn and his Nate's temporary home on the lower level of the building and my dog threw himself into my arms.

"Oh, Arf. Arf. Good boy. My good boy."

"He's been walked and fed," Glenn said. "He's been well-behaved, as always. But we could tell he knew you were in trouble."

A tear dribbled down my cheek, and a rough tongue wiped it away.

On our way upstairs, I passed the door of the neighbor I barely knew. "Tomorrow," I said. "Tomorrow, we'll get to know each other."

And then it was time to call my Nate. Didn't matter what time it was, frankly. I wanted desperately to hear his voice. To assure him I loved him, trusted him, needed him in my life no matter what the terms or where he was.

That's what love is. I sat on the floor and called my guy, stroking the dog's head in my lap. I was a fortunate cookie, indeed.

OVER the next few days, more of the story emerged. When Abigail had been diagnosed with cancer, she'd rewritten her will to leave the Gold Rush to Oliver and Terence jointly. Oliver had known and agreed. It was Abigail who'd encouraged him to take control of the property. Terence had not been attempting blackmail, as Bobby had charged in the argument I'd overheard in the comic book shop. Rather, he'd hoped to find the drawing his mother had hidden and not had time to retrieve. The police made a copy, which Oliver and Abigail gave Roxanne to help complete her survey of the building. The project would take months, and there was a good chance she'd be able to hire Reed as her intern.

Oliver assured her that no matter what they did with the hotel, the pharmacy would be preserved. The old man had not been able to bring himself to destroy it. Despite his bitterness, he'd understood its historic importance to the community and beyond. And perhaps, I mused, keeping it intact had allowed him to nurse his grudge.

The chop found with Dr. Chen's drawing had in fact been his seal, and Detective Spencer gave it to Glee.

Glee had experience with converting older buildings into modern hotels and was willing to offer her advice, if that's what Abigail and Oliver chose to do. Aki Ohno and her friends advocated for senior housing or assisted living. Once a community activist, always a community activist. No decisions had been made. After all, Oliver told Seetha when they finally made it to the symphony, and she told me the next day, the Gold Rush had been waiting patiently for decades. It could wait a little longer.

When Roxanne reported hearing noises while she worked,

Oliver had quickly realized that her unpredictable schedule meant she and Terence were prowling the hotel at the same time. He'd grasped at his father's love of Bruce Lee for an explanation. He apologized profusely, and she accepted with the grace I'd come to expect from her, and even a touch of humor.

As for why Terence had rented the lion dancer costume, we surmised that he wanted to be part of the community at the Lunar New Year. To dance and bring good fortune.

Glee spoke with Gloria Wong about researching the family history and genealogy. Gloria and my friend at the city would help sort out the multiple deeds and identify what Dr. Chen had owned and what Fong aka F.H. and Francis had bought when, in the block surrounding the Gold Rush. I had little doubt that forcing a man to sell you a five-story building with a working hotel above a successful clinic for a hundred dollars was a bad sign. Nate wondered if they might uncover evidence that Fong had taken unfair advantage of other families as well. Time would tell, as it often does.

Now cleared of any suspicion, the would-be buyers had set their sights on another building, one without so many ghosts.

Hayden arrived for the Wednesday morning staff meeting, his first, with a serving tray.

"What? What did you bring?" Cayenne asked.

"Pimento olive puffs, made with smoked cheddar and a dash of smoked paprika. I developed the recipe myself." He uncovered the tray and passed it around.

"You're going to fit in just fine," Sandra told him, and I agreed.

Reed had joined us for the meeting. "Dad and Granddad and I are taking a tour of the pharmacy as soon as the cops okay it."

"Prepare to have your mind blown," I said.

"Granddad's been going over the medical records Glee and John Webster brought, trying to solve the mystery of old Mr. Wu's first wife."

"And?" I was surprised how desperately I wanted Dr. Chen to be proven blame-free in the death nearly a century ago of a woman I had never met.

"Based on her pulses and the herbs Dr. Chen gave her, he suspects a heart condition caused by malaria or some other infection she never knew she had. If she'd known, if she'd had symptoms, it could have been treated. But with the stresses of travel, then detention, by the time she saw Dr. Chen, it was too late."

"Such a tragedy."

"Also, I probably shouldn't tell you this, but my dad says Abigail is doing fine, despite all the stress. He's treating her regularly to keep things in balance, but the moment he senses any serious change, any sign that she's coming out of remission, he'll send her back to the oncologist. You know he believes Eastern and Western medicine work best together."

Keeping the elements in balance. Always a good thing.

DETECTIVES Spencer and Tracy came by to give me an update.

"No cookies today, Detective," I said to Tracy after our conversation. "Care for an olive puff?"

He grunted. And ate three.

I'D SET a few of Hayden's olive puffs aside for Sandy Lynn and delivered them midafternoon. I had to wait my turn as she wrapped wedges of triple-crème brie and Rogue River blue for customers.

The spunky cheese monger looked happy, but tired.

"Pepper, you used to work in HR, didn't you? I thought I could run the shop on my own, but if it's like this in January, I'll never be able to handle the busy season. Can you help me hire someone?"

So much for leaving the past alone.

Then I headed to the comic shop Down Under. At my suggestion, Oliver had contacted Dave Hudson to appraise the contents of Bobby's shop, as neither he nor his mother wanted to run the place. They'd also asked him to inventory the collection stashed in the Gold Rush, once the crime scene was released. Whether it belonged to Bobby or Abigail was a legal question, but the proceeds of a sale might go a long way toward paying his legal fees—and Abigail's medical bills. And maybe, if the boxes held what Bobby believed was hidden there, seed money to help restore the Gold Rush.

"Passion," big Dave said to me now, "is healthy, even when other people don't understand."

In all my talk about needing a hobby, this was the piece I'd been missing. There's no point spending hours learning to knit one, purl two if you don't truly, deeply enjoy making things with yarn.

"And then there's obsession," he continued. "Comes from the dark side. Driven by something other than love. If you aren't careful—and the obsessed rarely are—it'll kill you."

Wise words.

"By the way, I've been thinking about the traffic tangle." Dave reached under the counter and brought out a roll of paper, laying it flat so I could see the Market streets, drawn to scale. He added a toy car and a couple of delivery trucks. "Not that I'm obsessed or anything."

I laughed right down to my toes.

THANKS in equal parts to Keith Chang's enthusiasm for our spices, my role in solving the murder, and Aki and Paula Ohno's words in the right ears, the Spice Shop got a surprising uptick in business from restaurants in the CID. Even Rose from the Red Lantern called me. And the next weekend, when the Market wrapped up the city's two-week celebration of the Year of the Rabbit with a parade and food walk of our own, I invited Keith to serve dim sum in the Spice Shop. My staff added a few goodies made with Sandy Lynn's smoked cheddar. If the Year of the Rabbit proved lucky, the Fortunate Sun might develop some new business, too.

Watching the lion dancers snake down the street, with barely a vehicle in sight, made my heart swell. Some traditions are meant to be shared.

Oliver and Seetha sauntered in, hand in hand, matching grins on their faces. Fitting, with Valentine's Day fast approaching.

"Who knew my dad was a world expert on the Green Hornet?" Oliver said. "Bruce Lee's first role on American TV. It's hot again. Do you know how cool that would have made me as a kid?"

"I think you're pretty cool right now," Seetha said. Ah, the flush of new love.

"I heard from Roxanne," Oliver said, "that you give a mean Bruce Lee yell. You should take up kung fu."

"You were looking for a hobby," Seetha said.

"Smarty pants."

I had plenty of questions for Oliver, but they could wait. This was a day to celebrate the successes of the past and the promise of the future. That's what Cadfael would do. I had decided that the Buddha in Roxanne's medicine cabinet was her Cadfael, her reminder to stay on track. Maybe I'd ask her someday. Or not.

A last-minute change upended her plans to take in the parade. She texted her apologies. *The expert from San Francisco is coming today to see the pharmacy. You understand, I know.*

I replied that I did. A string of dots formed on my screen.

I want to come to the Market next week, if you have time to give me a tour, she said. *And go Down Under, to the import shop*, she wrote. *It's time to put the past behind me.*

Amen, sister. Amen.

ARF AND I walked home past the old INS bldg. So many stories. I made a mental note to ask my friends at the city preservation office about a plaque. There are times when the past deserves to be remembered.

As we walked away, I glanced up at the roof, sticky-uppy things of some kind in the planter boxes, waiting for spring. Azaleas?

A little bud of an idea began to take root in my brain. A future hobby? Maybe.

WE WERE having dinner on the houseboat, one of the last gatherings before my parents flew back to Costa Rica. My brother and his family were there, Arf and Charlie stretched out on the floor together.

"We bought a house today," my mother said as I was about to take a sip of wine.

"What? Where?" I lowered my glass. "You didn't tell me you were making an offer."

My dad gave the address.

Carl and I stared at him. At them both. They were brimming with delight. With glee.

"That's our old house," Carl said. "In Montlake."

"Yeeeep," Dad said. "Good house. Perfect house."

"I saw that listing," my brother went on. "Even if you didn't offer the full ask, it was nearly twice what you sold it for."

"Yes," my mother said. "But darling, you invested the money so well that we can pay cash."

Twice in one day, I howled with laughter. Howled until I cried.

When I recovered myself, I raised my glass. "A toast to the perfect house. To a fortunate life."

I would be sorry to see them go. I would be sorry to see Reed leave the shop, as I'd been sorry to lose Matt. But I knew the importance of following your passion, no matter how young or old you are when you find it. Passion, after all, had led me to the Market and the Spice Shop, and the loft and the dog. To my Nate, out on the ocean.

I didn't need a hobby. I had a life filled with people and work I loved. And that is the true spice of life.

Recipies and Spice Notes

The Seattle Spice Shop Recommends . . .

THE SPICE SHOP TEA

Created by the Spice Shop's original owner, this tea has quenched thirst among Market-goers for decades! Serve hot or iced.

> black Assam tea leaves
> green cardamom pod
> allspice berries
> dried or fresh orange peel

For one cup, using an infuser, combine a heaping teaspoon of black Assam tea leaves, a slightly crushed cardamom pod, two allspice berries, and about 1/8 teaspoon dried grated orange peel (or fresh if you've got a willing orange). Steep 3-5 minutes, remove infuser, and pretend you're in the Spice Shop with Pepper, Sandra, and Arf!

PEPPER'S FIVE SPICE BLEND

> 1 tablespoon star anise, about 3–5 stars
> 1½ teaspoons whole cloves
> 1 tablespoon fennel seed
> 1 tablespoon cinnamon or cassia (about 3 sticks, which work well)
> 1½ teaspoons Szechuan or black peppercorns

Crack the stars, cloves, and cinnamon sticks with a mortar and pestle, a meat grinder, or the flat of a heavy knife. Combine all ingredients and grind to the texture of cornmeal or ground black pepper in your spice grinder. Store in an airtight container.

Note: If you don't have a spice grinder, you can use your coffee grinder. Make sure to clean it before and after by grinding dried rice in it to pick up the coffee residue, then wiping it thoroughly.

CAYENNE'S FIVE SPICE FRENCH APPLE CUSTARD CAKE

Cayenne spiced up this classic apple custard cake to demonstrate the versatility of the Chinese Five Spice Blend. The alcohol will bake off, leaving a hint of flavor to complement both apples and spice.

1½ pounds Granny Smith apples or a mix of Granny Smith and McIntosh (3–4 large apples, depending on size)
1 tablespoon Calvados (apply brandy), brandy, or white rum
1 teaspoon lemon juice
2 tablespoons Chinese Five Spice, divided
1 cup plus 2 tablespoons all-purpose flour, divided
1 cup plus 1 tablespoon granulated sugar, divided
2 teaspoons baking powder
½ teaspoon salt
1 large egg plus 2 large yolks
1 cup vegetable oil
1 cup milk
1 teaspoon vanilla extract
powdered sugar for topping (optional)

Heat oven to 325 degrees. Lightly coat a 9-inch springform pan with cooking spray and place pan on a baking sheet.

Peel and core the apples. Cut each in half and place cut side down on the cutting board. Cut each half in 4 pieces, then rotate and slice into pieces about 1/8-inch thick.

Place apple slices on a microwave-safe pie plate; cover with plastic wrap and microwave until apples are pliable and slightly translucent, about 3 minutes. (This softens the apples in the finished cake.)

Toss apple slices with Calvados, lemon juice, and 1 teaspoon Five Spice, and cool about 15 minutes.

In a medium-sized bowl, whisk 1 cup flour, 1 cup granulated sugar, baking powder, salt, and remaining Five Spice (1 tablespoon plus two teaspoons).

In a second bowl, whisk the whole egg only, oil, milk, and vanilla together until smooth.

Add the flour mixture to the wet ingredients and whisk until just combined. Transfer 1 cup batter to a separate bowl and set aside.

Add the 2 egg yolks to the remaining batter and whisk to combine. Gently fold in the apples. Transfer batter to the pan, using a spatula to spread evenly to edges. Shake lightly to ensure an even layer and smooth surface.

Whisk remaining 2 tablespoons flour into the 1 cup batter. Pour on top of batter in pan. Spread evenly and smooth the surface. Sprinkle remaining tablespoon of sugar evenly over the batter.

Bake until the center of cake is set, a toothpick or tester inserted in center comes out clean, and the top is golden brown, about 65 minutes. Transfer pan to wire rack; let cool for 5 minutes. Run a knife around sides of pan to loosen the cake; remove the springform and let the cake cool. Dust cooled cake with powdered sugar, if you'd like.

Serve slightly warm or cool.

APPLE AND SMOKED CHEDDAR SCONES

Cayenne created these tasty treats using smoked cheddar from Say Cheese! Use the strongest smoked cheddar you can find, as the smoky flavor mellows in baking. Apple and hickory smoked cheddar are both wonderful! If smoked cheddar isn't available near you, use a sharp cheddar.

> 1 pound firm tart apples (2–3 apples, depending on size)
> 1½ cups all-purpose flour
> ¼ cup sugar
> 1½ teaspoons baking powder
> ½ teaspoon salt plus additional for egg wash
> 6 tablespoons butter, chilled and cut into ¼-inch cubes
> ½ cup smoked cheddar, shredded
> ¼ cup heavy cream
> 2 large eggs
> 1½ tablespoons sparkling, turbinado, or granulated sugar, for topping

Heat oven to 375 degrees. Line a rimmed baking sheet with parchment paper or a silicon baking sheet.

Peel and core the apples, then place them cut side down on your cutting board and slice them about 1/4-inch thick. Turn and cut into quarters, so you end up with apple chunks. Place chunks in a single layer on the baking sheet and bake until they take on a little color and feel dry to the touch, about 20 minutes. They will be about half baked. Allow to cool slightly. Leave oven on.

Stir together flour, sugar, baking powder, and salt. Set aside. Place butter in the bowl of an electric mixer, and add the apple chunks, cheese, cream, and one egg. Add flour mixture gradually and mix on low speed until the dough just comes together. Do not overmix.

Dust your cutting board with flour and place the dough on top, then sprinkle with a little flour. If your dough doesn't look fully mixed or feels sticky, knead it gently just to combine all the ingredients. Press into a circle, about 8 inches across and 1 ¼ inches thick. Cut circle into 8 wedges. Turn the parchment paper over to line the baking sheet. Transfer the wedges to the baking sheet, leaving 2 inches between each scone.

Beat remaining egg in a small bowl with a pinch of salt. Brush the scones with the egg wash and sprinkle them with sparkling sugar. Bake until firm and golden, about 25 minutes. Transfer to a wire rack and cool about 10 minutes.

Makes 8 scones.

SANDRA'S CHEDDAR ROSEMARY CRACKERS

Sandra loves to experiment in the kitchen, and the presence of another creative cook in the shop has only inspired her!

¾ cup unsalted butter, at room temperature
8 ounces smoked, sharp, or extra sharp cheddar, grated (about 2 cups)
2 teaspoons finely chopped fresh rosemary (4–5 sprigs)
½ teaspoon kosher salt
½ teaspoon freshly ground black pepper, cayenne, or paprika
2 cups unbleached, all-purpose flour
cold water

In the bowl of an electric mixer, beat butter and cheddar on medium speed. In a separate bowl, stir together the rosemary, salt, black pepper (or other spice), and flour, and gradually add to the cheese and butter, mixing on low. Add 1–2 tablespoons cold water and beat until mixture is well combined.

Turn half the dough out on to a sheet of waxed paper, parchment paper, or plastic wrap. Shape into a log with your hands, then use the paper or wrap to smooth the log and wrap it. Repeat with the remaining dough. Chill 30 to 60 minutes.

Heat oven to 375 degrees. Line two baking sheets with parchment or silicone baking sheets. Slice the logs 1/4-inch thick and lay slices on the sheet, about an inch apart.

Bake until firm and lightly golden around the edges, 10–12 minutes. (The bottoms won't turn golden like a typical cookie.) Cool briefly on baking sheet, then transfer to a wire rack to cool completely.

Makes about 4 dozen. These keep nicely, well wrapped, for about a week, and freeze well.

CHEDDAR PIMENTO OLIVE PUFFS

Hayden created these cheesy treats to surprise his new coworkers. He'll fit right in, and so will you, anytime you serve these delightful two-bite appetizers.

    1 cup sharp or smoked cheddar cheese, shredded
    3 tablespoon butter, melted
    ½ cup flour
    dash of kosher salt
    ½ teaspoon cayenne or paprika, sweet or smoked
    12–15 pimento-stuffed green olives, drained

Heat oven to 400 degrees.

In a medium bowl, combine cheese and butter with a fork. Add flour, salt, and cayenne or paprika and mix into a rough dough. Use your hands if necessary. Use your hand or a spoon to scoop up a tablespoon of dough and wrap around an olive. Roll into a ball and place on baking sheet. Repeat with remaining dough.

Chill one hour.

Bake 12–15 minutes or until golden. Serve warm.

LENA'S HUNGARIAN MUSHROOM SOUP

Nothing says comfort like soup, especially the soup your mother made. Lena's immigrant mother made this soup for her and her sisters whenever they were sick, but Lena and Pepper make it any time they long for a little old-world flavor. Adjust the spices based on your preference and the strength of your paprika. To serve over noodles, make a stew by thickening the roux with an extra tablespoon of flour, then boil up a pot of wide egg noodles while the stew simmers.

2 tablespoons butter
1 large yellow onion, finely chopped
1 clove garlic, minced
12 ounces cremini or white button mushrooms, or a mix, sliced
3 tablespoons unsalted butter
2 tablespoon all-purpose flour (plus 1 tablespoon, for a stew)
1 cup milk (whole or 2%)
2 cups beef broth
1 tablespoon tamari or soy sauce
1½ to 2 tablespoons Hungarian paprika
1½ teaspoons dried dill or 1½ tablespoons chopped fresh dill
1 teaspoon kosher salt
¼ teaspoon freshly ground black pepper
½ cup sour cream
chopped dill or parsley, for garnish
extra sour cream, for serving
egg noodles (optional, for a stew)

In a heavy stockpot or Dutch oven, melt 2 tablespoons of butter. Add the onions and cook until translucent and just beginning to brown, 4-5 minutes, stirring regularly. Add the garlic and cook another minute. Add the mushrooms and cook until the mushrooms begin to release their juices, about 3-5 minutes. Transfer the mushroom mixture to a bowl and set aside.

In the same pan, melt 3 tablespoons of butter and add the flour, stirring continuously for 4-5 minutes or until the mixture is a rich, caramelized brown. Add the milk, broth, and soy sauce, stirring until the mixture is smooth. Add the paprika, dill, salt, and pepper. Stir in the mushroom mixture. Bring to a boil, reduce heat to low, then cover and simmer for 15 minutes, stirring occasionally. If you're using noodles, cook them now.

Stir in the sour cream and heat through.

Ladle into soup bowls or over noodles in pasta bowls. Garnish with a spoonful of sour cream and a sprinkling of chopped dill. Serve with a green salad, crusty bread, and your favorite red wine.

SPICE UP YOUR LIFE WITH PEPPER AND THE FLICK CHICKS LONGEVITY NOODLES

If all this talk about Chinese food makes you crave stir fries and noodles, remember that Pepper shares her recipes for Broccoli Beef and Cold Sesame Noodles in The Solace of Bay Leaves.

In Chinese tradition, the extralong noodles served at the New Year symbolize our hopes for good luck and a long life. They can be hard to find; lo mein or egg noodles are an easy substitute. Stir-fry shrimp or chicken with sesame oil and a little soy sauce to add protein, if you'd like, or serve with stir-fried baby bok choy or snow peas for a reminder of all things fresh and green.

And of course, Pepper believes that any meal you enjoy with people you love is a sure sign that good luck has already found you!

For the sauce:

    2 tablespoons soy sauce
    2 tablespoons oyster sauce
    1 tablespoon sesame oil
    1½ teaspoons freshly grated or jarred ginger
    2 teaspoons white pepper or finely ground black pepper
    red pepper flakes or chili pepper sauce, to taste (optional, for
        those who like a bite)

For the noodles:

    2 tablespoons each sesame and vegetable oil
    4–6 ounces fresh shiitake mushrooms, thinly sliced (or crimini,
        if you can't find shiitake)

1–3 ounces dried shiitake mushrooms, rehydrated (package
    sizes vary)
4–6 green onions, sliced, white and greens parts separated
5 cloves garlic, minced
10–12 ounces longevity noodles or lo mein (egg) noodles
    (package sizes vary)

In a small bowl, whisk together the sauce ingredients. Set aside.

Bring a large pot of water to a boil. Boil the noodles for 3 minutes.
Drain.

Return the pot to the stove and heat the sesame and vegetable oil
over medium-low. Add the mushrooms and sauté 3-4 minutes, stirring
to prevent sticking. Add the garlic and the whites of the onions. Sauté
until the garlic is golden and the onions have begun to soften, another
3-4 minutes.

Add the drained noodles and onion greens. Stir to combine and
cook an additional minute. Pour the sauce over the noodles and stir
gently, so the sauce coats the noodles without breaking them.

Slide the noodles into your serving bowl.

Serves 4 as a main dish, 8 as a side dish.

EGG TARTS

Smooth, glossy, slightly sweet filling in a pastry cup—what could be more delicious? Egg tarts are a staple of dim sum carts and Chinese bakeries, and easy to recreate at home. Mini tart pans make the baking easy!

For the dough:

2 cups all-purpose flour
⅛ teaspoon salt
12 tablespoons unsalted butter (slightly softened)
2–3 tablespoons cold water

For the filling:

½ cup granulated sugar
1 cup hot water
½ cup evaporated milk (at room temperature)
3 large eggs (at room temperature)
1 teaspoon vanilla extract

In the bowl of your food processor, or in a large bowl with an electric mixer or sturdy spoon, combine the flour and salt. Cut the butter into pieces and add to the flour and salt. Pulse to combine. Add 2 tablespoons of cold water and pulse until dough begins to come together. Add more water if necessary, starting gradually, up to 1 tablespoon. Remove dough from bowl and form into a ball or disc. Wrap tightly and refrigerate 15-20 minutes.

On a lightly floured surface, roll the dough into a rectangle, roughly 6 x 15 inches. If the dough is difficult to work, allow it to warm up a few minutes, until it's pliable. Fold the top third of the dough to the center, then fold the bottom third up to create a three-layered package about 6 inches wide and 5 or 6 inches long. Turn and roll again, into a 6 x 15-inch rectangle. Fold, wrap, and chill 30-60 minutes.

Meanwhile, make the filling. In a small bowl or large glass measuring cup, dissolve the sugar into 1 cup of hot water. Allow to cool for several minutes. In a medium bowl, whisk together the evaporated milk, eggs, and vanilla. Add the sugar water and whisk thoroughly. Strain into a bowl or pitcher with a pouring spout. (This process removes the bubbles and any egg solids to create a smooth filling.)

Heat the oven to 350 degrees.

Roll the dough about 1/8-inch thick. Cut in 4-inch circles, rerolling the scraps, and place rounds in mini tart pans. Leave about 1/4 inch of dough above the edge of the pans to allow for shrinkage. If the dough breaks or cracks, press it back together with your fingers or patch with leftover dough.

Pour the filling into the tart shells to just below the lip, dividing evenly. Bake about 30 minutes, until the filling is just set and the crust is a light golden-brown. Test for doneness by inserting a clean toothpick into the middle of one tart. If it feels firm and the toothpick doesn't wobble, the tarts are done; if liquid pools, bake a little longer.

Allow tarts to cool for about 10 minutes before serving.

Makes 12–16 tarts, depending on the size of your pans.

READERS, it's a treat to hear from you. Drop me a line at Leslie@
LeslieBudewitz.com, connect with me on Facebook at LeslieBude-
witzAuthor, or join my seasonal mailing list for books news and
more. (Sign up on my website, www.LeslieBudewitz.com.) Reader
reviews and recommendations are a big boost to authors; if you've
enjoyed my books, please tell your friends, in person and online. A
book is but marks on paper until you read these pages and make
the story yours.

Thank you.

Acknowledgments and Historical Notes

A CITY'S RICHNESS LIES IN ITS NEIGHBORHOODS. THEY HAVE their own history and traditions, their own architecture and identity. They evolve, adapt, stumble, and recover, and getting to know them was one of the joys of living in Seattle as a college student and young lawyer, and remains one of the joys of visiting—in real life and on the page.

My Gold Rush Hotel is fictional, built on what was, when I last saw it, a parking lot in Seattle's Chinatown–International District. I first started thinking about sending Pepper to the CID after visiting the Wing Luke Museum, located in the historic Kong Yick Building, in 2016. In creating the Gold Rush, I also borrowed from stories of the Panama Hotel and Hotel Louisa in Seattle, and the fascinating history recounted in *Building Tradition: Pan-Asian Seattle and Life in the Residential Hotels*, by Marie Rose Wong, PhD.

The Wing Luke Museum, named for Seattle's first Asian city councilor, is a treasure trove in the heart of the CID. It also maintains a permanent exhibit devoted to Bruce Lee, the martial artist, actor, and philosopher who lived in Seattle from 1959 to 1964. Bruce and his son Brandon are buried in Lakeview Cemetery on Capitol Hill. But while Bruce Lee remains a powerful presence in the CID and throughout Seattle, rumors that he haunts the place are entirely my invention, just for fun.

Although Uwajimaya and the Tai Tung restaurant are real, all other businesses in my version of the CID are fictional.

I first discovered the purple prism skylights of Pioneer Square and the doors and windows partially buried by the regrades as a wide-eyed college freshman. I picked up a few facts about the regrades and their effect on the streets, alleys, and buildings of Pioneer Square and the CID from *Seattle Walks: Discovering History and Nature in the City* by David B. Williams. More history came from a brochure promoting the reclaimed Nord, Maynard, and Canton Alleys, published by 4Culture, the cultural funding agency for King County. *Building Tradition* by Marie Wong, mentioned previously, is a fascinating account not just of the residential hotels in the CID but of the history of the community. Property ownership in the CID, as in Chinatowns and other Asian communities around the country, was complicated by the Chinese Exclusion Act and other laws designed to limit the ability of Chinese and Japanese immigrants to own property. As a result, some buildings, like the Kong Yick, were owned by corporations; by buying shares, individual investors acquired merchant status, easing the restrictions they faced. I have ignored all that by assuming Dr. Chen and old Mr. Wu were American citizens, at least on paper.

Two books provided helpful personal accounts, photographs, and historical research: *Divided Destiny: A History of Japanese Americans in Seattle* by David Takami, and *Reflections of Seattle's Chinese Americans: The First 100 Years* by Ron Chew and Cassie Chin. I pored over photos and stories on the websites for the Kam Wah Chung Chinese Heritage Site in John Day, Oregon, and the Mai Wah Society and World Museum of Mining, both in Butte, Montana. Although it covers a slightly different time period and region, I got lost in the pages of the memoir *Long Way Home: Journeys of a Chinese Montanan* by Flora Wong and Tom Decker.

I am grateful to our friend Gloria Wong, Flora's daughter, and Gloria's husband, David Snyder, for reading the manuscript and commenting. Thanks to Gloria and our friend John Webster for lending me their names.

The story of Dr. Henry Locke's training is based on the experience of my husband, Dr. Don Beans, who studied in the early 1980s with a Chinese Canadian doctor who preferred to teach a white American man rather than train his own daughter. Fortunately for me, in this case, the student did not marry the teacher's daughter!

Although Washington, like several other states, has changed its laws to refer to "Acupuncture and Eastern Medicine," I have used the terms I think my characters would use. My thanks to Tamara Venit-Shelton, PhD, professor of History at Claremont McKenna College and the author of *Herbs and Roots: A History of Chinese Doctors in the American Medical Marketplace*, for answering my questions about the practice of Chinese medicine in Washington State in the 1930s.

A note on the name Chinatown–International District or CID: That's the present-day name, used by both the city and residents, although the name and boundaries have evolved over time. In general, it encompasses areas once known as Chinatown, Japantown, and Koreatown. Little Manila came later, and more recently, Little Saigon.

Of course, mistakes are inevitable, and they are my own.

As always, I ask you to forgive me if the city on the page does not match the city of your memory or experience. Cities change, and I have occasionally renamed or relocated a business to better suit the story. At this writing, the permanent relocation of the totem poles in Victor Steinbrueck Park and the proposal for a new transit substation in the CID are still under discussion.

The heart of the cozy is the community. I hope this story demonstrates the importance of communities like Chinatowns and International Districts, still vibrant and resilient, and still vulnerable. In many cities, as in Seattle, these neighborhoods were among those hardest hit by the pandemic, racist attacks, and other public safety issues. If there's one near you, or you have the chance to visit in your travels, please show your love. And by love, you know I mean "eat."

At the 2022 Malice Domestic convention celebrating the traditional mystery, reader Sandy Lynn Sechrest made an incredibly generous donation to the children's literacy programs run by KEEN Greater DC-Baltimore, for the right to name a character in this book. She's from Wisconsin, so naturally we decided she would run a cheese shop in the Market, and to spotlight one of her favorites and mine, smoked cheddar. If we've addicted you to the stuff, our work is done.

As always, I am inspired by everything I eat, the offerings from spice shops I've visited, especially World Spice Merchants in Seattle, and my creative sisters at Mystery Lovers' Kitchen, the blog where mystery writers cook up crime and recipes.

It takes a village to make a writing career. Thanks to Debbie Burke for another terrific read and critique, and to Dan and Zhamal Harvey for many years of conversations about life in the fishing business. Marlys Anderson-Hisaw and her crew at Roma's Gourmet Kitchen Shop in Bigfork, Montana have supported me since my first mystery was published, hand-selling books like crazy. Amanda Bevill and the World Spice staff have been my dream partners. Kit Dieffenbach spent an hour sipping tea on a friend's front porch, recalling his years selling his jewelry in the Market, and later, showed me some of his favorite haunts. Dan Mayer, Ashley Calvano, and the other book lovers at Seventh Street Books have helped bring the Spice Shop books to life and put them in the hands of readers. Jo Piraneo of Glass Slipper Design keeps my website looking spiffy and designs my bookmarks. Pepper has her BFF and I have mine, Lita Artis, who listens, ground truths, and even tests recipes.

Special thanks to my husband, Dr. Don Beans, for his vast knowledge and experience of acupuncture and Chinese medicine, and all the late nights watching Bruce Lee movies.

About the Author

LESLIE BUDEWITZ IS PASSIONATE ABOUT FOOD, GREAT mysteries, and the Northwest, the setting for her national best-selling Spice Shop Mysteries and Food Lovers' Village Mysteries. As Alicia Beckman, she writes moody suspense set in the Northwest.

Leslie is a three-time Agatha Award winner: 2011 Best Nonfiction for *Books, Crooks & Counselors: How to Write Accurately About Criminal Law and Courtroom Procedure* (Linden/Quill Driver Books), 2013 Best First Novel for *Death al Dente* (Berkley Prime Crime), first in the Food Lovers' Village Mysteries, and 2018 Best Short Story for "All God's Sparrows" (*Alfred Hitchcock Mystery Magazine*). Her books and stories have also won or been nominated for Derringer, Anthony, and Macavity awards. A lawyer by trade, she has served as president of Sisters in Crime and on the board of Mystery Writers of America.

Leslie loves to cook, eat, hike, travel, garden, and paint—not necessarily in that order. She lives in northwest Montana with her husband, Don Beans, a musician and doctor of natural medicine, and their gray tuxedo cat, whose hobbies include napping and eyeing the snowshoe hares who live in the meadow behind the family home.

Visit her online at www.LeslieBudewitz.com, where you'll find maps, recipes, discussion questions, links to her short stories, and more.